"Let's get out of here."

Finn was rarely taken off guard, so the obvious invitation in Rowan's words caught him up short. "Where do you want to go?"

"Have you ever been to the British Museum after-hours?"

He had, in fact, been there on more than one occasion, but he wasn't about to tell her that. "Now, what would a nice girl like you be wanting in a place like that?"

"What happened to that adventurous spirit, Finn?" Rowan moved in, the light scent of her wrapping around his senses as the heat of her body assailed him through his suit. "You know, the one that had you making those idiotic jumps off your office building?"

"And the guards with guns?"

She waved a hand. "Easy."

"What are we waiting for, then?" Finn held out a hand, barely suppressing the urge to wrap her in his arms. "Lead the way."

House of Steele: Elite investigators taking on the most difficult assignments all over the world.

Dear Reader,

Welcome back to the world of the Steele siblings. Liam, Campbell, Kensington and Rowan formed the high-end security firm—the House of Steele—to cater to a wealthy clientele the world over. Each has a unique skill set used to get the job done for their elite, exclusive clients.

In *The London Deception,* the youngest Steele, Rowan, is forced to confront her past in the form of sexy Finn Gallagher. Now a modern-day female Indiana Jones, Rowan trots the globe, rescuing antiquities.

Finn needs Rowan's help. He's authenticating a major find in Egypt's Valley of the Queens and needs her expertise. What neither of them anticipates is to be revisited by an enemy more dangerous than either ever suspected.

I had so much fun writing *The London Deception.* I've always had a fascination with ancient Egypt and I hope you'll forgive me some artistic license as I played with the history of Ramesses II and his wife Nefertari. While they are real, I've taken liberties with their sculptures and burial chambers for the sake of the story.

I absolutely loved writing this book and the very real challenge of taking two damaged souls and redeeming them through the power of love. Love of family, love of a significant other and, maybe most important of all, love of self.

Best,

Addison Fox

THE LONDON DECEPTION

—

Addison Fox

HARLEQUIN® ROMANTIC SUSPENSE

Recycling programs
for this product may
not exist in your area.

ISBN-13: 978-0-373-27844-2

THE LONDON DECEPTION

Printed in U.S.A.

HARLEQUIN®
www.Harlequin.com

Books by Addison Fox

Harlequin Romantic Suspense

The Paris Assignment #1762
The London Deception #1774

*House of Steele

ADDISON FOX

is a Philadelphia girl transplanted to Dallas, Texas. Although her similarities to Grace Kelly stop at sharing the same place of birth, she's often dreamed of marrying a prince and living along the Mediterranean.

In the meantime, she's more than happy penning romance novels about two strong-willed and exciting people who deserve their happy ever after—after she makes them work so hard for it, of course. When she's not writing, she can be found spending time with family and friends, reading or enjoying a glass of wine.

Find out more about Addison or contact her at her website—www.addisonfox.com—or catch up with her on Facebook (addisonfoxauthor) and Twitter (@addisonfox).

For Alice

Valued critique partner, trusted confidante, dearest friend.

I'm so blessed you left a message.

Chapter 1

Twelve years ago—London

The bullet missed her ear by the grace of God and a stone in her shoe.

Unwilling to tempt fate twice, Rowan Steele belly crawled across the roof of the Knightsbridge townhome, reluctant to find out if her assailant was going to try again or just come after her.

She needed a more secure location.

Now.

Not for the first time did she curse her innate fear of guns or she'd have nicked Grandfather's World War II service pistol and stuck it in the waistband of her black pants before sneaking out earlier. A raw, choked laugh welled in her throat at the irony.

Guns she ran in fear from. Climbing London rooftops as a means to rip off the contents below? Bring it on.

A shout echoed from the street, muffled in the light fog that coated the city. When she'd arrived ten minutes earlier, she'd considered the fog a blessing, but its rapid swirl and increasing weight had her reconsidering that decision.

Who the bloody hell would be shooting at her?

And how did they even know she was up here?

Rowan kept moving, her breath heavy, even as the questions swirled through her mind faster than the fog around her body. A small nook sat between two chimneys—sitting room and study respectively—and she moved determinedly onward over the rough tiles to give herself a moment to regroup in relative safety.

Obviously the jewelry extraction—the evening's main event—was off.

Now she just had to figure out how to get off the roof undetected.

The small space enveloped her as she slid her body between the twin columns of old brick and took her first easy breath since the gunshot. Voices still echoed from the street, but they'd grown fainter and she didn't think it was only from the fog.

Her plans for the evening ran through her mind's eye on the same steady loop she'd not been able to get out of her head since her first visit to the townhome six months before. Her dear friend Bethany Warrington couldn't stop talking about her mother's latest gift from her father—a diamond-and-ruby bracelet purported to have been worn by Queen Victoria.

While Bethany might have been dear, she was altogether too dim and had blithely provided the combination to the jewelry safe her mother kept in her bedroom as she'd fiddled her way through it three times before successfully cracking it on the fourth.

Since the bracelet was basically sitting there for the taking, Rowan could hardly ignore the windfall and had plotted how she'd get in and out when Bethany's family took their annual jaunt to the Côte d'Azur.

On a rather huge level, Rowan knew what she was doing was wrong. Even if she could work her way past the clear directive in the Ten Commandments, she also knew by her actions she betrayed a friend.

Yet the impulse to take—to take and take and take whatever she could get her hands on—wouldn't be sated.

And no matter how much she wanted to, she couldn't change that simple fact.

Just like her parents.

They'd been taken from her by that same God who'd laid down those Commandments and she couldn't quite get past the need to strike back at Him and anyone else who got in her way.

In those moments when she stole something—be it a piece of jewelry worn by royalty or a pack of chewing gum carelessly left on the edge of a desk at school—she *felt*.

And in all the other endless hours, she simply marked time with that sickening well of grief in the pit of her stomach that wouldn't close, even as month piled on month to the tune of nearly four years gone.

It was that same pit of grief—and the desperate urge to fill it—that had her creeping out of her hiding place as the voices on the street below stayed quiet.

Rowan allowed those emotions to carry her along the path she'd originally mapped out. The large tree that stood in the small garden two doors down from the Warringtons' had provided the rooftop access and it had been easy enough to work her way across the roofs until she got to number twenty-three.

It was now the work of a minute to shimmy down the back wall on the thick ivy vines that wrapped the back of the house and enter through the former servants' entrance. A servant-free entrance due to the fact that most were on their own holiday and the remaining three in residence had been given the night off.

Rowan crouched before the door, her pick tools in hand. The lock was complicated—she'd expected no less on a home this dear—but she knew she could do it. Especially after all the practice she'd put in on her grandparents' town house.

After completing the last tumbler, she got back to her feet and opened the door. With careful strokes, she tapped out the alarm code Bethany had also shared and watched the red light flash over to green.

Rowan stood still for one moment, drinking in the quiet air of the house. Anticipation hummed in her veins and she took the briefest moment to savor it.

To savor being alive.

Then she relocked the door and headed up the kitchen stairwell to the third floor. The hallway carpet runner was soft under her feet as she moved into the bedroom Lady Warrington kept for her own use.

Night reflected through the windows, sheening the bedroom to a bright silver as Rowan slipped into the room. She slid open the double doors of the walk-in closet and went straight for the small safe built into the wall. The muted smells of fine leather, rich fabrics and the light scent of Chanel assailed her with a memory of her own mother's closet but she ruthlessly tamped it down.

She *would* do this.

And any sympathy for Bethany or her mother needed to be ignored.

Just as with the pick tools, the thin leather gloves that

covered her hands weren't a deterrent, and she quickly sped through the safe combination from memory. Even without knowledge of the combination, Rowan knew the moment each tumbler fell into place. Call it a sixth sense, subtle anticipation or the superb hearing her family regularly teased her about; the answer didn't really matter.

Rowan *knew*.

On the last spin, she settled on the number sixteen— fittingly the same as her age—and reached for the safe's handle. The door swung open, revealing all of the beautiful contents inside.

Rowan looked past them, despite the fact they called to her, whispering what a conquest it would be to remove everything. Instead, she pressed on, the piles of velvet containers housing bracelets, rings and necklaces all ignored until her hand settled over the black pouch in the rear of the safe. The cuff was heavy in her hands and she already imagined the wink of diamonds as she pulled the pouch from the safe.

Already, she felt the way the hard metal would encase her wrist as she hid the bracelet under the too-long arm of her school sweater, daring fate to rat her out.

To uncover her dark, desperate need to feel something.

Despite her fantasies, Rowan was eminently practical and knew any further daydreaming would need to wait for home. With one last look at the layers of velvet boxes still in the safe, she let out a small sigh and reached for the thick metal door.

The scream welled in her throat immediately at the heavy hand that came over hers while another dragged heavily against her mouth, muffling any noise.

"Thank you, darling. You've made this terribly easy." The dark voice crooned into her ear, the sounds of England unmistakable in the cultured tones. His breath was warm against her cheek.

She struggled against the hold—and the uncontrolled shiver at the light breath—but her captor was prepared, his elbows tightening against her shoulders to keep her still. Raw fear flooded her mouth with a harsh metallic taste as the simple urge to flee surpassed every other thought.

Was it one of the Warringtons' servants, lying in wait? Another thief?

A cop come to catch her?

The thoughts tumbled one over the other, in time with the heavy thud of her heartbeats, and it took Rowan several seconds to realize her captor hadn't moved.

He'd made no effort to touch her further and she felt only his hands on her body, no press of a gun or knife.

"If I move my hand, will you listen to me?"

She nodded, the voice oddly seductive in the dim light of the closet.

"Since I don't fully believe you won't scream, let me give you one more piece of advice, Peach."

She stilled, the strange sense that he spoke the truth filtering in through the fear as the odd endearment sent a shiver down her spine. What was likely a simple way to address her in lieu of her name felt different somehow.

On his lips the name felt lush. And seductive?

While she wasn't all that familiar with the sensation, she'd read more than enough romances to wish for a little seduction in her life. Had giggled with her girlfriends over the very same.

"That gunshot you blithely ignored in favor of heading in here? The man with the gun and two of his friends are still outside the house. So I suggest you do nothing to alert them to our presence."

Whatever sensitive emotion had momentarily gripped her fled at the very real threat that awaited both of them. The man lifted his hand and Rowan took her first easy breath since he'd captured her. Although he'd removed the cover over her mouth, the press of his body still held her in place facing the safe.

"Wh-who are they?" Her breath hitched on the words and she winced at the weakness.

"I don't know but I suspect they're after the same thing we both are."

"The bracelet?" Her voice was stronger and she squared her shoulders under his grip.

"The very same."

"How would they know about it?"

"Seems as if Lord Warrington purchased something that wasn't really for sale."

"He stole this bracelet?"

"*Steal* is such an ugly word when there is a payment involved. He claims he purchased it rightfully, but it's been whispered in several places he knew full well the bracelet rightfully belonged to another."

The cryptic answer stilled her and Rowan tried once more to turn in his arms. "How do I know you're not with them?"

"I work alone." The words were swift and immediate and she didn't know why she believed him, but she did.

"I can feel the brush of your ski mask against my head. Can I just turn around to talk to you? I clearly won't be able to identify you."

A light laugh drifted over her as the velvet pouch was snatched from her hand and then the heavy press of his body vanished. Rowan wondered briefly at the loss of warmth before the thought fled and she turned to face her captor.

Her very first impression was one of broad shoulders encased in black. The tight shirt he wore tapered to slender hips and long legs that made her think of the gangly height of her older brother Campbell. The wool mask she'd felt whisper against her head covered his face; odd that something she'd normally think of as scary or menacing only left her curious to see the face underneath.

Rich hazel eyes glittered from the holes in the mask's face and she forgot herself for the briefest of moments when her gaze locked with his.

On a hard shake of her head, Rowan focused on the problem at hand. What *was* the matter with her? "Who's out there?"

A quick light flashed across his eyes before being replaced by a hard glint that matched his next words. "A few blokes who want what's in here and thought tonight would be a good night to case the joint. Just like you and me."

"How could they know that?"

"How'd you know that?"

The words were nearly out—that she knew the family—when she bit them back on a hard clench of her teeth. He might be a friend for the moment, but the man clad head to toe in black wasn't to be trusted.

"Come on, Peach. Close that safe door and let's figure out how we're going to get out of here." The name whispered across her nerve endings once more, and Rowan tamped down on the delicious clench that seized her belly.

Rowan closed and locked the safe as directed. "There are servants' stairs at the end of the hall at the back of the house."

"They've got three guys. One's no doubt back there." The masked man never turned as he reached for her hand and dragged her from the closet. He gestured with his free hand as they crossed the broad expanse of Lady Warrington's room. "Over there. Behind the curtains."

"We can't hide behind the curtains. They'll find us for sure."

"No, they'll find us in the hallway, which is likely where they're headed now."

"They can't get in that fast."

"Of course they can. Especially since they've probably breached the back door you so kindly left unarmed." He turned to look at her. "You do realize you're not the only person in London in possession of lock picks?"

Once again Rowan was forced to clamp down on a retort, the truth of his words striking deep.

Why hadn't she quit when she was ahead?

The gunshot had been scary enough. She'd known once she got to safety between the chimneys that it was time to get out of there.

So why had she assumed the threat had vanished?

The image of her hand closing over the velvet bag holding the bracelet popped into her mind like a lure, but for the first time in four years the thought of possessing something not hers fell flat.

Her captor—partner in crime?—pushed her behind the heavy curtains decorated with large, rather unattractive cabbage roses that hung along the wall of Lady Warrington's bedroom. Rowan felt the dusty air swirl around her as the man fluffed the thick floor-to-ceiling pleats into place.

"Shhh, Peach."

"Why—"

The question was cut off by his hand as he covered her mouth and she caught the vague image of him shaking his head in the darkened space.

And then there were no words—not even breath—as

the thick, old door to the bedroom slammed open, knocking against the wall.

"She in there?"

"No one's in here." A Cockney accent reached her ears, although it was muffled slightly through the curtain, and Rowan prayed the voice belonged to a man too dumb to do a thorough search of the room.

The voice that belonged to the man who hunted her pressed on. "This was her destination."

"Place looks untouched, guv."

Rowan could only thank the heavy rug that covered the floor didn't show footprints the same way plush carpet would have, and her esteem for Lady Warrington's decorating skills rose a notch.

"Did you search it?"

"Look. She's not here, I tell ya. Let's look at the safe." The muffled sound of footsteps crossing the room, then the nearly soundless swing of the closet doors broke the silence. "Look. Safe hasn't even been touched."

"Maybe she cracked it."

"Little bit of fluff like her?"

"Don't underestimate her. Size has little to do with skill."

A low grumble echoed from the closet and Rowan had to strain to hear the response. "She was on the roof not ten minutes ago. How'd she get in here, crack the safe and get away?"

The idea that the gunshot had happened less than ten minutes ago surprised Rowan. If she'd been asked, she'd have surely said she and the man in black had been in the closet for at least twenty minutes, yet it had been merely a quarter of that.

"What if she's still prowling the outside? Or got away's more like it." The assurance dripped from the second man's voice and Rowan could only offer thanks he was so eager to assume she'd fled the scene.

"Check the room. I'm going to work on the safe."

The moment of good fortune—the one that had bloomed so briefly—shriveled and died as heavy footsteps thudded in the direction of her hiding place.

Finn Gallagher reached for the small, slender hand next to his and willed her to understand his intentions. The urge to flee straight-out was strong, but he knew there was the slightest chance the idiot on the other side of the room wouldn't discover them.

Slim, but a chance.

Besides, he'd gamble on stunning the grunt with the element of surprise, leaving him to only have to deal with the one in the closet. And if there was a third, as he'd originally calculated?

Finn mentally shook his head. *Deal with it if it comes, boyo.*

Wasn't that what his old man had always said?

While not quite comforting in his current predicament, the old man had always been a wise bugger. He'd do best to take the advice and sit still, maintaining an even breath and a steady focus.

He squeezed the girl's—could she really be more than sixteen or seventeen?—hand once, then dropped it to brace for discovery.

And had to wait the length of time it took the moron taking orders to cross the room and poke the curtain.

"Run!" Finn hollered the order as he threw a punch about where he estimated a head should be. The heavy grunt from the other side let him know he'd come relatively close as the girl streaked away from their hiding place.

Finn used the brief moment of confusion to reach down and throw the curtain over his opponent's head, pushing forward at the same time as if in a rugby scrum. He caught the slender black form run across the room from the corner of his eye, satisfied she'd at least cleared the immediate threat.

Although her movement had turned his attention for barely a second, it had given his assailant enough time to struggle to a standing position. Finn saw the hard glint in the seasoned professional's eye and opted for an old trick he'd learned on the playground.

He kicked first, telegraphing the motion with his eyes, and used the man's off-kilter frame as he dodged the foot to slam another punch into his face. The heavy thud of bone on bone rang up his arm but Finn ignored it as he took off after the girl.

"Teddy! She's headed your way. Get her!" The shout rang out from the closet as the first thug clamored out. Finn knew "Teddy" must be the third thief. A renewed sense of urgency gripped him to make sure the girl was all right, even as the thought he didn't know her—and really shouldn't be investing this much time in protecting her—flashed through his mind.

Then an image of her wide blue eyes, strangely guileless for the fact she had just been removing a piece of jewelry worth well over a million pounds, intruded on his waffling thoughts.

Could she really be that innocent?

Of course, if she was the age he'd assessed, the answer was quite possibly a yes. He'd only been in the game a few years himself, but he'd lost his own innocence a hell of a long time ago.

Which made it that much more puzzling she'd be so immediately appealing.

Finn kept moving, the heavy bracelet he'd shoved in his fake pocket—inside an interior pouch he kept wrapped around his leg—took a bit of getting used to as he straggled his way across the room. The cuff of the bracelet was awkward against his flesh and he fought to adjust the wrap around his thigh.

As he hit the back servants' stairwell, Finn knew the few moments of hesitation to adjust the bracelet were going to cost him. A thick hand reached out and snagged his shirt, the tug enough to slow him down. Finn stopped hard and pushed toward the hallway wall, knocking the man off-balance. It was only when he felt the hard edge of a gun that Finn knew he was in real trouble.

The thick, heavy beats of his heart kept his focus sharp and he turned hard on his captor, using his body for momentum. He grabbed the weapon with one hand while executing a swift uppercut with the other. The thug gave as good as he got, his skills no doubt honed on the streets the same as Finn's, but the movements did dislodge the gun, and the heavy piece banged against the wall and fell.

Satisfied he'd removed at least half his problem, Finn used the wall to his advantage, slamming the man into it. A painting mere inches from the guy's head quivered with the impact, but Finn barely saw it as hands flashed up to slam him in the chin.

A scream echoed from the bottom of the stairs, effectively breaking through the ringing in his ears.

The girl.

Indecision ripped through him as he continued to struggle with the man in the hallway. The gun was a very real threat and leaving his opponent in favor of traipsing after the girl was only going to give the thug time to get the weapon—and the upper hand.

As another scream tore through the air, Finn made his decision.

With one final slam to his opponent and a brief prayer the hard wall would stun him enough to slow him down, Finn dropped his hold and raced down the stairs.

Rowan screamed as hands came over her shoulders, dragging her backward. She kicked and scrambled, desperate to get out of the hold as her racing heartbeat threatened to swamp her. Her breath was already coming in heavy pants, the urgent need to get to safety drumming through her system.

"Where you think you're going?" The man's breath was warm and clammy in her ear before he turned his head and hollered up the stairs, "Got her!"

Who were these guys? And what had Bethany's father gotten himself into?

"Think you're going to take what's ours, did you?"

"It's not yours." She struggled against the tight hold, suddenly conscious of how different this man's grip was from the man in black.

Where he'd pinned her in place to explain what was happening, this thug was all about the lascivious press of his body against hers.

And then the disgusting press of his body was gone as if it had never been as the man was literally dragged off her.

"Keep running!"

Rowan turned at the voice, a mix of relief and sudden ease swamping her.

The man in black was still fighting for her.

It was that very thought that had her defying his orders. "I can't leave you!"

"Get out of here." The words came out as a barely

concealed grunt as he struggled with her former captor. Eyes roaming over the hallway, she caught sight of a small corner of the kitchen through an open doorway. A heavy frying pan sat on the edge of the counter.

Rowan moved at once, the pan in hand as she raced back to the hall. The two men continued to fight, each locked in a death grip, and she braced her feet, waiting until the movements of the two bodies would put the dangerous thug in the line of her swing.

Be bold, Rowan Steele.

The words flashed through her mind. They were her father's admonishment before she ever did anything she didn't want to do or was afraid of. First days of school. A big footy tournament. A big test.

The words—forgotten these past years in her grief—were suddenly a very real reminder of the strength inside of her.

Arms rigid, she swung the pan as hard as she could. A zing of satisfaction matched the ringing in her arms when the thug went limp midfight. The man in black took advantage immediately, pressing on her shoulder to get her moving.

At the heavy thud of footsteps on the stairs, they both turned.

The other thug—the one from the closet—shot off another round from the bottom of the stairs. The bullet went wild, but he never had a chance to get off a second shot when the frying pan was snatched from her hand, then went flying, end over end toward the man's head.

The pan hit hard, knocking the man off his feet as another shot went wild.

"Wow."

The man in black stared at her for the briefest moment

before he shrugged and grabbed her free hand. "Let's get out of here."

She followed him out the same back door she'd used to enter the house. "Wait!"

The impatience was evident in those broad shoulders and the quick rocking from foot to foot, but he stopped for her. "What is it?"

"Give me a minute." Rowan reached for the small, slim plastic bag she kept in her back pocket.

"We don't have time for this."

"Just wait."

She flipped the small bag inside out as she waved him through the door with her other hand. "Go in front of me."

"What is that?"

"Petroleum jelly."

His low whistle echoed in her ear at the same time their felled thug let out a large roar. "Time to go, Peach."

Rowan gave the knob one more swirl from the bag before slamming the door behind her and fled down the back steps. "Come on down here. Through the old mews."

He reached for her hand to drag her out the back garden toward the main road. "They'll follow us that way."

"Not when we go up."

"Up where?"

"The vines. All the houses back here have thick ivy. We climb it."

"Absolutely not."

If the situation weren't so dire, Rowan might have laughed at his clear affront. "You've got a better idea?"

"We keep on and make a run for it through the alley. Same way I came in."

"They're going to follow us that way."

A shout behind them confirmed the truth of that and the man shrugged. "You sure about this?"

"Positive. There's a tree a few doors down for the descent. It'll be more secure than the alley."

Another bellow echoed from the direction of the kitchen, and Rowan knew the thug had found his progress stymied with the doorknob. A quick smile flashed in the man in black's eyes as he laced his fingers and put his hand out to give her a boost up the ivy. "Real nice trick back there, Peach."

"Thanks." Rowan put her foot in his hands, but stopped, the question she'd wanted to ask back behind the curtain flaring up once more. "Why do you keep calling me that?"

"Because you're lush and ripe, like a fresh peach."

The cavalier words—delivered with a wicked smile that was visible even through the mouth of the mask—caught her up as a flood of warmth rushed through her.

She knew it was reckless.

Pointless, really, and terribly dangerous, but like the bracelet she couldn't resist, she could no more stop the impulse than she could stop her heart from beating. With the quick fingers she was known for, she had his mask halfway off his face and her lips against his in the span of a breath.

Whatever surprise he might have had at her move was quickly tamped down by the hard press of his lips and the quick heat of his tongue as it swept through her parted lips.

A streak of heat flooded her belly before racing to the end of her limbs, and Rowan had the very real sensation of feeling her knees go weak.

He lifted his head, his lips bright with wetness in the moonlight, but it was his eyes that truly captured her. The gaze that had teased mere moments before glinted with something else. Something elemental. Something that called to her and made all those empty places inside—the ones that clamored so loudly in their silence—still.

And for the first time in four years, Rowan Steele felt an emotion that was stronger than the emptiness.

Voice gentle, he nodded toward his still-laced fingers. "Come on, darling. Up you go."

Rowan placed a booted foot in his hands, their eyes meeting once more. In the moonlight she saw what had only been an impression earlier when she'd thought him as gangly as her brother.

Likely because he was.

He was barely a man, no more than nineteen or twenty if she estimated correctly. The half of his face she could see—over his hard jaw and past the thin scruff of beard—held a softness. Even more than that, she had the distinct sensation that he wasn't quite done filling out the body that would ultimately be his.

With a hard push and the determination to find out who he was when they reached safety, she launched off his laced fingers, grabbing the ivy. She worked her way up the side of the house, hand over hand. He did the same on several strands next to her, his grunts the only sounds breaking the silence.

She cleared the second floor and turned to see him still struggling on the first. "Hand over hand and use your feet on the wall."

"Bloody vines are breaking under my weight."

"Grab a thicker handful."

"I'm try—"

The protest bubbling in his words never fully formed as the thug they'd left in the kitchen came into view beneath them. Rowan screamed as the pistol lifted, even as her body moved on, desperate with the urge to flee the threat.

They were so close.

And then they weren't.

The boy who climbed next to her shook with the impact of a bullet. His fingers loosened against the ivy.

His body slid down the wall, his gloved hands barely hanging on to the vines, before collapsing in a heavy slump on the ground.

Tears burned her eyes but she climbed on, torn between going back to him and the all-consuming need to get away.

To leave the nightmare behind.

The last image she saw before she ran over the London rooftops was that slumped figure—clad in black—lifeless on the ground.

Chapter 2

Rowan Steele fired round after round at the Lower West Side gun range that had been her main practice site for the past decade. The fear of guns she'd long carried had never faded, but Rowan refused to be ruled by it.

And she took some solace when the multitude of holes in the center of the paper target's chest indicated she'd mastered a technical proficiency, if not an emotional one.

The distinct feeling of being watched washed over her and she laid the gun down on the platform in front of her before turning around.

Straight into the eyes of her brother Campbell.

"What are you doing here?"

He shrugged, his long frame on the lanky, slender side of muscular. "Same thing you are. Staying sharp."

"You haven't been back from Paris all that long. I'd

have thought picking up a gun was the last thing you'd want to do for a few more weeks."

The hollow laugh was as empty as his eyes. "Why the hell do you think I'm here?"

Rowan nodded, well aware the events he and his fiancée, Abby, had faced the previous month were still far too fresh for both of them. The half brother Abby didn't know she'd had was gone, but his attempts at terrorizing her were going to take time to fade. Add on the fact that the man had died at Campbell's hands and she knew he and his new love were both working hard to get past the pain and look forward to their future.

She was just so damned happy they'd found each other and had a future to get on with.

"Abby going to take lessons?" She kept the question casual as she pulled a fresh magazine from her pocket.

"She's not interested. And I'm only here to keep Kensington off my back." Campbell grimaced before adopting a high tone meant to mimic their sister. "All those who work for the House of Steele are trained with the highest degree of security and protection skills."

"So we are."

"I'm surprised to see you, actually. I thought you were headed to evaluate that Egyptian collection coming into the new museum in Seattle."

"Kenzi's got a different assignment she wants me to take on."

Campbell's eyebrows lifted over a speculative blue gaze. "I thought Seattle was a pretty lucrative gig."

"Apparently whoever she's got dangling is willing to triple the usual fees."

"Which is code for run far, run fast." Campbell's mouth slid into a frown. "Kenzi knows better than that. You look at the file?"

"Not yet."

"Whatever it is, there's no way it's worth it."

Rowan didn't completely agree with Campbell—they took on the hard jobs others weren't capable of—but she wasn't going to argue the point. Her brother had a right to be a bit raw after recent events. She heard the protective instincts that threaded through his words.

Campbell *would* bounce back, and in the meantime, she'd keep her own council on the new opportunity. The House of Steele stood out as a resource because they *did* take on the hard jobs. And they had very few peers because no one had their combination of connections, skills and bankroll to get it done.

It still didn't mean triple their already-exorbitant fee didn't ring a few bells.

"You get what you pay for."

"You always do." Campbell moved into the stall next to hers and removed his gun from a protective case. "Just remember you get what you take, too. You don't have to take this job."

"I know."

Although Kensington managed the majority of the jobs they took on, no one *had* to work on anything. Her sister did know how to force the issue—and had done so on more than one occasion—but at the end of the day they all had an equal vote.

Pushing aside the imagined contents of what awaited her when she finally got around to her email, Rowan resumed her stance and spent the next twenty minutes in companionable silence with Campbell.

She loved all her siblings and knew she was fortunate for the relationship she had with each of them, but what she had with Campbell was special.

Kensington took her position as oldest female sibling

seriously, pushing the matriarch role even when it wasn't necessary. And Liam used his status as oldest sibling *and* oldest brother to get away with whatever he chose whenever he chose.

But Campbell.

They understood each other.

Each was the youngest of their sex and both had made some dodgy choices in their youth. Although neither spoke of those times, she knew between the two of them they'd contributed to the majority of their grandfather's gray hairs.

Maybe it was the companionable silence or a weird melancholy she hadn't been able to shake since learning of Campbell's near miss in Paris, but as they wrapped up their things, she wasn't ready to end the evening. "You up for a cup of coffee or a drink?"

"I'd love to."

The breath she'd been holding came out on a rush. "Great."

"We're not far from Meatpacking. How about that new bar that opened. Johansen's?"

"Sure."

The high-tech glass-and-chrome interior of the bar welcomed them a half hour later after a brisk walk in the late October air and Rowan settled into her back-lit booth seat.

Campbell waited a beat until their waitress was out of earshot before leaning forward. "What's going on?"

"Nothing."

"You sure about that?"

"Can't I have a drink with my brother?"

"Of course you can. Doesn't change the fact I want to know what put the shadows under your eyes."

"It's nothing. It's just been a busy few weeks, that's all."

"No, that's not all and it's not nothing. Why aren't you sleeping? Is it the dreams?"

She briefly toyed with brazening her way through a bluff, but the blue eyes that bore into hers saw too much and knew too much for it to be worth the effort.

"Yes, I've been having the dreams again. They started up after you got home. After we understood what really happened in Paris."

"I'm fine, Ro." Campbell reached across the table and gripped her hand. "Abby and I are both fine. And it's behind us."

"You killed her brother, Campbell."

"I know."

"That doesn't just go away, so don't act like you're all fine with it."

"I know it's not that easy. And I am working on it. We both are." He looked up from their joined hands. "So why the hell are you the one having bad dreams?"

The urge to tell him about that long-ago night rose up, clamping her throat in a tight grip. With stoic determination, she pushed down on the urge. For nearly half her life, she'd kept the secrets of what she used to do.

The stealing. The deliberate and purposeful removal of prized possessions from others. Even the emotional void that she'd lived with for so long and which she still sunk into from time to time if she wasn't vigilant.

But underneath it all were the images of that horrible night.

The twisted body as it lay along the base of the house, unmoving. The gunshots directed at her that she'd barely missed. The lingering hunt through newspapers, police files, internet searches—whatever she could get her hands on—to find out if someone had been murdered outside the Warringtons' Knightsbridge home that spring night in London.

Rowan had always carried the slim hope that the boy who was barely a man had escaped with his life. She and Bethany had stayed friends, and the ensuing excitement and rampant sympathy at school for the traumatized house she and her family came home to had sparked endless rounds of discussion and speculation. On several occasions, Rowan probed if they'd found anyone, or any blood, or if anyone had gotten away.

The answer was always no.

Despite the hope she carried that he was all right, Rowan simply couldn't erase the images of that last night. And even now, she could feel his lips on hers if she closed her eyes.

Could remember the distinguished lilt of his voice when he spoke, his lips pressed to her ear.

Could feel the moment her heart had begun beating once more with a passion for life that had lay dormant since the death of her parents.

"Have you considered a vacation?"

Rowan zoned back into Campbell's words as their waitress laid down their drinks. "I'm taking part in that dig in the Valley of the Queens next spring."

"That's work, Ro. Not vacation."

She smiled at the endearment as she picked up her wine. "I love what I do, which makes it a vacation every day. Besides, who wouldn't want to get their hands on the new cache that was found this past spring?"

Campbell shook his head but his smile stayed broad. "What is wrong with us? I'm dragging Abby to a conference next month on the latest upgrades in internet security. Want to know the worst part?"

"What?"

"Abby's actually excited about it."

Rowan couldn't hold back the smile—or resist pointing out the obvious. "She is one of the world's leading experts in communications technology and she runs a multinational company. Does this really surprise you?"

The quick smile that was his trademark flashed. "No. And when you consider I find it oddly sexy, well, there you have it. We do what we love."

"That we do." She was so pleased to see that smile. Relieved, really. If he could smile that way, it meant he was on his way back to normal. "And for the record, we all think she's your match in every way. It's so obvious it's almost scary. I just can't believe Kensington never thought to introduce you two before."

"We weren't meant to meet before."

The words were oddly prophetic and Rowan chewed on them long after he'd walked her back to her Chelsea apartment, then went on to his own home.

Was there a time and a place? A moment when two people were supposed to meet or were meant to click? She'd always been a bit middling on the whole fate-takes-a-hand thing, but Rowan also knew there were simply things in life you couldn't explain.

Moments of extreme awareness that could save your ass, like dodging a bullet without even realizing it was coming.

Or acting on impulse and kissing someone you had no business touching.

She'd also visited enough parts of the world to know that superstition and the belief that some broader, guiding hand was in control had many a follower.

Despite all that—or maybe in spite of it, Rowan mused—she had never been able to fully abandon the notion that you also made your own life and made your own luck. Sitting around waiting for something to come to you was about as valuable as waiting to win the lottery.

Action trumped all.

Which was why her curiosity about the new job Kensington had on the line had her padding into her home office after changing into a pair of oversize, comfy sweatpants and a long-sleeved T-shirt. The heat kicked on as she walked into the old maid's room that she used as an office, and Rowan smiled at the sound. The crisp October air had grown colder in the past weeks and she was already thinking about the coming holidays.

She navigated through the secure log-in to the House of Steele database and pulled up the files Kensington had sent earlier. And forgot every single worry or care in her mind as she read the details her sister had layered over several pieces of source material.

The three-time payday was a lovely gesture, but as Rowan reread each piece of information on Finn Gallagher and his company, Gallagher International, she knew deep in her heart she'd have done the job for free.

Finn rechecked his email as he lingered over a bourbon, irritated there had been no further correspondence from Kensington Steele. He'd requested services from her firm three days ago.

What was she waiting on?

Even as the question floated through his mind, Finn knew the answer. She was vetting him as thoroughly as possible, just as he would have done with any business partner he was considering working with.

The fact he already kept close tabs on the entire Steele family, watching them from afar, was a different matter entirely.

The sounds of the bar—a favorite of the London art crowd—swirled around him in dulcet tones as he allowed himself a few brief moments to think about Rowan Steele and her family. He was fascinated by what the Steele siblings had built. Although their firm wasn't highly publicized—there was no website or social-media feeds for them—those in the know knew exactly how to find them.

The House of Steele was a discreet resource, and from what he'd heard, observed or pulled through casual gossip, the Steeles always got what they came for.

It was a track record he couldn't help but admire.

"Gallagher." Finn stowed his phone in his interior coat pocket and glanced up at the greeting before standing to extend a hand.

"Good to see you, John. Join me for a drink."

John Bauer—a well-placed administrator at one of the world's top auction houses—took the seat opposite. "Don't mind if I do."

Finn ordered a bottle of wine he knew John set stock by and settled in for a lively discussion. As evenings went, it wasn't what he'd planned, but if he were honest with himself, he had no idea what he'd planned. The restless feeling that had gripped him the previous week when the job came in had sharp claws and he hadn't been able to settle.

The conversation with John would give him some much-needed company while also ensuring he'd go home rich with information he didn't have when he began his evening.

With a congenial smile, Finn opened with a quick stroke to John's ego. "Heard you're the favorite for the maharaja jewels."

"We certainly hope so. The Brunei government has been rather cryptic on who they will choose, but I think it will be us." Finn saw the cat-in-the-cream smile and knew the deal was far nearer to closed than the words suggested, but gave the man his illusions.

He'd get far more out of him if John thought he wasn't as quick on the uptake.

"I wish you the very best on it."

The conversation swirled with the wine, and Finn settled in for a discussion that would follow tangents and fragments of tangents until they finally swung back around to where he wanted.

"Speaking of inside lines, heard you've got your eye pretty firmly focused on the antiquities market."

"It's a sound strategy." Finn kept his words casual as he poured out the rest of the bottle between them. "I've always had a personal interest in Egypt, so it's rather easy to meld the two with my business goals."

"Big news that cache found last spring in the Valley of the Queens."

"It's extraordinary. And tied up in red tape, squabbling and a whole host of attitude from the academic community. My firm is helping to mediate as well as authenticate the find."

"You don't say."

Finn nodded. "Handling this one personally myself."

"You know—" John broke off, speculation rampant in his gaze. "Rumor has it you're an Indiana Jones type. Scouring the world for lost treasures. Keeping the less savory blokes from looting the ruins and all that good fun. Gallagher International's just a front for all that."

Finn kept his smile broad and his tone wry. He knew as well as anyone technology and modern communications had made it virtually impossible to remain fully incognito. But he was surprised by the depth of John's gossip-fueled knowledge.

"Do I look like I like khaki pants and fedoras?" Finn extended his sleeves for good measure, pleased when his cuff links winked in the light of the bar. "And I'm not sure I've ever touched a bullwhip."

John's smile—and the wine that fueled the haze behind his gaze—was broad. "And this is clearly how gossip gets started. You're a young guy. People know you've got a sense of adventure. The rest steamrolls from there."

"I'm a businessman with diverse interests. But I have to say I'm sort of pleased to know I have a reputation."

John had the wherewithal to decline another bottle, and it was only as Finn was headed home, the thick fall air clearing his head from the wine, that he congratulated himself on the approach he'd taken with the House of Steele.

If John's comments were any indication, people in the know had begun to speculate on his motives. He ran Gallagher International with an impeccable track record, and his skills authenticating for the major auction houses were known to be among the best. State-of-the-art and thorough authentication of artifacts, the ability to secure permits and licenses to excavate, and the mediation services he'd indicated earlier.

All had proven far more lucrative than the choices of his early, misguided days.

And all had provided an outstanding cover for his older, somewhat wiser, still-misguided choices.

The only question left to his mind was whether or not Rowan Steele was going to go along for the ride.

Rowan sat in the conference room they kept at headquarters and pored over the map of Egypt she'd had since her college days. The map was well used—full of pencil markings, notations and a fair number of rips and tears—

but she loved it and the history of her life that was tied to every one of those external markers.

She'd instructed Kensington to take the meeting with Finn Gallagher and knew she needed to be on her game. The man had rearranged his entire schedule to get to New York overnight for their face-to-face, only reinforcing the job was one of his highest priorities. As if the payment he'd offered didn't already offer a sizable clue.

Although she hadn't slept much this week, the time with Campbell the other night had eliminated the nightmares, and when she did sleep, her mind was blessedly free. For the first time in more days than she could count, Rowan felt somewhat back to her old self.

Kensington bustled into the room on sky-high, pencil-thin heels, her normally serene expression haggard. "That's what you're wearing to this meeting?"

"I'm fine." Rowan glanced down at the peasant blouse she'd donned with a pair of jeans. "What's your damage today?"

"Finn Gallagher is offering us a rather lucrative gig, Rowan. You can't take it a notch above bohemian chic?"

"I think your sister looks rather beautiful, Ms. Steele."

They both turned, and Rowan would have bet her face was a match for Kensington's dropped mouth as they both took in the large man that stood in the doorway.

"As do you in your corporate chic. I hope you'll forgive my coming straight up. Your assistant let me in." He stepped into the room and crossed to them, his arm outstretched. "Kensington?"

Rowan gave her sister the edge in quick recoveries and saw the polished veneer that returned once more to her porcelain skin. "Mr. Gallagher. Glad you could join us."

"Finn, please."

The man turned toward her, and Rowan felt the first

blast from his intense gaze. Rich hazel eyes winked at her, slight crinkles edging the corners, and she felt herself immediately sucked in.

Especially when another pair of hazel eyes rose up in her mind to swamp her with the memory of a moonlit night full of danger and death.

Pull it together, girl.

The admonishment did little to remove the memory, but it was enough to have her gathering her manners and extending her hand. "Lovely to meet you."

"Likewise."

The cultured tones of his native Britain met her ears, and another remembrance struck hard and fast. This man's voice was deeper than the one that haunted her memories, but still effective at turning her insides liquid.

Kensington gestured him toward a seat, and Rowan took a moment to gather herself while his attention was diverted. She'd been in the presence of men with British accents before. She'd also been in the presence of men with hazel eyes.

So where was this sudden flash of memory coming from?

And why was it so strong and nearly debilitating in its intensity?

Sure, the dreams had been particularly bad of late and she hadn't been sleeping well, but even insomnia wasn't an excuse for such a reaction. Maybe it was the prospect of spending time in his all-too-attractive company if they agreed to the assignment.

Or so Rowan hoped.

They all helped themselves to coffee and a small fruit-and-breakfast-pastry tray before resuming spots at the table. Rowan hung back, lingering over the preparation for her coffee, intrigued by the seat Finn selected.

In her experience, powerful men always gravitated to the head of the table, so it was fascinating when he selected a seat in the middle. It was even more fascinating to watch as he removed his suit jacket and rolled up the sleeves of his white dress shirt, the thick muscles of his forearms capturing her gaze.

"Finn, I appreciate your taking the time to meet with us." Kensington started in, her "client tone" firmly in place. "Your request is an interesting one and frankly not something a lot of firms have the expertise to pull off."

"Which is why I made the outreach to you in the first place."

"And which we appreciate." Kensington volleyed right back. "It doesn't change the fact you're requesting services from us that are, at best, unorthodox and, at worst, highly dangerous."

"The danger should be minimal, especially for someone of your sister's expertise."

For the first time since the discussion began, Finn's gaze settled fully on her. Rowan felt the shift in attention immediately, a heavy rush of heat filling her center at his scrutiny.

"You seem awfully sure about that, Mr. Gallagher."

"Finn." He corrected her with a smile. "Please."

"Whatever I call you, it doesn't change the fact you want me to accompany you into a highly charged political situation. Those assigned to excavate the site have a variety of interests. What makes you so sure they're all willing to play well with others?"

"I make it my business to know the odds. To understand where there's real danger and where there's simply a lot of smoke."

"And I make it my business to pick the proper partner when politics are involved," Rowan parried.

"I am the right partner."

"I've already been approached on this project by the British Museum. I'm scheduled to spend time on the excavation site in the spring."

"Partner with me and you can get there next week. All your clearances will be taken care of. Immediate access, Ms. Steele."

Rowan smiled, the formality an interesting touch, especially since they'd already dispensed with surnames at his directive. "I've spent my career building my reputation with the Egyptian authorities, the world's major auction houses and the academicians who want to ensure history is preserved."

"As have I."

"Yet you want me to pose as your business partner, aid you in authenticating the cache and potentially aid in the removal of said cache if the situation becomes untenable."

"Yes."

She shook her head, the movement enough to flutter the light material of her blouse where it gaped at her throat. "You don't need me for that. Your reputation is sound and you've already got the job. Why bring in an outsider?"

Finn knew she had a point, but damn it, he needed her on this. "I want an expert. An outside expert who can see things that I can't."

"The intel that's come back already suggests it's a straight excavation job on a site that's already been studied for a century. It's about to play host to several teams of experts. Why bring in one more?"

While he'd expected her skepticism, he didn't expect the overt push back. He'd been involved in the project for the past two months, and no matter how he looked at it, he couldn't hold back the sense that he needed another resource with him. The parties in play—the British Museum, the British and Egyptian governments, and several interested auction houses—all had ulterior motives in mind.

But were any of them truly worried about the preservation of the priceless artifacts the experts were pulling from the tomb?

"The site's always been considered the most dynamic of all the tombs in the Valley. A discovery anywhere is big news, but a discovery like this has drawn the interest of any number of unsavory interests."

"The British Museum is hardly going to let an *unsavory* character—" the slightest edge of humor tinged her words "—walk out of there."

"They will if they don't know who to keep an eye on."

Her eyes widened and any hint of teasing had vanished. "You think an insider is going to try to take the pieces?"

"I need to be prepared for that eventuality. I can't authenticate anything if it's removed before I take possession of it. And I won't take a risk that someone switches in a fake."

"So why do you need me?"

"You know the items. You know Egyptian artifacts. You know the players. I need a right hand to help me remove anything that might be at risk."

"Then perhaps you're unfamiliar with my work and my reputation. I'm no thief, Finn."

Chapter 3

*O*n the contrary.

The words popped to mind immediately—along with the memory of Rowan Steele clad head to toe in black— but Finn kept them to himself as he took in the twin looks of concern staring at him across the old cherrywood conference table.

Perhaps he'd miscalculated.

He'd originally thought his summons to the Upper East Side brownstone that acted as headquarters for the House of Steele was about sizing him up for the job and deciding if they wanted in.

What he saw brewing was something else entirely.

The question wasn't if they wanted in on the job. They were simply calculating the odds of whether or not they wanted to hitch their wagon to his.

"I wasn't implying anything of the sort, Rowan."

"Yet that's exactly what you've asked of me and are

willing to pay our already significant fees several times over should I agree to accompany you."

"If I determine the cache that's been discovered is at risk, I'll do what I need to do to protect it."

"Even if taking it means you'll be in violation of the UNESCO Convention?

"Yes." The vivid blue of her gaze never wavered from his, and he had to admire her gumption. "I have no intention of keeping any of the contents should it come to removal. But I will not see them looted by thieves in the middle of the desert."

"What makes you qualified to make that decision?"

"I'll know it should the situation arise."

Rowan shook her head, but he didn't miss the faint smile that ghosted her lips. Heat arced between them as he smiled back and enjoyed the slight widening of her lips before she morphed back into skeptical adversary on the other side of the conference room table.

She was even more beautiful than he'd remembered. Although he'd kept tabs on her since that night in London, he had forcefully tamped down on allowing that interest to be anything more than that of a smart businessman who possessed full knowledge of his competition.

Whenever he'd thought of that night—those youthful moments that defined his path for adulthood—he thought of Rowan Steele.

Her presence at the town house had been as shocking as it was unexpected. But it was the young woman who had revealed herself to him that night who had intrigued him, while also ensuring he'd never forgotten her.

He'd sensed pain. A deep-rooted recklessness that drove her actions and which she wasn't quite able to control.

It was that recklessness—and the corresponding sensation of looking into a mirror where his own actions and choices reflected back at him—that had dogged him throughout his recovery from the gunshot wound he'd sustained that night. Rowan had forced him to acknowledge he was on a path that wasn't going to ensure a very long life span.

She'd also ensured he had quite a mystery to solve once he'd healed from his injuries. Although he'd begun focusing on his future, he'd made it his business to figure out how a highly skilled young girl had come to be on the Warringtons' roof.

"Tell me more about the excavation. In your own words."

Rowan's question pulled him from his thoughts and he focused on the reason he'd sought her out. "A small tomb was discovered next to Nefertari's burial site. The cache of objects is believed to depict the great love between Ramesses II and his wife, Nefertari. Several of the jewels already discovered are believed to be her wedding set."

"Why do you believe it's been overlooked? Nefertari's tomb is the best known in the Valley of the Queens. Scholars have been over and around every inch of it."

He'd turned the problem over and over in his mind and hadn't yet come to any firm conclusions, but was anxious to discuss them with her. "At the risk of seeming uneducated, I'd consider it a sign of technological advancement combined with a stroke of pure dumb luck."

Rowan's smile was back. "I'm not quite sure the team from the British Museum who made the discovery while rephotographing the tomb would appreciate that characterization."

"You know the team?"

"Well enough. Baxter Monroe has always been a supporter of my work."

Finn suspected Baxter Monroe was also a supporter of

Rowan Steele's rather delectable ass, but kept his thoughts to himself. "We'll agree to disagree."

Kensington took that moment to step in. "Finn, while I have every confidence in my sister, you can't ignore there's possible risk."

"Which my firm is prepared to minimize. In addition to Rowan's sterling reputation, I have legitimate reason to be on-site because Gallagher International has been selected to authenticate the dig by the Coalition of Antiquities."

Clearly unconvinced, Kensington pressed again. "So why isn't your firm fully handling the site?"

"I am personally handling the site, not my staff. I need an expert on this and someone who knows the players in the region. Rowan has that. Her recent history of successfully retrieving various antiquities thefts is impressive. I think her presence will offer a degree of deterrence to those who'd like to see the cache distributed to the highest private bidder."

"Why don't you cut to the chase?" Rowan interrupted whatever it was Kensington was about to say next. "You want me to spy on-site and schmooze with my contacts. None of which will do us any good if everything goes sideways."

Finn felt the deal slipping away, the hard glint in her eyes telegraphing what would no doubt be a refusal, and he puzzled at the strange sense of disappointment sweeping through his bloodstream. He knew from the start this was a difficult request. Knew the tensions between the various political factions involved in the tomb discovery were a hard sell.

So why did the rejection feel personal?

"The deal's not going to go sideways. But if you want reassurance, why don't you pay a visit to the Gallagher International offices? I'll take you through all our research to date. The original reports from the team at the British Museum overlaid with topography of the region, our intel on all of the major crime rings currently involved in antiquities theft and full background on each of the players currently involved in the site."

"And if I say no?"

"Then you'll miss out on the opportunity to be on-site for the full excavation inside the tomb, the opportunity to authenticate the jewelry and private items already discovered in the cache along with anything else we find. Oh, and unfettered access to Nefertari's tomb, which, as you know, isn't granted to just anyone, nor is it granted all that often."

A merry little twinkle lit up her eyes, the only real expression of her agreement. "I'm in."

Rowan took a small measure of satisfaction at the matched looks of shock on both Finn's and Kensington's faces. While she knew the surprise was for vastly different reasons, she was pleased to have knocked both off guard.

Sure, the dangers at the site were real, but so were the dangers on any job she took on. She would go through her normal meticulous preparation in advance, and then it would be up to the situation to fall where it may.

But there was no way in hell she was missing out on that tomb.

"Then it's settled. Can you be in London in two days?"

"Of course."

"I'll see you then. In the meantime, I'll forward some additional documentation for you to review."

Kensington maintained her usual small talk, then ushered Finn Gallagher from the conference room, their voices fading down the hall. Rowan heard the vague mention of contracts and an early transfer of funds to pay for her travel but tuned the majority of it out.

She was headed back to Egypt.

And she was headed there with a man who put her back up all the while intriguing her.

Finn Gallagher was a puzzle. The same early behavior that impressed her with his seat selection—a clear indication he held both her and Kensington in equal regard—had continued throughout the meeting. He made his points without apology, yet she got the distinct impression he fully understood what he was asking.

And he scored major points for his very real skepticism of Baxter Monroe.

She'd always hated the museum's head of Egyptian artifacts and thought the man operated with a pomposity that bordered on ignorance. She also knew for a fact the man had spent little time on the dig site despite his lavish claims to the contrary. The discovery was the result of his poor behavior in the tomb on a random visit that had oddly paid dividends, but rather than acknowledge his team, he was now blithely taking credit for the work of his staff.

Oh yeah, she wanted in.

And when you added in the petty joy that would come from the chance to get on-site and beat the museum to the catalog of the find as well as its overall authentication, she'd be damned if she stayed out of this project.

"I'm not sure if I think you're terrifyingly brilliant or brilliantly terrifying." Kensington walked back into the room and crossed toward the credenza on the far wall for more coffee.

"Can't I be both?"

"I thought you were going to brush him off like lint."

"Aside from the fact that I don't think Finn Gallagher brushes easily, there's no way I'm passing this up."

"Ro." Kensington took her seat once more, a sudden seriousness painting her features as her blue gaze turned solemn. "You need to be careful."

"I will be."

"Really careful. There are a lot of players in this one with a lot invested in the outcome."

"I'm invested, too. This is a major discovery."

"That's my point."

Rowan fought to keep the frustration from her voice, opting for what she hoped was a more persuasive tone. "This is the perfect blend of my professional expertise and the types of assignments we take on here. I'd be a fool to pass it up."

"Please just promise me you'll be careful."

"I'm always careful."

"No, you're not." That serious expression was back, and much as she wanted to argue with Kenzi, on some level Rowan refused to lie.

She did take risks and she always had.

While she had given up stealing after that night in the Warrington house, she'd never given up the thrill of the hunt. And archaeology had given her an outlet for that.

Great finds.

The potential for danger.

And the deep understanding of how the mind of a thief worked had come in handy on more than one occasion.

Because she knew how to case a place—how to find its weak points and devise a plan to get in and out—she knew how to find the thieves that regularly attacked locations of value.

"I'd say it's a family trait we all have in spades."

* * *

Jared Wright reviewed the report from the Valley of the Queens and marveled at the sheer stupidity of his contact at the Cairo Museum. He'd ensured a local was on the job within days of the discovery of a cache of royal jewels, yet it didn't seem to be helping. The team from the British Museum had the inside track and had managed to get the site locked up tight as a drum.

He needed a way in.

His phone beeped and he glanced down at the screen. The words *New Player* flashed before the screen faded to black. He did a quick screen swipe and typed in his ten-digit password—you could never be too careful—before accessing the message.

J:
Some old friends are headed to Luxor. Seems the duo on the Victoria Project are back in business together. Talk soon.
M

The news had a ready sense of anticipation flooding his veins as he reread the message.

Although he'd kept tabs on the two kids who'd taken the Queen Victoria bracelet years ago, he'd never done more than keep watch. The boy hadn't been worth his time and when he'd discovered a few weeks after the heist the kid had had the fortitude to live, he'd given him the benefit of the doubt. They'd never found the bracelet when they searched him and he was too small-time to ultimately be worth his time.

The girl, on the other hand…

It had taken some doing to track her down, but when he finally figured out who she was, he backed off all the way. He was building an empire and it would have done him no good to go up against the Steele family. *Especially* if he'd garnered the scrutiny and attention of the British government should the girl have gone missing. No, Jared had washed his hands of the entire mess.

Oddly enough, the bracelet had never hit the market and he also suspected that night had been the last heist Rowan Steele had ever tried. None of his surveillance had turned up her involvement in anything further, and when she finally went off to college and then spent several years on archaeology sites, he stopped focusing on her.

His network kept tabs and that was all that was needed.

The fact she was working on the Valley of the Queens project wasn't all that surprising. The archaeology community was strong, and Rowan was well respected.

But what was she doing reteaming with Gallagher?

Jared turned the puzzle over in his mind as he tapped out a response.

FOLLOW THEM.

He already had a buyer lined up for the results of the tomb; chief among the coveted items was a set of bracelets and a necklace made entirely of lapis lazuli, purported to be Nefertari's wedding set.

And what a strange coincidence it all was.

Jared shook his head, setting the phone back on the desk as he stood to pace. He'd learned long ago there weren't any coincidences.

So the real question was, who was playing who?

Rowan stared out the window of the external elevator as she was whisked the twenty stories up for Gallagher International's main offices. The London skyline spread out before her and she saw the Gherkin in the distance, the large, egg-shaped building that had become a fixture in the city's skyline a decade before.

The elevator came to a smooth stop and she stepped out onto plush carpeting. She had to give Finn credit, the selection of office space in London's most recent architectural accomplishment, the Shard, gave a sense of quiet flash and competent business acumen. And she was thrilled to make her first visit to the impressive building.

Her brother Liam had BASE jumped it while it was under construction and she'd been jealous at the time. Now after actually visiting—and considering the size and shape of the building—she decided she'd leave the truly idiotic yearnings for adventure fully to her oldest sibling.

Finn waved at her from a glass-enclosed office. She watched him work his way from the office, down a short hallway before moving into the reception area to greet her. The wide-open space—the windows on the far side of the building were visible through the glass of Finn's office—was impressive.

And lent a curious air of trust at the truly open design.

She watched him move, the vague sense she'd felt in the conference room a few days before taking better shape in her mind.

He was an attractive man—powerfully so—and an impressive one, too. His shoulders filled out the Savile Row suit to perfection and she could see the slim taper of his waist where the jacket hung open before he closed it with a dapper twist of a button.

His chiseled jaw, thick sandy brown hair and ready smile gave the vague sense of an impish child even as the fine lines of the suit suggested he wasn't someone to be toyed with. When she also considered the clear signs of intelligence that sparked in his voice with every comment, Rowan could only admit Finn Gallagher was one impressive package.

She'd have to be stupid not to feel some sense of attraction to the man.

And she was very rarely stupid.

That long-ago night on Bethany Warrington's roof flew through her mind but she ignored it in favor of focusing on the warm hazel eyes that drew her attention first.

"Rowan. Thank you for coming."

His large hands enveloped hers before he leaned forward into the customary European kiss on both cheeks. The lightest slide of his beard—the day's growth just beginning to show—met her lips and she couldn't deny the rush of attraction that slid down her spine at the masculine scent that surrounded her. A touch of cedar over the fresh scent of the outdoors.

Delicious.

Just like the man himself.

She allowed herself the briefest moment to enjoy the contact by making a full turn around the lobby. "Impressive office space. I wasn't even aware the building was fully occupied yet."

"We got in early. I knew what I wanted in terms of space and it's been everything I've hoped it would be."

She didn't miss the flash of pride that lit his eyes and couldn't argue with the sentiment. There was something thrilling about seeing the results of your efforts and hard work.

That thrill had been the most unexpected joy after she'd come back to the land of the living. The transformation had taken time—and a lot of work with a therapist to understand her inner urges to steal—but she'd made a commitment to her grandfather and she wasn't going to change it.

And she was proud to know she'd come out the other side. "What's that smile for?"

She glanced around the office once more before smoothly sharing her more casual thoughts from the elevator ride. "I was just thinking of my brother. I'm pretty sure he BASE jumped here."

"We both did."

"You jumped off the building?"

"Yep."

"Together?"

"No. Despite knowing his reputation, I've never met your brother."

"Why would you do something like that?"

He shrugged but she saw that spark of pride flare up once more. "Because it was here."

"I suppose that's as good an answer as any."

They both lingered for a moment, awareness filling the small space between them. Rowan had changed for the visit, her peasant blouse and jeans traded for a plum-colored power suit that would rival anything in Kensington's closet, and she was suddenly aware of the tight stricture of her skirt as she fought to keep her breath even.

The moment lingered a few seconds longer before the rich tones of his voice broke the silence. "I'm happy to take you on a tour or we can head on down to the labs."

The focus on business helped and Rowan clung to that like a lifeline. Her anticipation for the office visit had grown over the past few days as she'd read several reports he'd sent in advance. His facilities were state-of-the-art, some of the equipment so new she'd only read about it. "I'm sure the labs will frame up the majority of my questions. Why don't we start there?"

He extended a hand toward the hallway he'd come

through. "Let's take the stairs. They're next to the windows, so you can at least get a view of Tower Bridge and the Tower of London before we go down to the lab."

"Nothing like a midday view of one of the city's most notorious spots for executions." She'd meant it as a joke more than anything else—a moment to break the tension that gripped both of them—but his reaction caught her up short.

Those compelling hazel eyes widened momentarily in surprise before narrowing in thought as they strolled toward the bank of windows. "That's funny. I usually have a completely different reaction when I look at it."

"You don't think of beheaded queens and kidnapped princes?"

He stopped and turned toward her as they stepped up to the outer glass window to look out at the city below. "I realize they're a part of the Tower's rich and storied history, but I can't honestly say that's the first thing that comes to mind."

"What does come to mind then?"

The distinct notes of passion and the slightest touch of avarice—like a man viewing his lover's body for the first time—lit up the depths of his eyes, turning them a rich moss-green. "The Crown Jewels, of course."

Chapter 4

Finn searched for any hint of awareness in Rowan's vivid blue eyes, but there were none. All he saw reflected back was that same bright curiosity that had captured him from the first.

There was a vibrancy about her, the energy humming under her skin strangely intoxicating. He'd met few people in his life who seemed as if they burned for their next adventure, excitement for life thrumming in their veins. It practically pulsed off Rowan Steele like a live wire sparking in the rain.

"What makes you think of the Crown Jewels first?" Her voice broke his reverie and Finn pulled himself back to their conversation. "Doesn't the history intrigue you?"

"Absolutely. Political executions, state secrets and kidnapped royalty are fascinating and all deeply important during the point in time in which they happened. But all of them take a backseat to the Crown Jewels."

"How so?"

How did he explain it?

While he led a life of material wealth, he'd never considered himself ruled by it. He was as comfortable with a backpack and a pair of sturdy boots as he traipsed through the jungle as he was in his expansive London flat, several floors up from the office. He likely smelled better when he stayed home, he thought with a rueful smile, but he enjoyed both equally. "Those jewels represent something far more lasting than the people who wear them."

"Yes, but political intrigue and the lives of rulers live on in our history books."

"Of course, but people still come and go, no matter how famous, how royal or politically savvy. They're footnotes in history books, memories written down and told. But those jewels remain forever."

"Is that why you love antiquities? The link to the past?"

"And to the future." Finn gestured toward the door to the lab. "Come on, I'll show you what we've got."

He leaned forward into the retinal scanner that sat next to the lab door, then pressed his palm to a small pad. The lock snicked softly, the red light sitting above it flashing to green. "After you."

"Impressive security."

"Necessary security."

"No doubt." She walked ahead of him and he couldn't keep his gaze from skimming over her thin frame. The suit she wore fit her perfectly, and it was easy to see the lithe strength underneath the plum-colored silk. Her skirt fell to a tasteful length above her knee—a shame it wasn't shorter, Finn couldn't help thinking—before exposing spectacular calves that flowed into four-inch heels.

The entire package screamed competent businesswoman, but he also knew her reputation. That same backpack-carrying, boot-clad vision he kept of himself was an apt description for Rowan from all accounts. The reports of her exploits for the past decade indicated the woman was as comfortable in pearls and an evening gown as she was in a tank top, shorts and hiking boots.

And she switched effortlessly between both sides of her life.

A sharp intake of breath pulled his attention off her body as she swung around to look at him. "This is yours?"

"Yes."

She danced backward on her heels, the excitement he'd sensed before amping up as she practically ran to the long steel counters that lined the perimeter of the room. "You can do carbon dating here?"

"Yes."

"Do you have an electron microscope?"

"Off-site. While this building offers many wonderful advantages, it's too high to realistically ground the equipment. We house the microscope off-site with another lab we have about twenty kilometers outside the city."

"Wow." That single word, full of reverence, had his body tightening in anticipation.

Had he ever seen a woman that excited about a piece of technology? Moreover, had he ever felt like a conquering hero simply because he owned one?

Fascinated, he watched as she worked her way down the rows, her smile broad and her questions pointed as she stopped to talk to a few of his researchers before she returned to his side.

"I realize you're considered foremost in your field, but even you can't possibly have enough work to keep the lab busy? There aren't enough dig sites to keep a facility this size active."

He led her toward another set of doors, her attention

shifting toward him as they walked. "We take on work from museums, auction houses, educational facilities. It's been a key piece of my business strategy, to provide a top-notch facility so they can outsource their lab needs."

"Smart."

"And highly lucrative. The investment in equipment has paid dividends several times over."

Finn gestured toward a waiting elevator. "You ready to go up? I'd like to go over my plans for the trip."

"You mean the trip where we may or may not steal several ancient artifacts?"

A vivid light twinkled in the depths of her blue gaze and Finn fought the urge to move toward her. "That'd be the one."

"Perfect. I've got a few ideas of my own on that, starting with a way around that toady Baxter Monroe."

He gestured her back off the elevator and toward his office. "You don't like the intrepid leader of our dig? We will be working under him for the next few weeks."

The light snort would have been clue enough, but it was the vitriol that dripped from Rowan's words that had him taking real notice. "He couldn't dig his way to anything but more dirt if it weren't for all that family money he throws around. He's useless, and I don't speak that harshly about many people."

"What has he done to get your back up?"

"He nearly destroyed a series of relics in Iran a few years ago. He claimed his experience in Egypt made him a natural for any work in the Middle East and handled several ancient Persian relics like a two-year-old on a sugar bender. The man is a menace and for the life of me I can't understand why the museum keeps him on staff."

Finn couldn't hold back the smile as he opened his office door, standing back so she could walk in first. "So that means you have no interest in attending his launch party this evening?"

Rowan turned on her heel, the move as smooth as her near-pirouette in the lab. "Launch party?"

"He holds one before every major project starts."

"You party with the man?"

"Hardly. I have about as much respect for him as you do, perhaps less since I was called in by the prime minister to mediate that little Iranian situation he created. But I'm a firm believer in that old adage."

Her eyebrows arched over those fierce blue eyes, that sharp gaze sexy as hell. "Let me guess. 'Keep your friends close'?"

Finn nodded, an image of Baxter Monroe firmly in his mind's eye. "'And your enemies closer.'"

Rowan glanced around her well-appointed hotel suite as the bellman made quick work of her bags. She had to give Finn Gallagher credit, the man did know how to impress. Her suite at the Savoy was subtly appointed, yet it spoke of wealth and influence. It was also eminently practical, since Monroe was holding his launch party here at the hotel.

She'd had the requisite twinges of guilt at not informing her grandparents she'd be in town, but had tamped down on them at the evidence Finn expected her time on the job to include evening events.

She tipped the bellman and ushered him out before turning her attention toward the evening's events. The concept of a launch party stuck in her stomach like a ball of lead, but she willed it aside. The event had no bearing on the serious work that should be taking place in the Valley of the Queens, but it would do what Finn had suggested.

Allow her to size up her enemy.

The fact the event was a social one *and* on Baxter Monroe's turf was a small side benefit, guaranteed to make him relaxed and approachable. The very daring neckline of the gown she'd brought with her was another plus and she knew she had another weapon in her arsenal.

The phone buzzed from the depths of her oversize purse and Rowan dug it out, pleased she caught it in time before the caller went to voice mail. "Hey, big sis. You checking up on me?"

"Of course." Kensington's tone was sharp and matter-of-fact. Rowan couldn't keep the smile from blooming on her face as she imagined her sister seated behind her ruthlessly organized desk. "I wanted to see how your meeting went with Gallagher."

"The man can do his own carbon dating. I practically had an orgasm in his lab just thinking about it."

"Don't you think you should save that until you know him a bit better?"

Rowan did laugh at her sister's dry tone before she outlined all that she'd learned while visiting Gallagher International. "So tonight's a party with the museum crew."

"I won't even ask your feelings on that. You may be three thousand miles away, but your voice drips with loathing and a scathing disdain I can only admire."

"It's an archaeological dig, for Pete's sake, not a party. The fact Monroe's even throwing one is further proof of what a world-class jerk he is."

"Yes, but you *will* mingle and be charming."

Rowan fought the urge to grit her teeth. "Am I anything but?"

"Did you bring a dress?"

"Yes, I brought a dress."

"Because I told you to."

"I'm hanging up."

"Wait! Rowan, please." When she hesitated, Kensington pushed on. "Be careful tonight. Something's felt a little off about this from the first."

"You don't trust Finn?"

"We don't know him to trust him. But I do know I don't trust the situation."

"I hardly think I'm in much danger attending a party at the Savoy."

"Just stay sharp."

The urge to tease her sister or tell her to quit the melodramatic directives was high, but something held Rowan back. Whether it was a sixth sense or something else, she didn't know, but the light brush of nerves along her spine had agreement rising up in her tone. "I will."

"Love you."

"Love you, too, Ken-zoo." The tease was nearly as old as she was, a funny back-and-forth she had had with her sister since they were small. Another wave of nerves layered over the first as they disconnected the call, and Rowan fought to shake it off.

There was nothing to be worried about. Nothing at all.

Rowan was still trying to convince herself of that an hour later as she wended her way through the lobby of the Savoy toward a small gathering room chosen for the party. While Kensington had the sisterly ability to mix smug satisfaction with older-sibling order giving, Rowan had to admit the snug black cocktail dress she now wore in place of her plum suit was an inspired last-minute packing choice.

A packing choice she'd have overlooked had it not been for her sister, she admitted to herself as she came to a stop inside the entryway.

The same lush accommodations she'd experienced upstairs were even more impressive here. Various servers circulated through the room, their trays full of champagne or canapés. The crowd stood in elegant conversation circles, evidenced by the muted hum of voices that rose up around her as she moved farther into the room.

"Ms. Steele," a low voice whispered in her ear, a split second after she'd felt the sheer heft of his body sidle up against hers. "You look beautiful this evening."

"Thank you." The words nearly stuck in her throat as she caught full sight of Finn Gallagher in a crisp black suit. Broad shoulders filled up her gaze as she turned to face him and once again she was struck by the incredible vision he made.

He had nearly flawless features; the only criticism she could even muster up was that they were almost too sharp—too harsh—to be handsome. Yet even as she thought it, her conscience fought her, reminding her it was that very trait that screamed masculine perfection.

She could picture him in the jungle just as easily as she saw him in the designer suit that covered his impressive form. Regardless of the situation—rugged or refined— both telegraphed the exact same thing. Finn Gallagher would be a formidable opponent.

A man who inevitably got what he came for.

And why did the suddenly delicious thought flutter through her mind that she would love to be the object of that intense focus?

She'd been raised around strong men. Both her father and her grandfather were formidable in their own right, and her brothers, Liam and Campbell, had followed family tradition. While each of her brothers had their own individual style, both epitomized the strong, self-assured male.

Having been brought up that way, she respected men

who knew how to go after what they wanted. She respected them even more if they admired that trait in her.

One look into Finn Gallagher's deep hazel eyes and she saw flashes of that respect layered under the distinct notes of male appreciation and attraction, and it drew her in.

"I know he's not your favorite person, but Baxter did order the best champagne." Finn held a full flute of the pale liquid toward her. "It'd be a shame to let it go to waste."

"True." She accepted the glass, bemused when Finn lifted his flute in toast. "Now you're going to force me to celebrate Monroe's generosity, too?"

"I'd prefer to think of this as a toast to our partnership."

Rowan lifted her glass. "May it bear the most ancient of fruits."

She didn't miss the subtle lift of his eyebrows over the rim of his glass, but other than that, Finn didn't cop to any other response. She took a sip of her champagne, the bubbles light and crisp on her tongue. "Damn, but he did choose the good stuff."

"How else do you suppose he's going to impress a room full of his top patrons?"

"Is that how you got in on the dig?"

"I don't need to wine and dine slimy toadies like Baxter Monroe to sell my services." He hesitated for a moment before flashing a quick, wolfish grin. "I do, however, spend considerable time wooing his bosses."

"No one argues with the moneyman." Rowan thought about her afternoon visit to Gallagher International. "Or the man with the fancy research lab."

"Spot-on you are."

"I think I'm beginning to get a picture." Rowan took another sip of her champagne as she glanced around the room. "You ensure the top museum brass have an unlimited supply of what they need, namely money and access to research services, and in exchange, it allows you to keep tabs on Monroe and his activities."

"Spot-on again."

"And keeping tabs also ensures you have a place on the digs, whether Monroe wants you there or not."

"Now you're just showing off." The cocky grin was back, along with that distinct layer of respect in his gaze. "Well, then. Are you ready to go have some fun?"

"At this event?"

"Of course."

She paused a moment, pleased when Finn's gaze darkened with that tantalizing attraction that hummed subtly between them. "There's a phrase in America. It's called poking the bear in his den."

"You're suggesting Monroe's the bear in this delightful Mark Twain-esque colloquialism?"

"Yep."

Finn extended his arm and Rowan took it, his hard strength more than evident through the sleeve of his suit jacket. She fought the urge to cling to those delectable muscles, instead nodding in the direction of Baxter Monroe. "Allow me to lead the way."

Finn gave himself the momentary gift of simply drinking her in, before he moved them deftly through the ballroom. The woman cut an incredible figure, the black dress clinging to each and every curve she possessed. If her plum suit from earlier had twisted him in knots, the black cocktail dress had him engulfed in flames.

She was stunning. Her pert features—already maximized by the short cap of hair that covered her head—stood out without the need for much fuss. Her makeup was minimal, the natural flush of her cheeks a sign of her vitality. The gamine cut of her hair had a secondary benefit—her neck and shoulders were fully exposed. The slender curve of her neck drew his gaze and he imagined pressing a line of kisses there, flicking his tongue lightly against her skin with the sole purpose of making her shiver.

The image gripped him as he placed his near-empty glass on the tray of a passing waiter. Finn laid his hand over hers, pleased by the light jolt that rattled through his body at the contact. The shudder of her arm where it threaded through his only reinforced she was as affected as he was.

He took pleasure from the thought, surprised when a quick flash of memory rose up swift and strong. The same woman, clad all in black, pressing her lips to his.

He wanted to kiss her again. Wanted to see if the lush memory he'd kept all these years was nearly as satisfying as he remembered. Wanted to know if there was a way to replicate something that sweet and innocent, yet carnal and almost desperate with need.

"I wasn't sure you'd make it." Baxter's voice broke the moment, and thoughts of kissing Rowan Steele vanished at the very clear evidence they were both "on." The hand that had reflexively tightened on his arm with attraction tightened once more, this time in a subtle anger that practically vibrated from her.

He disengaged their linked arms, shifting his hand to the small of her back, and pulled her a fraction of an inch closer, whether in protection or possession, Finn didn't know. "Baxter."

Monroe turned to face Rowan. "And Miss Steele? I understand you'll be joining us in the Valley of the Queens. I'm delighted."

"Likewise."

"When did you arrive in town?"

The forced conversation spun out and Finn was amused to watch how elegantly Rowan played her mark. She kept up the polite facade, never breaking eye contact or the subtle hints of flirtation until she went in for the kill. "I understand the site's discovery was something of a surprise."

Baxter's laugh did nothing to hide the stiff lines of his face. "Hardly. What would give you that idea?"

"Just some things I've heard."

"That's hard to imagine. The museum was doing routine restoration in Nefertari's burial chamber. We've always had reason to believe there was something else there and the time was ripe to explore. It's as simple as that."

"Fascinating." Rowan shook her head, her voice still layered in polite platitudes. If Finn didn't see her vivid blue, predatory gaze with his own eyes, he'd likely not have believed the small, genteel woman was capable of what came next.

"Yes, it is."

"And here I thought this incredible discovery was all because you got your panties in a twist and tossed a small, pointed archaeology trowel across a priceless burial chamber."

"Of all…" the man sputtered, the pale skin of his neck growing red.

"You then forced one of your lackeys to go pick it up before anyone could possibly snap a photo of the tossed object. Isn't that right, Baxter?"

"Gossip and innuendo."

"Yes, well, in my experience, nearly all gossip and innuendo has a grain or two of truth in it."

The red flooding Baxter's face shifted as his rolling

gaze locked on to Rowan's. "If that's true, then surely you're well aware of the rumors that follow you, Miss Steele."

Finn fought the immediate and urgent need to get in between the two of them as Rowan leaned into Baxter's personal space. "Then you *are* familiar with my reputation. I'm delighted to hear it. I expect you'll be on your best behavior when we go to Egypt, then."

"I'm interested in preserving the site and whatever we recover from the chamber."

"As am I."

"Then we're obviously on the same page."

"See that we stay there."

Baxter avoided any pretense of a polite departure as he turned on his heel and crossed the room toward the bar. From the widening eyes of the bartender, Finn could only assume the drink request was given in a harsh bark.

With a sly smile he couldn't have held back if he tried, Finn turned his gaze toward Rowan. "I can't say I understand your motives but I do like your style."

"I told you I didn't like him."

"There's subtle disdain and then there's barely veiled hatred."

"I prefer to think of it as a preemptive strike." Rowan's smile was broad as she gestured toward the door. "Let's get out of here."

Finn was rarely taken off guard, so the obvious invitation in her words caught him up short. "Where do you want go?"

"Have you ever been to the British Museum after hours?"

He had, in fact, been there on more than one occasion, but he wasn't about to tell her that. "Now, what would a nice girl like you be wanting in a place like that?"

"I can think of a few things."

He could think of several himself, but again, Finn thought it wise to avoid that topic. "The museum opens tomorrow morning at 10:00 a.m. sharp. I can have a car arranged to pick you up, deliver you and wait for you as long as you'd like."

"What happened to that adventurous spirit, Finn?" Rowan moved in, the light scent of her wrapping around his senses as the heat of her body assailed him through his suit. "You know, the one that had you making those idiotic jumps off your office building?"

"There were far fewer cameras recording that idiocy."

"We can get around those."

"And the guards with guns?"

She waved a hand. "Easy."

"What are we waiting for, then?" Finn held out a hand, barely suppressing the urge to wrap her in his arms. "Lead the way."

Chapter 5

The party played out just as Jared Wright had expected it would. Several hundred stuffy intellectuals standing around eating canapés, talking about the world and doing very little living in it. He stood at the fringes and couldn't fully hold back the sneer at how they all sipped their wine and put on pompous airs, their conversations swirling as if the fate of the world hung on their overeducated heads.

If they only knew.

His gaze shifted to Baxter Monroe. The man had one job to do, and from the miserable look on his face after he stalked away from Finn Gallagher and Rowan Steele, he had slacked off on the job. Damn it.

He'd spent years getting Monroe right where he wanted him, along with several top brass at the museum. Jared knew his deep pockets were a perfect match for certain…*appetites,* and he'd invested wisely. But none of it did him any damn good if his point man fouled up the job in Egypt.

Shifting his gaze from Baxter Monroe, he watched the couple slip from the small ballroom. It was curious to see them back together after all this time. Did it mean anything?

His contacts had indicated the two were working together, but their body language suggested something more intimate. Suggested they were a pair.

Although he'd disregarded the notion years before that they had worked the Warringtons' as a pair—and all intel gathered after the debacle with the Victoria bracelet suggested they hadn't—he couldn't deny something seemed to simmer between the couple.

Interesting.

He slipped his phone from his pocket and issued instructions to one of his men waiting, even now, in his car.

Guests departing now. FOLLOW THEM.

"Wright."

John Bauer's bright and clueless smile greeted Jared as he looked up from his phone. "Good to see you, John."

"Didn't expect to see you here. I called your office earlier this week. Thought you were out of the country."

"My meetings wrapped early and I jumped at the chance to spend a few days at home."

John's gaze drifted around the room as he snagged a glass of champagne from a passing waiter. As soon as the man was out of earshot, John moved a fraction closer. "I dropped the suggestions to Gallagher like you asked me to."

"Did you, now? How were they received?"

"With laughter, just as you thought. Seems as if your friend would prefer his extracurricular activities didn't receive any notice. Brushed off the Indiana Jones reference with a sly smile and a glib line."

Jared took a sip of his own champagne. "Understandable."

"My firm is looking forward to the upcoming sale of whatever is recovered from the Valley of the Queens. Auctions full of Egyptian artifacts draw special attention."

Jared nodded, the not-so-subtle reference to the man's upcoming take in exchange for his assistance more than clear. "I can trust you to handle the next phase of things here in London?"

"Of course."

"I look forward to the auction. I'm sure it will be the highlight of your schedule next summer."

Rowan watched Finn from the corner of her eye and wondered at his reticence to accompany her on their late-night adventure. Despite the stupidity of suggesting they break into the British Museum, the taunt had seemed like a strong tactic to suss him out.

For reasons she couldn't fully define, something about the man seemed familiar.

Too familiar.

Which was only further proof her lingering fascination with the young boy who'd fallen during the Warrington job had taken on near-mythic importance in her mind.

Rowan did her level best to brush off the strange thoughts, unwilling to dwell too closely on indiscretions best left in the past and instead pulled a small laminated card from her purse.

"Good evening, Miss Steele." The guard who stood at the museum's entrance nodded his head, waving them both through. "Mr. Gallagher."

"So this is what you meant?" Finn waved his own card, identical to hers, before he shoved his back into his wallet.

"You've got one, too."

"Of course."

"They don't give these out to just anybody."

"Well, then." Finn leaned in and squeezed her shoulders, the sensation shooting a small line of sparks down her spine. "It's a good thing we're not anybody."

Rowan shook her head but couldn't hold back the smile. "And here I thought you were up for a small game of breaking and entering."

"But it's so much easier to simply have special access."

Rowan knew he was right, but couldn't stop the kernel of disappointment that her ploy to figure out if he was the young man from her past had backfired. No matter how many ways she tried to look at it, she couldn't shake the fact that Finn Gallagher pushed her buttons and made her remember things best forgotten.

Because try as she might to ignore it, something about him made her think he *might* be the boy she'd left at the bottom of the Warringtons' back patio all those years ago.

Of course, it wasn't exactly something you asked a person. *Oh ho, there. So I was wondering if you ever tried to rob a Knightsbridge townhome.*

To borrow a phrase her grandfather was rather fond of, not bloody likely.

"What was so urgent we needed to come here tonight?"

Rowan moved at a steady clip through the Great Court, her heels tapping lightly on the marble floor. Darkness flooded the sky above them, visible through the glass panels in the roof. "Room 4 is one of the most popular areas of the museum."

Finn nodded, his understanding immediate. "And you'd like a private viewing?"

"Let's just say I love my fellow man in principle, but when I can jump the line, I'm all too willing."

She felt the light caress on her shoulder as they came to a stop in front of the Egyptian Sculpture Gallery. Although the museum boasted several popular rooms housing Egyptian antiquities, this one was by far the most favored—and most visited—due to the fact it housed the Rosetta stone.

"You shouldn't need to wait." He traced her collarbone with the tip of one finger and Rowan could have sworn her stomach had just dropped out of the center of her body.

Attraction washed through her system in hard, chopping waves of need, and her legs trembled as they stood at the entrance to Room 4. Their gazes locked as he dropped his hand from her shoulder, and Rowan couldn't hold back the rush of disappointment at the loss of contact.

With what she hoped was a casual move, she took a step closer. "It's always more fun to have something unique and special all to yourself."

His gaze darkened, the hazel flashing over to a deep golden-brown. Once more, his hand returned to her shoulder, this time settling at the base of her neck. With gentle movements, he leaned in, his lips whisper soft against her ear. "I couldn't agree more."

Another wave of delicious shivers racked her system, and even as her body leaned toward his, more than willing to enjoy the moment, her mind screamed at her in protest.

What had possibly possessed her to go down this path? They were business associates, working on a high-profile—and potentially dangerous—job. She needed to keep her wits about her, and instead she was letting her hormones do the talking.

"Let's get to it, then."

Humor had the corners of his eyes crinkling as he smiled, but he gave no other reaction as he stepped back. "Lead the way."

Rowan walked past the Rosetta stone, stopping briefly to look at one of the world's most famous artifacts. The words on the stone registered in her mind as she read the decree from King Ptolemy V. *"In the reign of the young one..."*

"Can you read it?" Finn's question pulled Rowan from her perusal.

"Yes."

"All three languages?"

The briefest flush of embarrassment had heat creeping into her cheeks. "I'm not great at Demotic, but yes, I can read all three."

"That's incredible."

"You don't read hieroglyphics?"

Finn shook his head, the regret clear in his voice. "I've never learned. I'm incredibly impressed you can."

The genuine appreciation in his gaze lit her up, and the warmth of embarrassment changed into something else.

Excitement.

While she didn't lack for male attention, her agile mind and constant travel didn't lend itself to many long-term relationships. And she'd discovered all too early that few men wanted to sit across a dinner table discussing Egyptian relics, ancient Persian dig sites or Mayan ruins.

And no one she'd ever met had ever quite lived up to the young man in the mask who'd kept her safe on the worst night of her life.

"Is this why we're here?"

"No." Rowan shook her head, pulling herself from the distracted thoughts. Comparing Finn to old dates—or to a young man from a long-ago night—ran the risk of putting too much emphasis on the personal aspects of this trip and not nearly enough focus on why they were together. The find in Nefertari's tomb was under threat of theft and they needed to be prepared to defend it.

That was the reason she was here, and she'd do well to remember their trip required her full focus. "The bust of Ramesses II is at the end of the room."

"Of course. The *Younger Memnon* statue. And Nefertari's husband."

"Exactly."

"You think there's something on the statue?"

"It can't hurt to take a look. Nefertari was one of several wives, but she was purported to be the woman he loved."

"The statue's been studied extensively. Do you really think there's something there?"

"There are hieroglyphs running down the back of the statue. As I remember, it's basically the name and title of the king, and there's a dedication to Amun-Ra. I'm curious if there's anything else."

"He was quite the prolific king." Finn's large form kept pace with hers as they moved through the large hall. Priceless statues surrounded them and it pained her to pass by them so quickly, but it wasn't time for a leisurely perusal.

"He fathered eighty-five children."

His grin was quick, his white teeth flashing in the subdued night-lighting in the room. "That, too. But I meant that he was also politically savvy. He understood the benefit of putting images of himself all over Egypt. Hence the volume of statues that bear his likeness. And he also had one of the longest reigns in Egyptian history. Well over sixty-five years."

"You know your Egyptology."

"Right back at ya, Miss Steele."

"It's fascinated me since I was little." They came to a stop at the base of the statue, and as the bust of Ramesses II rose above them, she thought of her youth. Of the hours she'd spent poring over the books and photos in her grandfather's library and the great joy she found visiting the museum on rainy Sundays, her hand wrapped in his.

Egyptology was a passion they shared, and Alexander Steele could always be counted on for a rousing discussion on ancient antiquities or the interpretation of historic texts. "And I come by it honestly. My grandfather is a rabid hobbyist."

"I'd wager most archaeologists can trace their fascination to their earliest school days, learning about the pyramids."

"Everybody loves a good pyramid. Add a mummy or two and it makes it even better."

Finn tugged on his tie, the move shockingly sexy as he stared up at the immense bust and head of the ancient pharaoh. "Hollywood's version does tend to focus a bit too heavily on the curse aspects, and decades of books and movies have framed how the public thinks of Egypt. Curses and mummies and ancient viziers bent on destruction."

Finn's words faded to a dull roar as Rowan simply drank him in. The tie was gone and his crisp white shirt was open at the collar, exposing his throat. A light chill ran the length of her spine at the strong frame of his jaw and the firm lines of his neck. Goodness, the man was gorgeous.

Brushing off that damnable pull of attraction, Rowan

pulled her phone from her purse and opened up the camera icon. She *had* to get her head in the game. Had to *focus*.

"You okay?"

She looked up from her phone screen at the concern in his voice. "Of course. Why?"

"You looked upset all of a sudden."

"No." She mentally hunted for a topic, settling on something he'd just mentioned. As responses went it was fairly lame, but it kept her from admitting the truth. Somehow telling him she was fantasizing about running her lips over his neck while unbuttoning his shirt wasn't the best way to kick off their partnership. "I think you're right about the public's perception of Egypt. It's why this gallery is the most popular in the museum. Everyone loves to imagine the Egypt of myth, full of flowery and dramatic overtones."

"I don't think the Egyptian tourist board minds much."

"No, but it does diminish the region's rich history."

"That's why we do what we do."

Rowan was caught by his comment. "How do you mean?"

"The myths of ancient Egypt might have been what got me into what I'm doing, but it's the reality of preserving pieces of history that keeps me in the game."

"That's rather poetic."

That grin flashed once again. "It's also rather lucrative, so I can hardly complain. I'm one of the lucky people who gets to combine what I love with my career. It doesn't get much better than that."

"No, it doesn't." She took a few steps around the base of the statue until she could look up at the vertical rows of hieroglyphs that ran along the back of the statue and extended her phone toward Finn. "You're taller. Can you take some photos for me?"

Even with Finn's added height—nearly a foot on her—the statue was considerably higher than both of them. He took the phone, his large fingers brushing over hers as he took the small device. All her effort to disregard his effect on her fled at the warmth of his touch.

Electricity ran the length of her arm and she couldn't stop the desperate urge to look at him. Those large shoulders, framed by the tailored cut of his suit jacket, held her attention longer than was necessary. Nor was it professional.

But it was the raw hunger in his gaze that prevented her from looking away. His observation was that of a lover—complete and absolute—and Rowan fought another shiver as that sultry stare came to rest on her lips. Something flashed in his eyes—regret?—before he turned away from her and lifted the phone. "Let me take a few and you can look at them to see if they're what you need."

"Of course."

Even though the statue was still too high to get a full-on photo, Finn's longer reach enabled him to get the majority of the writing in view. "Here. See what we've got and if you can do anything with these."

Rowan flipped through the images Finn had captured, discarding a blurry one and another that didn't fully capture the hieroglyps in the frame. It was as she came to the last two photos, though, that she knew he'd captured what she needed. "These are great. I've got the full inscription."

"What's it say?"

"Pretty much what's been reported. His name and title are included along with a dedication to Amun-Ra."

"That makes sense. Worship of Amun-Ra was at its height during the reign of Ramesses and his father, Seti the first."

Rowan expanded the images on the phone, manipulating the screen until she could see several of the glyphs near the bottom. "The last few glyphs suggest something more personal."

"Can you read it?"

"It's a little faint and I'd like to compare it to some textbooks."

"This statue has been evaluated top to bottom, for nearly two centuries. It's not possible that no one's figured the words mean anything more than a listing of his accomplishments and a prayer."

A dull excitement throbbed in her veins. It was the knowledge that something was just out of reach. "No one's discovered the secret cache in Nefertari's tomb before, either."

"You think there's something more to it?"

The jovial camaraderie she'd felt from Finn since they'd entered the Egyptian hall had vanished, replaced with something darker. More serious.

"If I'm understanding the glyphs correctly, this provides incontrovertible proof that Nefertari was his beloved wife."

"But history has always been clear on that. He had several wives, as was custom, but Nefertari was his great love."

How did she explain what was a sense more than anything else? "Yes, but it looks like marriage markings. Likely the same markings we'll see on the wedding cache. It'll be a key piece in the authentication."

"We already know that. The one thing everyone's been clear on from the beginning is that the tomb is original and, up until now, undiscovered." Finn's eyes narrowed. "What aren't you telling me?"

"So you know how I was sort of making fun of how Hollywood has glamorized Egypt?"

"Sure. Ancient pharaohs and mummy resurrections and the like."

"Well, if I'm reading everything correctly, among other things there's a curse on the wedding cache."

"You can't seriously expect me to believe you believe that."

Finn watched those slim shoulders stiffen before she let out a delicate shrug. "It's not about what we believe. It's about those who are trying to get their hands on it."

Whatever he'd expected, Rowan's harebrained revelation had turned every expectation he'd had for the evening on its ear. "Why don't you start at the beginning? We're not here for fun this evening, are we?"

"No."

"Rowan—"

She held up a hand. "Look. Can we get out of here first? We've been on every camera in this place for the last twenty minutes."

"You think someone's watching us?"

"We can't discount it."

"If you were worried about being watched, we could have played this a hell of a lot differently." His words came out on a growl, and the fierce stabs of anger at the idea she might be in danger surprised him in its ferocity.

"How so?"

Whether it was that simmering frustration or his sheer inability to stop thinking about getting his hands on her, Finn didn't know.

And he no longer cared.

With quick movements, he had his hands at her waist, pulling her close as he pressed her back against the base of the Ramesses statue. Those incredible blue eyes widened for the briefest moment before he saw acknowledgment—and welcome—in their depths.

And then her arms were around his neck and his mouth was hot on hers and there wasn't any room for rational thought.

Need flooded his system in harsh, pounding waves at finally having her in his arms once more. He'd thought about her for years—those odd moments that would grab him by the throat and shake him with the intense sense memories of their fated evening together—but the reality was far better.

Phenomenally better.

Finn sunk into the kiss and allowed all those pent-up years to take over. Her small, slim body wrapped around his, welcoming him and driving him crazy. Her soft, lush lips pressed to his, open and demanding as she matched his movements. Her champagne-tinged tongue parried his thrust for thrust.

And when a small sigh escaped the back of her throat, floating up around them in the dark and quiet of the museum, Finn knew his sanity was on a crash course with oblivion.

Those same lips that were driving him crazy curved against his in a smile as she pulled back. "Was that what you had in mind?"

He bent his head and pressed his forehead to hers. "For days now." *Years, really.*

"We should probably get out of here." Her gaze drifted in the direction of the nearest mounted security camera, one of hundreds. "I think we've given a proper amount of distraction."

"I'm not quite done yet."

He pressed his lips to hers for one more kiss. One more taste of that incredible mouth. One more moment with her arms wrapped around his waist and her indigo-blue gaze open, honest and wanting.

"Finn—"

She broke off the kiss once more, and even as he knew it was for the best, he wanted more. Wanted all.

"We need to go."

"Of course."

Finn followed beside her, his hand resting against her lower back to ensure they kept up the show for anyone who might be watching until they reached the Great Court. "We got what we came for."

"And avoided a throng six deep of tourists." Her light-hearted jest fell flat as they walked, that spark of attraction between the two of them drowning out even the simplest of remarks.

"So we did."

They once again reached the entrance, and the night guard greeted them. "That was quick."

"Thanks again, Josh. I just wanted to show Mr. Gallagher a piece of Egyptian art."

"No problem, Ms. Steele. We look forward to having you both back."

Josh's man-to-man grin as they walked past confirmed he hadn't missed the little show the two of them had put on in the Egyptian Sculpture Gallery. Although his body still bore the traces, Finn couldn't argue with the results. He and Rowan had looked to the casual observer like lovers on an evening outing. Nothing more.

Nothing more.

So why did the thought twist him up and make him want more. A lot more.

"It's a nice night. Would you like to walk?"

Rowan's comment pulled him from the throes of frustration and Finn focused on her upturned face and bright smile. "It's a bit cool. You sure?"

"Of course."

"Here." He stripped off his suit jacket and handed it to her, not ready to believe the thin material that clung to her like a caress could be all that warm.

"Finn, I'm fine."

"It's still a bit of a walk. Humor me."

He waved his driver on, instructing the man to wait for him at the Savoy before starting the walk toward the Strand. The heft of the museum faded behind them as the London evening wrapped around them, and Finn couldn't fault Rowan for the suggestion of a walk. The night breeze was doing wonders for his head, airing out the sudden haze of madness that had descended the moment he'd pressed his lips to Rowan Steele's.

Just like before, on that night so long ago.

Like a love-struck lunatic, he briefly wondered if she remembered, even though it had been more than evident she hadn't recognized him.

And what'd you expect, boyo? You were wearing a mask and she probably thinks you're dead. That's a fairly finite combination.

Of course, he'd moved on—both their lives had demanded nothing less—but try as he might he'd never fully forgotten her. Kissing her tonight only reinforced his first impression.

"Real nice trick back there, Peach."

"Thanks. Why do you keep calling me that?"

"Because you're lush and ripe, like a fresh peach."

A first impression that was now reinforced with the

passage of time and a woman who was more than worth his interest.

The lightest sound—nothing more than a scrape of shoe, really—pulled him from his thoughts and had the hair on the back of his neck standing on edge. With deliberate movements, he pulled Rowan under his arm, shielding her body as best he could with his.

"Finn?" Irritation spiked in her tone as she turned her narrowed gaze on him.

"Shhh."

"What is it?" Her eyes widened but she lowered her voice to the barest whisper.

"Not sure."

The light scrape of a shoe grew louder, even as he could see the streetlight on the next corner blinking brightly in front of them. They needed another half a block and they would be among more people.

If they had that long.

The footfalls grew even heavier and Finn knew he couldn't wait until they hit the corner. With a hard turn, he spun on his heel, coming face-to-face with a thin, scrappy thug. "What do you want?"

"Nothing, mate. It's a nice night for a walk. Heading to the pub."

Finn made no move to touch him, nor did the man respond in kind, but he couldn't stop the beat of discomfort that thudded in his veins. "Then be on your way."

"Easy. Easy." Flat green eyes—the only distinct feature in the man's face—crinkled at the corners as his gaze shifted to Rowan. "She's a sweet bit of fluff, now, isn't she?"

"Be on your way."

The guy ran a hand over his jaw. "I'm not sure I can do that."

Finn leaped at the man's words, unwilling to wait another moment to see what the guy had planned. He plowed a hard fist into the thug's midsection and watched the man double over. He stayed on the balls of his feet but backed up slightly.

"Finn! Watch out!"

Rowan's scream had him moving backward another few steps, and it was only that movement that prevented him from feeling the pointed edge of the thug's knife.

"Want to play rough, mate?"

"Rowan! Go get the cops." He never turned—refused to move his eyes from the threat—as he shouted out the words.

"I can't leave you."

"Get the hell out of here, Peach!"

He heard her momentary gasp of shock before the thin man leaped once more, the knife glinting in the dim, ambient light of the street.

Finn sidestepped several thrusts of the knife, his quick footwork the only thing keeping him in the game. The slender man was fast and slippery and he'd yet to get another hold or punch on him. The sound of shouts lit up behind him, and the heavy footfalls were enough to spook the thug, who took off running.

Before he could give chase, one of the cops Rowan had summoned was off after the man, and another cop had a firm hold on his shoulder.

"I'm fine." Finn lifted his hands. "I'm fine."

The cop led them to the small stoop of a nearby building and gestured for them both to sit down. He ran through a list of questions, the fine cut of their outfits and the cop's assessment of where they'd been that evening going a long way toward his ready assumption it was a standard mugging attempt.

Finn shot Rowan a sharp look to play along but he needn't have bothered. She was well ahead of him.

"I did see him eyeing my clutch."

"Of course, ma'am." The officer made a few more notes before handing Finn a card. "I'm afraid there's not much more we can do tonight, Mr. Gallagher. I've got your information, and if you think of any further description, please call me."

Finn nodded and helped a still cold and aloof Rowan to her feet. The cops walked them the short distance back to the main thoroughfare before loading them into a car to drive them the remaining distance to the Savoy.

"So much for a quiet evening."

"Oh, I don't know." Rowan's voice held all the warmth of razors as she stared out the window as the cop turned into the hotel's front entrance. "I'd say it was strangely illuminating."

She allowed the cop to help her from the car and left him to make his own farewells. "Thank you for your assistance, Officer."

The man nodded and Finn practically had to run to keep up with Rowan's steady clip through the lobby. "I'll walk you up, darling."

"That won't be necessary."

He kept pace, stabbing his index finger at the button for the elevator. "Oh, but I insist."

"Don't put yourself out." She turned her back on him as the doors slid open, tossing her final salvo over her shoulder as she stepped into the empty elevator car. *"Peach."*

Chapter 6

Rowan wasn't surprised when Finn followed her into the elevator, but she hadn't counted on his rising anger or the delicious sensation of having his large form towering over her in the small space.

"I can explain."

"I sure as hell hope so."

"Rowan. Listen—"

"No." She waved a hand, unwilling to listen to some smooth explanation or some sort of misguided apology. "Whatever words you think you can cajole me with, you might as well save them." The elevator doors slid open on her floor and she stomped off, far from caring about how rude it was to leave him behind.

She was angry.

And irrationally hurt, which was the only possible reason tears pricked the back of her eyes as she struggled with her electronic key.

"Here. Let me." Finn reached over her shoulder and took the slim card from her shaking fingers. The lock switched to green and snicked open.

She crossed into the elegant suite and dropped her purse on the small couch that sat on the far wall, dashing at the moisture in her eyes before he could see the tears. She then stripped off the heavy suit jacket she still wore.

Rowan refused to face him and instead kept moving toward a bottle of water on the desk that ran alongside the couch.

"Rowan. We need to talk."

"You think?"

"Come on. Please."

She did turn at his words, the bottle partway to her lips before she dropped her hand. "What can you possibly say that will make any of this okay?"

"I couldn't tell you."

"You chose not to tell me. There's a difference." The urge to yell at him—a fierce need she'd held in during the entire ride back with the cops, then up to her room—faded in the light of the truth.

He's alive.

The young man she'd thought died saving her was alive and well and living a life of prosperity and success in London.

"Do you know how I've wondered about you? For twelve long years I've wondered if you died that night. I've lived with the pain of knowing I put you in danger and got you killed."

"I'm fine. I'm here."

"And you never even thought to tell me. To contact me or give me some hint that you were okay. That you'd lived."

"It's not that easy."

"Well, it sure as hell isn't hard." She set the bottle on the desk before the urge to throw it across the beautiful suite got the better of her. "A piece of me died that night and you couldn't even let me know anonymously that you were all right!"

"I couldn't contact you."

"What happened to you?"

"I got shot and I survived. It's that simple."

"I can't believe they let you get away. Just let you walk right out of there, dripping blood and holding on to the bracelet they'd come for." She thought back to that night—the memories still so vivid she could have sworn they'd happened the week before instead of more than a decade prior.

"I'd left a few traps of my own. You brought petroleum jelly to grease the door. I brought something a bit harsher."

"What kind of traps?"

"A few smoke bombs I could set off remotely. Some things in the street designed to trigger several alarms. I only needed to create a few moments of confusion in order to get away."

"So you fled? How did you get medical attention?"

"It was a flesh wound, mostly. I bandaged it up until it got better."

"You what?" The image of him tending to himself had her sympathetic urges welling up and she ruthlessly tamped them down. "It still doesn't excuse you never contacting me."

"I thought about it, but I knew you wouldn't leave me alone if I contacted you. And if you tried to find me, you'd put yourself right back in danger. It was easier to let you think I was dead."

Whatever understanding she'd tried to muster up during his retelling fled on swift feet. "I've spent twelve years convinced I've had your blood on my hands, and you thought the easiest answer was to ignore me and let me suffer with that? And that somehow it's all my fault?"

"You'd have suffered a hell of a lot more if those jackals knew you were back in the game."

"How would you know that?" Even as the words left her lips, the reality came crashing in. "Of course you knew. You've kept tabs on me. Watched me."

"Watched out for you."

"I didn't need watching out for. I have an entire freaking family devoted to that very sport. What I needed from you was to know you were alive."

The hostility that licked at her belly and tinged her words found its match in the harsh words that dripped from his lips. "Like you wouldn't have done just as I predicted. I hardly see you out of the game, Rowan. You may have switched teams, but you're still as foolhardy as ever. And still determined to mess with the world's most unsavory characters to meet your own goals. Your own ends."

"I'm part of a legitimate business and I put my skills to good use. I'd hardly be here, ready to depart in a few days to Cairo with you, if that weren't the case."

"None of it changes the fact you take chances."

The oddest urge to cover her ears and stomp her feet gripped her, and Rowan fought it back. She wasn't a child and she refused to act like one, even if every word out of his mouth contradicted something he'd said prior. "So you refused to contact me but you've kept tabs on me and quite extensively, I suspect."

"Of course I have. I needed to know if you were ever going to come after me. I had to be prepared for that eventuality."

Another laugh followed on the first as she tried to

take in the sheer audacity of his choices. "Yet you came to me for this job in the Valley of the Queens. Of all the people you could have contacted, you chose me. I'd say all your efforts to maintain distance were for nothing, wouldn't you?"

Throughout his confession, he hadn't moved from his place across the room. It was only when she stopped speaking that he moved closer, as if testing the waters of her anger, waiting to see if another maelstrom awaited him.

And when he finally spoke, his voice was quiet. "I need you on this."

"Well, we all need lots of things. I needed to know you weren't dead, but I didn't get that level of consideration or care."

"I understand you're angry, but if you could try to see it from my perspective…"

"You understand nothing."

Those tears she'd fought so hard against welled up before she could hold them back. "You have no idea what that night did to me. I'd lost my parents a few years before and then to see that happen to you. To think I was responsible."

Finn had her in his arms before she registered his movement, his arms wrapped around her as her cheek pressed to his chest. The steady beat of his heart thudded under her ear, and even though every instinct urged her to pull away, some small part of her wanted to curl up right there and never move.

The young man who had touched her heart all those years ago was here. Alive. Those strong, heavy beats inside his chest proved it.

Finn held Rowan against his chest, his hands tracing lazy circles over her back. While he had never doubted she remembered that night so long ago, he had no idea the depths of guilt she suffered over the evening.

She had nothing to feel guilty about, especially since he'd been more than responsible for his own actions. Hell, it was his fault they'd been discovered in the first place. If he hadn't spent those endless moments flirting with her inside Lady Warrington's closet—and how was it he still remembered the name of the mark?—she wouldn't have had to face the evening's eventual outcome at all.

He'd have gotten her to safety and saved himself a hell of a painful gunshot wound to boot.

Yes, he'd kept tabs on her, but it hadn't been easy. The healing had taken longer than it should have because he had to care for the wound himself. And then identifying the slip of a girl who'd cased the house and broken into a safe like a pro took even longer. When he'd finally discovered who she was—the granddaughter of one of England's greatest Parliamentarians—he knew he needed to keep his distance.

So he'd stayed far, far away.

Rowan had left a mark, though, and it was far deeper than the pucker of skin that marred the flesh under his ribs. She was a puzzle and he loved puzzles. Loved figuring out how to solve a problem.

Why would the daughter of such a prominent family resort to stealing? And how the hell had she gotten so good at it?

"You can let me go now."

The light press of her hands on his chest had him loosening his hold on her but not fully dropping his arms. "I'm sorry."

"Sure you are. Now. Because you got caught. Trust me, I know how remorse works."

"You think I haven't felt some responsibility all these years?"

"Whatever you might have felt is eclipsed by your overwhelming sense of being right. If you'd felt differently, you'd have said something. Would have found a way to get to me. Although—"

She broke off, an odd, speculative gleam alighting in her eyes. The normally vivid blue looked even brighter, if that were possible, still sheened with the residual effects of her tears.

"What?"

"It is curious you called me Peach. One would have thought a suave fellow like yourself wouldn't make such a stupid slip."

"Neither did we expect to be set upon while taking a short walk through a rather nice part of London." Finn tried to play it cool, but her words were accurate and, truth be told, the slightest bit mortifying. He prided himself on always maintaining control. On always having the last word.

So why would he make such a stupid, amateur mistake?

"Maybe so." Her steady gaze ensured she thought the mistake was anything but a slip, and Finn chose to leave her to her illusions.

Nothing had gone quite according to plan since Rowan Steele accepted the job on his team. If he didn't get his head back in the game, they risked more than a painful trip into both their pasts.

"I can't change my decisions up to now, but I can apologize for causing you pain. My only intention was to protect you."

"The people in my life seem awfully bent on doing the same. Must be the fact I'm short."

Finn didn't miss the sass in her tone, nor did he miss the small smile ghosting the edges of her mouth. "I'm not so sure about that. You pack an awful lot of punch in that small frame. I wouldn't underestimate you."

"Damn straight."

That crazy urge to drag her into his arms like some conquering caveman returned in full force and he figured he'd better cut bait while they'd moved to some semblance of a truce. "I'll see you tomorrow?"

"I need to visit an old school friend. I want to ask him a few things about those glyphs."

"I'll come with you."

"Still pushing your luck, Gallagher?"

"Consider it an opportunity to make it up to you. Prove we're full partners in this."

The slightest furrow marred her forehead before she nodded, as if coming to a decision. "Fine. You can pick me up here at eight. We'll go see William then."

"It won't be a surprise?"

"Will doesn't sleep, so I can text him now and arrive early and he won't mind."

The sudden, irrational urge to ask why she knew this man's sleep schedule struck him, but once again, Finn fought the urge to bait her further.

"Make it seven-thirty. I'll buy you breakfast on the way."

"I'm not all that pleasant before coffee, especially when a five-hour time difference is still nipping at my heels."

He leaned in, his intention to press a quick kiss on her cheek. Instead, he ended up lingering, his lips hovering near her ear. "I'll make sure you get a double shot of espresso, then."

"Good night, Finn."

The husky strains of her voice floated over him like a lover's caress and he forced himself to pull back, well aware the torture was his penance for years of silence. "Good night, Rowan."

It was only when he was once more in the hallway, the heavy door clicking closed behind his back and the secondary door lock falling into place, that he breathed a sigh of relief.

She was willing to see him again.

It didn't make up for what had come before, but it was a start.

Rowan opened one eye to stare at the clock as her cell phone trilled in her ear. She scrabbled for the phone, desperate to quiet the noise when her gaze alighted on the caller ID.

Her grandfather.

Bracing herself for the inevitable scolding—albeit one done with a loving hand—she engaged the call. "Good morning, Grandfather."

"What's this I hear from your brother you're in London?"

Damn Campbell and his big fat mouth.

"I just got here yesterday."

"And now it's today, and your grandmother and I still haven't heard from you."

"I was working, Grandpa." She switched to the more familiar address, hoping it would soften him up. *Not bloody likely.*

"Don't make me give you my lecture on balancing family and work."

"It's one I know by heart."

A heavy laugh echoed through the phone. "Well, then, you can make it up to us by having dinner with your grandmother and me. Tomorrow night at seven. She's dragging me to the ballet tonight."

"Culture's good for you."

"Not bloody likely. But we already contributed to the evening and she's assured me we can't not go." He heaved a great, long-suffering sigh Rowan knew was all for show before pressing his agenda once more. "So. Tomorrow night."

"You know I'd love to see you, but I am working and I'm not sure of what my schedule is." She thought of the preparations she and Finn still needed to make for their departure in a few days. "My client may need me."

"Seven. Tomorrow night, Rowan. There's always time to see your family. And bring your client, for all I care. I've never met Gallagher and I'd like to."

Rowan just lay there, shaking her head on the fluffy pillow. She would not ask how he knew who her client was.

She would not ask.

"Your grandmother loves that he's an Irishman, too. She's all aflutter to meet him. Has been nattering on about how he's one of the U.K.'s most eligible bachelors."

Thoughts of her kiss with Finn the night before assailed her in vivid Technicolor, but Rowan fought to keep them at bay. "I wouldn't know anything about that."

"You're young, single and healthy. Don't think I don't know it and don't be pretending you haven't noticed he's altogether the same."

"Grandpa!"

"Well." He stammered slightly and Rowan couldn't hold back the grin. "That's all I'm going to say about that."

"You miss nothing, Grandpa."

"It's only because my grandchildren honed that skill

to a sharp point. If you all weren't so hell-bent on giving your grandmother and me gray hair, I might have grown dull around the edges."

Much as she wanted to argue, Alexander Steele made a surprising amount of sense.

"Seven sharp. And make sure Gallagher comes along."

"I love you."

"I love you, too, sweetheart."

"Some days I'm not sure why. You put up with a lot." Rowan knew the events of the night before were close to the surface, but the words spilling from her lips still managed to surprise her.

"Now, now. What's this about?"

"I'm difficult."

"Hell yes, you're difficult. I wouldn't have you any other way."

She smiled, the ready affirmation going a long way toward improving her mood. "I'll see you tomorrow, then. Can I bring anything?"

"Just yourself, love."

They disconnected and she lay in the dark, unable to fall back to sleep. The lure of work and her bright, shiny laptop perched atop the desk tempted, but old memories beckoned in louder voices.

"The Warrington home was broken into the other evening."

"Bethany's house?" The words tripped off her tongue, full of surprise and no small measure of shock. Rowan thought they sounded rather genuine and she mentally applauded herself as she gazed at her grandfather across his large teak desk, a beautiful piece that had belonged to a ship captain in the British Navy.

Grandfather nodded. "Bethany and her family were

away, fortunately, but the damage has been done. Lady Warrington has lost a rather valuable piece of jewelry."

"The Victoria bracelet?"

Her grandfather's eyes had widened at her knowledge of the piece, his normal, unassailable poker face nowhere in evidence. "You know about it?"

"It's all Lady Warrington and Bethany have been able to talk about."

"That's funny. Bethany's father said they've been quiet about the acquisition. Didn't want such valuable knowledge getting out."

Rowan forced a bored note into her voice. "They should probably tell Bethany that. She was parading it around like it was a gift from a new boyfriend."

The word boyfriend *stuck in her throat, and Rowan swallowed the last word, images of a broken and twisted body taking root in her mind's eye. She fought the tightening in her throat and willed the tears away. She'd vowed to take the night at the Warringtons' to her grave, and she wasn't going to break forty-eight hours into a lifetime of silence.*

Even if her grandfather's gaze was preternaturally sharp.

That gaze shifted toward his paper and he picked it up, his tone casual. "You sure there's nothing else you'd like to tell me?"

"No, Grandfather."

Rowan was unaccustomed to blatant lies—she much preferred her subterfuge on the down low—but she had to see this through. She had no idea the bracelet was such a secret but she'd already pointed the finger toward Bethany.

All she needed to do was play it out.

"That's fine, then. You should probably run along to bed now. It's a school day tomorrow."

She nodded, the lump in her throat like a boulder. "Good night."

It was only when she'd reached the door of his study, her hand on the knob, that his deep, cultured voice—full of the lofty strains of Britain—rang out once more. "Taking things from others won't bring your parents back, Rowan."

Early-morning light framed the edges of her windows as Rowan pulled herself from the memory of that night in her grandfather's study. A long night that saw them still there as the sun came up, the paneled walls absorbing her confession of an endless litany of stolen items.

She'd never taken another thing from an innocent person after her conversation with her grandfather. When she did steal, it was a recovery and only because someone was paying for it.

Her days of assuaging her grief with the treasures of others had ended with the life of a young man.

Her grandfather insisted on therapy, which had ensured she stayed on the right path, but crawling up over the rooftops of Knightsbridge, a young man likely dead because of her, had stifled any and all urges to steal again.

With a resigned sigh, she threw back the covers and headed for the shower. It was strange how the past had shaped her future, even as she now understood some of that past was wrong. She'd spent twelve years living with guilt based on false assumptions.

Finn was alive. Alive and in possession of an identity. For so many years he'd simply been the young man in the mask, but now he had a name. A face.

A life.

She wanted to be angry. Knew she had a right to it,

but she also knew enough about herself to know her path had turned that night. It was only the horror of a shooting and nearly getting caught as they had that made her finally understand the risks she was taking.

Risks that she still took, but ones that held vastly different consequences, for both herself and her family.

She was still thinking about those risks an hour later as Finn greeted her in the lobby of the Savoy, once again gifting her with a kiss on both cheeks. The greeting was elegant and somewhat at odds with the man she knew him to be by his actions. The thought left her off-kilter, and for the briefest moment she couldn't help but wonder who was the real Finn Gallagher.

And then she pushed it aside, well aware she showed the real Rowan Steele to very few.

"Good morning. Where's the three-headed dragon you led me to believe would be greeting me, deprived of caffeine and sustenance?"

She grinned at that, those strange thoughts fading away in the glare of his bright gaze. "He already went a few rounds with my grandfather at 6:00 a.m. and ordered an espresso from room service."

"Let me guess. Someone told him you're in town?"

Rowan was grateful for the easy banter. It allowed her to bluff her way through the sudden heat that warmed her at his simple touch, even as she attempted to forget all the reasons why she was still mad at him.

"This time it was my brother Campbell."

"This time?"

"My grandfather has a surprising sixth sense about his grandchildren and at any given moment is craftily getting one of us to give up the whereabouts of the others. On the rare thing he misses, my grandmother does a stellar job running interference."

"You love them."

"To distraction. None of which eradicated my summons to dinner tomorrow evening."

"Enjoy the time."

"You're coming with me." It was only later, as she reflected on the moment, that Rowan could congratulate herself on two things.

One, that she'd ensured her gaze was level with his as she delivered the news of their impending dinner invitation. And two, that she'd somehow managed to catch Finn Gallagher unawares.

She knew full well it was unlikely to happen again.

Chapter 7

He didn't *do* dinner. Not with grandparents. Especially not with grandparents who were considered some of London's finest citizens and who would likely take him for a fraud at thirty paces.

Finn was still smarting from Rowan's pronouncement on the summons from her grandfather thirty minutes later as he laid several quid down to pay for their breakfast. The small café near the Savoy hummed around him, oblivious to his impending inquisition, and he grabbed his takeaway cup of coffee off the table with greater force than necessary.

He'd spent his life avoiding brushes with every form of authority imaginable and he had no great interest in changing that at this late date.

Of course, he wasn't a fraud any longer. He was a legitimate businessman with a successful company and interests that no longer needed to be hidden with secret ledgers or offshore accounts.

None of it changed the fact that Alexander and Penelope Steele were cut from the highest quality British cloth, while he was the son of a Northside Dublin man, transplanted to London for a fresh start after his wife died far too young.

A fresh start that had included a surprising number of old ways.

Rowan returned from the front counter, a box of pastries in her hand for her friend. "You look like you swallowed a mouthful of coffee grounds soaked in lemon juice."

"I do not."

"You just had a breakfast that could fell a truck driver. How can you be grumpy already?"

"I'm not grumpy."

Her small shoulders—set off by a thin cashmere sweater in pale green—twisted as she dragged on a lightweight jacket. "It's the dinner, isn't it?"

"No, it's not the dinner."

"Of course it is. You've been pissy since I mentioned it."

"I'm not—" Finn pushed back his chair, wincing as it hit the wall with a heavy thud. "I'm not pissy about dinner. I fail to see why I need to join you at a family function."

"I think my grandfather has some notion you're going to hit on me in Egypt."

He gestured for her to walk in front of him through the restaurant, holding his comments until they were once again out on the sidewalk. "I don't need to go nearly four thousand miles to do that. I already hit on you here in London."

"You pretended to hit on me at the museum to fool any onlookers."

"Then you weren't paying very good attention."

Rowan stopped and turned toward him. "What's that supposed to mean?"

"You tell me. You were right there in the moment with me."

"It wasn't flirtation. Or…or something more. We're working together, and by the way, I still haven't forgotten that you deceived me. It's going to take me some time to get over the fact you're not dead."

The words were so absurd Finn couldn't hold back a small grin. "I wasn't aware my company was so repugnant."

She shook her head but he didn't miss the small gleam that lit up her eyes. "Come on. Will's waiting for us. And if I didn't know better, I'd say the thought of facing my grandparents has you uncomfortable."

"I'm not uncomfortable. I'm unnecessary for this little dinner party."

"My grandfather doesn't think so."

"I know so."

"Nice attitude." She pointed toward the London Underground station. "Come on. This'll be quicker."

"I never take the Tube."

"Why not?"

"I just…don't." He'd sworn to himself once he made his first million he was never going to take the subway. Public transportation meant a common life. An unimportant life.

"About two and a half million people think otherwise."

"I have a car. And a driver."

"Save the environment and give him a rest for the day." She shook her head. "Sheesh, I never took you for a snob."

"I'm not." Even if his lifestyle suggested otherwise, Finn had to admit to himself.

She was already heading down the stairs, her voice floating over her shoulder. "Let me get this straight—you traipse the world over, sleeping in uncomfortable conditions and going days without bathing if it means you can get your hands on an antiquity, but you won't lower yourself to take public transportation."

Since he couldn't just stand and wait for her on the street, he followed her down. "Would you stop yelling it?"

"If the shoe fits, princess."

Finn hit the bottom step and followed Rowan to the ticket machine. Her joke hit a rather raw note and he wasn't sure what he could say to change her mind. "C'mon, Rowan, it's not like that."

Her fingers flew over the electronic screen. "I'm getting us both weekly passes so we can ride unlimited for the next few days."

"I have a car. This really isn't necessary."

"Oh, on the contrary. I'd say it's quite necessary." She dug a credit card out of a massive purse that hung off her shoulder, but he beat her to it, dragging his wallet from his pocket.

"I can at least pay for it." He swiped his credit card into the machine and was rewarded with two shiny tickets.

"See?" Rowan handed him his and dropped a quick kiss on his cheek. "It'll be painless."

Rowan was still laughing to herself as they changed trains at the Leicester Square station. "Only a few more stops."

"You're good at this."

"There's no better way to get around London. Not to mention it's a hell of a lot quicker than sitting in traffic."

He kept pace at her side but didn't say much else until

they'd completed their transfer, on the final train that would take them to Will. "You know London well."

"My parents brought us up in New York but we spent a lot of time here as kids. And then after…" The words trailed off and Rowan was amazed to find there wasn't the customary stab of pain that came with discussing the loss of her parents. "After my parents died, I spent the longest time here of all my siblings because I was still in school."

"How old were you when they died?"

"Twelve."

"That's awfully young to experience such loss."

"Yes, it was."

"You don't have an accent."

"Because I choose not to." His smile was broad as she adopted the cultured tones that had always lit up her grandmother's voice. "However, a well-employed British accent can take a woman far."

"Tell me about it. I can only be grateful the cultured tones of England have such an effect on people."

"I thought I detected the occasional hints of Ireland in your voice."

"Occasional is the right of it. I've lived here since I was a kid."

Rowan smiled. "Surely you must know the power of the accent. Nothing has an effect on people like the cultured notes of Britain. It's as if they sit up and take notice. They stand straighter and are much quicker to accommodate a request."

"American women certainly love them."

"And will shed their panties in droves at a mere 'hello' from a British gent."

He slapped a hand on his chest, his hand over his heart. "For which I am eternally grateful."

She laughed at the silly gesture, but couldn't deny

the truth of his words. She'd had several college friends who'd swooned at the mere sound of a British accent, and she could hardly deny the effect Finn's voice had on her.

Careful, girlfriend. Keep it up and you'll forget you're mad at him.

She wasn't over her anger at him—she'd not been lying about that earlier—but it was hard to stay overtly mad in the face of such simple acceptance and warm companionship. And while she had a powerful attraction to him, she also enjoyed his company. Finn was easy to talk to, and even the subject of her parents didn't seem so hard to talk about.

The public announcement system in the car trilled their upcoming stop. "We're next."

The easy banter faded as they exited the car with a multitude of others and walked the short distance to the college where Will taught.

"You think your friend can decipher the last few hieroglyphs on the back of the Ramesses statue?"

"I've no doubt he can translate them. I'm more interested in getting his take on what they mean."

"The UCL Institute of Archaeology has a world-renowned reputation. Why's he in the classroom and not out on sites?"

"He goes on the occasional adventure or two, as he calls them, but his decision to have a family changed his desire to wander the globe. He's also one of the school's premier lecturers and a postdoctoral research fellow, so he's got his hands more than full of archaeology."

"Would you give it up like that?"

"I don't think I'm wired that way."

"Even if you had a family?"

She was curious at Finn's question. Even more so by the lack of clues on his face as to what he was thinking. Most everyone came to the subject of family—and one's role within it—with a certain measure of personal opinion. It was a rare change to sense the absolute lack of judgment in him.

Rowan knew the loss of her parents had defined her life in a multitude of ways. The rush of adrenaline that fueled so much of her choices wasn't easily satiated in other ways—nor had she looked all that hard for alternatives. But she also knew some of her choices were defined by her age and station in life.

Would she change if she had a family?

She certainly knew she'd put her children first, bar none. But was that even in the cards for her? No matter how she'd envisioned her future, a husband and children always occupied a sort of vague, hazy corner of her mind.

Nice to have but terribly hard to imagine in reality.

"I haven't spent much time thinking about it. What about you? Would you give up the life?"

"I've never been one to tempt fate, so let's just say it's hard to imagine ever having to come to that choice."

Rowan tried to detect something more behind his broad smile but Finn gave nothing away.

So why did she suddenly feel as if the sexy banter and get-to-know-you chatter they'd shared all morning had lost a bit of its luster?

Marriage and babies?

Finn was still cursing himself for the wayward questions as he followed Rowan down the long hallway toward her friend's office. The evidence of higher learning surrounded them—a sensual mixture of the smell of old books and chalk, combined with the overtones of youthful excitement and anticipation.

When had he lost that?

He wasn't that old. Hell, he'd done more before thirty than most men would do in a lifetime, and he still had a heck of a long life left. Or at least he hoped he did.

So why did he suddenly feel as if all his choices were on a pointless collision course with fate?

"Here it is." Rowan stopped in front of a small office. "Will!"

A tall, thin man unfurled himself from behind a cluttered desk, and Finn was struck immediately by the warm light that filled the man's eyes as he pulled Rowan into a tight hug. Aside from the odd picture they made, since Will was roughly six foot six to Rowan's small, petite frame, there was a genuine warmth and a brotherly affection that spoke of long years of friendship.

"Rowan, my sweet." Those cultured tones of England they'd laughed about earlier coated Will's words before Finn received the brunt of his full attention. "Is this your friend?"

Rowan made brief introductions and it was only after Will had let go of his tight grip that the man spoke again. "I'm familiar with the work of your firm. The quality of the results is outstanding and we've placed a few students with your labs."

"I've been well pleased with anyone who's joined us from UCL."

The tall man grabbed several folders off his guest chairs and gestured for them to sit down. It didn't escape Finn's notice Rowan pushed the office door closed before she perched on the edge of a stool next to Will's desk. "Did you look at what I sent you?"

"I did. Let me pull it up again."

Will began typing on his keyboard, dragging up whatever Rowan had sent him already, and Finn gave himself a few minutes to look around the office. Will's small, disorganized space couldn't be more different from the glass-enclosed environment Finn worked in at Gallagher, yet there was a commonality in their interests that was evident almost immediately.

Several books he kept on a small, sleek bookcase in his own office took prominence on Will's shelves, and a monthly journal he had on his tablet sat in printed form on the top of a stack of mail on the desk.

Common interests, different choices.

Wasn't that really what he and Rowan had been discussing on the ride over?

"I've been through all the files you sent me." Will shot Rowan a lopsided grin. "You're lucky I don't sleep, although Debbie wasn't all that happy with you last night."

"I'll send her a big box of chocolate in thanks for the help."

Will's grin was lopsided. "I already tried it. No dice."

"I'll call her and apologize. I'm usually nicer at it than you are. Knowing you, you probably grunted at her as you dug through all the information." Rowan beat on her chest. "'Me archaeologist. You my woman.' All that flowery crap you're so bad at and all."

Finn couldn't hold back the smile at the funny conversation between Will and Rowan—conversation that batted back and forth faster than a match at Wimbledon.

"Did you look at the glyphs?"

"Yes, and we'll get to that." Will tapped a few keys on his computer, and Finn saw a new web page load on the screen. "But first, how up are you on the chatter going down over this dig?"

"I ran the Egyptology forum sites the other night, after I accepted the job from Finn."

Will nodded and Finn didn't miss the narrow-eyed

gaze. "You pay attention to the thread on the meaning of the jewelry."

"What thread?" Finn shifted to the edge of his chair to get a better view of the screen. "I took a look at the chatter as well and didn't see anything."

"It's buried pretty deep, but it's there." Will tapped a few more keys that brought up a message board. "Buried way down deep, but take a look."

Finn scanned the screen, his gaze alighting on the repeated use of the words *curse, fate* and *high priest.* "You can't be serious."

Will shrugged, his gaze never leaving the screen as he navigated through several posts. "I've never been big on that sort of thing, but it doesn't matter what I think. All you need is a fanatic with a mission and you've got a problem on your hands."

"What's it say?" Finn leaned farther forward but his progress was stopped by a towering stack of what appeared to be term papers.

"Oh, come on, Finn." He didn't miss the distinct notes of disdain in Rowan's tone. "You can't think anyone takes this seriously."

Will raised his voice to be heard over her protests. "The rumors say that the wedding jewelry discovered in the cache will reunite lovers, bring people back from the dead, that sort of nonsense."

"Anything else?"

A light flush crept up Will's neck, but he kept going. "The wedding texts are also purported to house a recipe for a fairly strong sexual stimulant."

"No way." Rowan's protests grew louder. "You think someone's going to rob the tomb for an ancient recipe for Viagra? Come on. I might not think Baxter Monroe knows his head from his ass, but he's still a scholar. That has to count for something."

Even though he had no great love for Monroe, Finn did acknowledge Rowan had a point. With that thought came another, swiftly on its heels. "What if it's a front?"

"For what?" Rowan looked up from her perch over Will's shoulder, where she read the posts.

"To raise interest. Pull things off course maybe and hide the real prize. Nothing perks up the media like a good dose of sex talk, in any form they can get it. Add that to ancient Egypt, which has a high degree of interest anyway, and you've got a newsperson's dream."

"It still doesn't make a lot of sense." Although she disagreed, Finn was intrigued to watch her work through the details out loud. Which wasn't all that different from watching her eat breakfast or ride the Tube or talk to Will.

She fascinated him.

A dull throb settled in the base of his skull at the increasing evidence of his interest in her.

Why had he thought this was a good idea? Rowan Steele might be one of the world's experts on the provenance of antiquities, but there were others. Well-qualified individuals who could work on the project and whom he'd have no interest in seeing, let alone talking to, after the authentication was over.

"This is modern times. The world's sort of moved past believing in curses. People are too attached to their technology to believe some supernatural force is going to sweep in and hurt them."

"So if we go with Finn's idea, what could it be a cover-up for? I leave you to ponder that." Will pulled them both back to the problem at hand as he pointed toward the screen. "Want to go over the glyphs on the back of the *Younger Memnon* statue?"

"You found something?" Whatever Rowan had been willing to argue vanished in the face of more details that would lead to better understanding the discovery in Nefertari's tomb. "Those last two glyphs on the statue?"

"You were right. They are about Nefertari." Will leaned forward, his gaze focused on the computer screen. "'Great king's wife, his beloved. The one for whom the sun shines.'"

Finn thought through the translation, but couldn't understand how there was anything new. "Those epitaphs for her have been found on other markings. It's not uncommon."

"No, but this last glyph is."

"So you agree with me?" Rowan had already moved to stand over Will's shoulder again.

"I agree the glyph's highly unusual, but I don't think it's tied to a curse. At least not overtly beyond the standard 'don't mess with the tomb or else' language."

"What do you think it *is* tied to?" The excitement threaded underneath her words was unmistakable as she pointed toward the computer screen. "Especially since it hasn't raised any questions up to now."

Will sat back in his seat with a heavy thud. "Because no one knew about the markings that hadn't yet been discovered in the tomb. They're the key. And the match."

"Ho there. For the lay people over here who don't read hieroglyphics." Finn waved his hands. "Want to tell me what's going on?"

Excitement practically telegraphed itself off Rowan's small form as she danced her way around the desk. "The glyphs are clues to Nefertari's lineage and the family who gave her to Ramesses in marriage."

Even without the level of knowledge Rowan and Will possessed, Finn knew the reality of what they suspected was more than extraordinary. Nefertari's heritage was one of the greatest mysteries in Egyptian history. "What does it say?"

Will spoke first, intoning the same inscription from before. "'Great king's wife, his beloved. The one for whom the sun shines. Descendant of all that is good.'"

But it was Rowan's voice, quiet and full of ceremony, that added the context that made it real. "That last glyph matches the first images sent back already from the dig site."

"Which means when we excavate more deeply into the chamber, we'll find the rest of the message." Finn pointed toward the screen. "Do you have the images sent back?"

Will flipped through a few screen before Finn stopped him.

"There. That one."

The picture was dull, the lighting not optimal in the photograph, but the evidence of what Rowan and Will both believed was easy to see. Finn pointed toward the lower corner of the screen, where the imagery faded off into hard-packed earth. "That's it, right? The advance team in there already believes there's about six more feet of wall to uncover."

"That's the spot." Color rode her cheeks into a vivid pink, and in that moment, Finn saw the love and excitement she had for her job. For how she made her life.

This was not a woman who'd be content to live behind the scenes or ride a desk.

Ever.

"We'll discover where Nefertari came from, Finn. One of the oldest mysteries in Egyptology will be explained."

The excitement he saw there—the near blind devotion to possessing that history—rose up and gripped him by the throat. He'd seen that same look once before, on the face of a young girl as she admired the rich patina of gold that overlaid a priceless bracelet worn by Queen Victoria.

And in the depths of that excitement, he saw the proof that she'd take any risk to attain her goal.

Finn was still off-kilter from their meeting a few hours later as they walked through St. James's Park. The jostling, packed subway car that had carried them back toward the city center hadn't helped his mood, but he knew the root of his discomfort went far deeper.

The October afternoon was a rarity in London with clear blue skies and a pleasant temperature that almost made their light jackets unnecessary. Despite the beauty of the day—and the beauty of his companion—he couldn't shake off the unease that rode hard against his shoulder blades.

Their meeting with Will turned up little except the man's promise he'd keep digging into whatever else had been found or cataloged to date at the site. He also promised to reach out to his private network to see what the word was on the cache.

Finn had been thrilled when this job came to Gallagher International. He knew it wasn't without risks, but the opportunity and the ultimate payoff were considerable. Hell, he'd cultivated a relationship with the British Museum—and put up with wankers like Baxter Monroe—specifically to get access to opportunities like the Nefertari tomb.

So why was he so itchy?

The two of them walked along a wide footpath, Rowan's smile broad and happy. She turned toward him and he was captivated by her warmth. "That was a productive morning."

"I owe you some serious credit for the hieroglyphs

on the Ramesses statue. While I enjoyed our late-night romp through the museum, I never expected those photos would pay off."

"They'll pay off even better when we get that wall fully exposed in Nefertari's tomb. It changes everything."

Was that the reason for his unease? That the job he'd prepared for had suddenly changed? "Come on, Rowan. You know we're not going to get much of a chance at it."

"Of course we will. We're the only ones who know it's there."

"Right. And the moment you uncover it, Baxter Monroe will shut us out of there so fast it won't be funny. We're there to authenticate the wedding objects, not manage the scholarly aspects of the dig."

"We're both qualified to do both."

"You're qualified. I'm just the guy who provides the authentication services when they hit the mother lode."

She stopped walking to face him, and Finn couldn't help but notice how the bright blue sky was nearly a perfect match for her eyes. "You think I'm letting Baxter anywhere near the wall? He thinks the jewels are the big deal. I'm going to go for that darkened corner no one thinks matters."

"That's not why we were hired."

"Who the hell cares why we were hired, Finn? It's the find of a century. Hell, two centuries. Speculation has always run rampant about who Nefertari was. With this discovery we'll know her lineage and even possibly how she came to be Ramesses's consort. Despite the fact he had several wives, she was the one he loved and trusted above them all. This may explain why."

Whether it was a combination of his strange unease from the morning visit to Will or the rising sense he was losing control of the work—work he'd deliberately brought Rowan in for—Finn didn't know.

And suddenly, he didn't care.

"It's still not the reason we were hired."

"So we change the game. React on the fly."

"Like you did in the Warrington house twelve years ago?"

"What the hell is that supposed to mean?" Those blue eyes that so captivated him flashed over to anger in a blazing heartbeat.

"You heard me. You barreled into danger at sixteen and you've obviously not gotten a hell of a lot smarter in the ensuing years. The dig isn't ours. Doesn't matter what you or I think about that—the museum owns it. They've got the permit on it. And it's the British Museum that's deigned to allow us on as hired guns. They want us to authenticate the cache, nothing more. Don't forget that."

"I can't believe you're copping out like this."

"And I can't believe I'm on the verge of asking you off the project."

Rowan dropped onto a nearby bench. "You can't do that."

"I can and I will, if you're unwilling to take my lead. This is Gallagher International's project. I brought you in as a subcontractor for your expertise."

The anger he wanted to hold on to flitted away at the sheer sadness that filled her face. "This is the project of a lifetime."

"It won't be if it gets you killed."

Something in his words must have broken through because he saw a subtle change come over her. The anger hadn't vanished, per se, but it was almost as if she picked it up and set it aside for the moment.

She tugged on his hand, pulling him down next to her

onto the bench. As he sat, his large frame dwarfing hers, he couldn't help but make the quick comparison between them. She was so delicate, like a tiny pixie.

A crazed pixie, if the thunderous look in her eyes was any indication.

"I'm willing to give you the benefit of the doubt for five minutes before I pull out my crazy-ass-bitch persona. But I warn you, it's pretty damn lethal."

"I'm not playing, Rowan."

"Neither am I. So let me have it. Something has you weirded out and I want to know what it is."

Well hell, how did he explain it?

It had all started in Will's office. What had started as subtle humor at Rowan and Will's strange sort of half language had morphed into something else as their discussion ramped up speed.

This project was historically significant yet the advance chatter was filled with curses and sex potions. Even the jewels themselves, while a significant find, had a strange air of distraction about them.

"I can't explain it any better than this, but I feel like we're all players on a chessboard, being dragged around at the whim of someone else."

"To what end?"

"That's what I can't define. But seriously, don't you sense something else is going on? What's this completely idiotic nonsense about a curse? It feels like a distraction."

"And you think someone's deliberately manipulating the distractions?"

"Yes, I do."

He heard the skepticism in her tone fade ever so slightly. "While I don't want to dismiss the power of intuition, we've both been on projects where the adrenaline runs hotter than others. It doesn't mean there's anything to worry about."

"I haven't had this feeling many times in my life, but I've got it now."

"Well, what happened the last time you had this strange woo-woo feeling?"

"I got shot."

Chapter 8

Rowan's initial urge to scoff at Finn's strange and sudden attack of nerves vanished at his words. Instead, all she could picture was his body, twisted at an unnatural angle and bleeding over the Warringtons' back porch, where she stared down from the roof.

"You want to run that by me again?"

"You heard me."

"That's the only other time you've had a bad feeling on a job?"

"Deep-in-the-gut bad? Yes."

And what in the hell was she supposed to do with that?

"The British Museum is spearheading this. One of the most respected entities in the world. You really think they're going to pull a fast one?"

"I think there are players involved we can't begin to understand. But even if I'm wrong about all that, can you honestly sit there and tell me you don't feel anything at all strange about what we know so far?"

"You're really bugged about the curse?"

"Not a curse in and of itself, but the fact that someone's using it as a distraction."

Rowan knew Finn had a point. What had been effective in the early days of archaeology—or in endless adventure movies—was in reality fairly impractical. Because of the sheer number of people involved in the dig, from crew to press to a sizable security staff, generating creepy, curselike environs would be nearly impossible. Further, since each week's discovered artifacts would be airlifted out of there and into labs, it made it harder to use one specific artifact to generate problems.

The transparency of technology made subterfuge a much more subtle game in this day and age—her brother Campbell understood that better than most—and preying on people's fears of the unknown was a difficult proposition.

"So we prepare with that in mind. From the very first meeting, you told me this trip wasn't without its challenges or its dangers. And I accepted that."

"And if the dangers aren't what we thought they were?"

"Then we make sure our escape plan is airtight."

He hesitated and she thought he was about to argue, but instead, he lifted a hand to her face. She felt the warmth of his palm where it cupped her cheek. The lightly callused tips of his fingers where he brushed a thumb over her lips.

A rush of heat and something very much like yearning flooded her body at his intimate touch.

"Does anything frighten you?"

"Of course not." She swallowed hard on the lie before reconsidering her words. "Yes, of course, I'm frightened. By a lot of things. But that fear can't stop me from doing what needs to be done. From doing the things that are hard."

"Is this some sort of youngest-child thing?"

She smiled, the exquisite torture of his touch on her lower lip only exacerbated when the movement of her lips dragged the pad of his thumb over the sensitized flesh. "According to my family, it's a Rowan thing, plain and simple."

He ran his thumb once more over her flesh, and she nearly gave in to the urge to move closer and press her lips to his, ending the madness. And then his gaze shifted and grew thoughtful before he dropped his hand.

"I'm sorry. For not telling you who I was from the beginning. And for letting you think I'd died that night."

"Why didn't you tell me? Or find a way to tell me?"

After she'd gotten over the initial shock of knowing he was alive, the fact he'd remained quiet for so many years was the real question left behind. Why hadn't he found her? Or given her some sense—even anonymously—that he'd survived.

"I couldn't put you in danger like that. Those weren't ordinary thieves that night."

"Who do you think they were?"

"Best I've been able to discover, they're part of a bigger ring of criminals. Something was going on in the Warrington house that night, and you and I happened into the middle of it."

"How'd you come to be there?"

It wasn't something she'd understood that night, but in the years that followed, when she'd dissected each and every moment of that evening, Rowan had come to wonder about his presence in her friend's house.

"My father was a less-than-respectable businessman."

"He's how you got into theft?"

"Yep. And I went on to exceed every expectation he

had for me." Finn turned to stare out over the expanse of the park, memories stamped on his face like a mask.

She was more fascinated to hear his tale than she thought possible, but waited until he was ready to continue his explanation of his past.

"My father was never a rich man, but after my mother died, we moved from Dublin to London. He had a cousin here who suggested he could get better work than he'd had back home."

"How old were you?"

"Five or six."

She wanted to ask how he'd handled the loss of a parent but sensed it was a big step for him to share the story of his father. Pushing too hard might have the opposite effect of getting him to open up, so she offered up a light tease instead. "Hence the more British-than-Irish accent you put to such good use."

The tease had her desired effect when a smile crossed his face before he continued, "Something like that."

He took a deep breath before returning to the story of his father. "Patrick Gallagher wasn't a bad man. Still isn't. But he's never been known for his smart choices. And the move to London only put more choices in his path."

"You lived with the cousin?"

"Off and on, depending on how well the old man was running. Turns out his cousin did some thug work for a local dealer. Small jobs, running numbers and picking up payoffs from local businesses. My father started there but when he demonstrated his quick fingers, he was put into service doing other things."

"He took the work, even though you were so young?"

She didn't think the question held judgment, but saw the way Finn's mouth tightened all the same. "It paid better than anything else he could have gotten, so yeah, he took the job."

"And you?"

"I was the anomaly of the neighborhood." He must have seen the question on her face because he added, "I loved school and I developed an ability to get in and out of a surprising number of scrapes."

"Because you're just that good?"

The smile was back, but it was what she saw reflected in the depths of his eyes that really grabbed her. A wisdom beyond his years. "Because I'm good and I listen. It's a powerful combination. You'd be amazed how many people forget just how important that second part is."

Rowan understood Finn's comment, her own experiences only reinforcing his point. People were so focused on their end goal they frequently stopped listening and paying attention to the clues that were often littered around them. From casual comments to the increasing electronic footprint individuals left in social media, clues were everywhere. She knew better than most that keeping a sense of the world around you could pay dividends.

And it had for her several times over.

Human beings gave away an inordinate amount of information about themselves day in and day out, so long as you were willing to listen.

"When did you do your first job for your father?"

"I'd been running a few cons on my own. Small things. Funny how no one expects the school's honor student to be the same one nicking stuff from lockers or sneaking into the school cafeteria's coffers."

"And then it got bigger?"

"More independent. I saw the people my old man was in with and I had no interest in following suit. I like being my own boss."

Rowan knew his choices, misguided as they were, were an indicator of the man who sat before her. "Did it bother you? The morality of it?"

"Sometimes, yes. More often than not, I'm sad to say, it was no. You?"

"All the time."

"Then why'd you do it?"

The urge to shrink away from the scrutiny was strong, but Rowan refused to hide from it. "I couldn't not do it."

I couldn't not do it.

Her words echoed in the warm, breezy air between them, and despite the vivid blue skies above, Finn felt a chill settle in his bones. "Why?"

"It was a whim at first. About six weeks after my parents died. A Friday afternoon near the end of the school day. I was new and didn't know many people. I was standing at my locker packing to go home. The girl next to me had hers open but she was paying no attention because she was flirting with the boy she liked. And there was a fresh pack of gum on the small shelf where she stored her books."

"And you took it?"

"I took it. And for the first time since my grandmother woke me up out of a sound sleep to let me know my parents were killed, I felt something. It wasn't much. A momentary triumph that had nearly faded by the time I got home, but it was something."

"How'd they die?"

"A car accident on their twentieth-anniversary trip. They'd gone to spend the week in the Welsh countryside. It's why we were at my grandparents' here in London."

His gut twisted at the thought of her loss. It was hard to lose anyone, but for it to be so sudden…

So absolute…

How did you recover from that? And as he imagined the small pack of gum, he realized that you didn't recover from that. You simply marched on, day after day, finding solace where you could.

"And after the gum?"

"I graduated to a variety of items at school. A pair of gloves. A new wallet in an open purse. Even a beaker from chemistry class. It was more opportunistic than planned."

"How'd you go from nicking odds and ends to breaking and entering?"

"How does anyone feed an addiction? They escalate their behavior, growing more and more reckless in search of the high to be gained."

Although he'd never equated the two, Finn had to admit Rowan's description of her slide into theft had a surprising correlation to addiction. The increasingly poor choices coupled with increasing risk. "Without the risk, there is no reward."

"Pretty much. And then one day I was visiting my friend Bethany and I saw my shot at a big score. She showed off the Victoria bracelet and I was enamored. If I could only have it. Possess it. A score like that would fill the empty places. It had to."

"Is that why you didn't turn back after getting shot at from the street?"

"Yep. I was all set to leave. I was hiding on the roof next to the chimney and I was simply waiting it out until I could crawl down again. And then, as the night grew quiet once more, I thought better of it. The good old 'Why not? I can stop tomorrow' that every addict tells themselves with fierce commitment to the idea."

The events of that night had never been far from his

thoughts, but her story brought them crashing back in vivid clarity. The moment when he realized someone had beaten him to the score. The even bigger moment when he realized the other thief was just a child.

He hadn't been far out of the schoolroom himself, but the sight of a teenager with her hand in the safe in the Warringtons' bedroom closet had thrown him for a loop.

Even now, twelve years later, he could smell the light scent of her as they stood hidden behind the curtains. He could also taste the raw fear that coated his tongue with iron as the thugs casing the house had entered the room.

Could he keep her safe?

And would they get out of the house undetected?

With the exception of that night, every job he'd ever worked he worked alone.

"Why were you there that night?"

Rowan's questions pulled him from his thoughts. "At the house?"

"Yes. That's the one thing I've never fully understood. There were a hell of a lot of us after the same thing that night. How'd it come to be?"

"The Victoria bracelet was a hot topic of conversation after it came on the market. Warrington purchased it from a less-than-reputable dealer, and I just kept tabs on the house and knew when they were going away. And you?"

"It really was all Bethany. I'd never have known about it if it weren't for her showing it to me. Girls do love to talk about pretty things, and Bethany was no exception."

"There were no girls in the circles I ran in, and plenty of men talked about that pretty thing, too."

"What about the others? The other thugs who set upon us that night?"

Finn shrugged, even as a small spark of electricity lit

up the back of his neck. "I always assumed they found out same as I did."

"What if you assumed wrong?"

Finn paced his study, the view of London from his window awe-inspiring. When he'd made the decision to move his business into the Shard, he'd purchased an apartment in the building, as well. Aside from the practicality of being so close to the office, the views were unparalleled.

Rare.

And the purview of a privileged few.

He'd come a long way and he never wanted to forget it. He had wealth and power and he had both because he'd worked his tail off. What he'd done before—acts that he'd felt minimal remorse for at the time—had become a mental albatross around his neck as he worked to change his decisions and make a better life for himself.

The scar that ran just under his rib cage and the occasional twinge of that flesh were a constant reminder of what he almost lost to youthful vanity and reckless immorality.

Thankfully, he'd long since retired the vanity.

Despite the inevitable consequences of growing up, he'd never been able to give up the spoils of that evening. Youthful folly or something to remember the evening by, he didn't know, and after a while it no longer mattered. He unlocked the safe in his study and pulled out the Victoria bracelet to once again look upon its beauty. The light caught the gold, and the rubies that ran the length of the thick cuff winked in the fading light that streamed into the room.

Why had he kept it?

At first, it had been a matter of self-preservation. Putting the piece out on the black market would lead the thugs he'd run from straight to his door. But over time and with his connections…

He could have moved the piece years ago, yet he'd hung on to it.

The piece changed his life—literally and figuratively.

A man wanted to hang on to that. To remember the effect of something so profound. He could divide his life, before and after the possession of the Victoria bracelet.

Before and after Rowan.

Why did it keep coming back to that? Over and over again, it came back to *her.* A slip of a girl who'd changed his life.

His phone vibrated in his pocket and he dug it out, surprised to see his father's number on the screen. "Dad."

"Boyo. How are you?"

"Doing fine."

"Hear you've got a big gig coming up."

The notes of Patrick Gallagher's Irish roots coated his words in a thick brogue, and even after more than a quarter century in London, Finn knew nothing would change that. "Word travels fast."

"For a man who likes to stay in the know."

While his father's ready knowledge of his business unnerved him ever so slightly, he couldn't hide the very real fact that his father also presented him with an opportunity to dig into who might be talking. "You know how much I love Egypt. And this is a big one."

"The whole world's watching, son. Can't pick up a paper without reading some bit of news or another about the find."

"As one of my subcontractors put it, everyone loves Egypt. There's even rumor of a curse floating around."

"Horseshit, I'd say."

"I agree, but if it sells more papers, the press certainly isn't going to argue."

His father laughed, deep and hearty, and Finn couldn't deny the small streak of sadness in how long it had been since they'd seen each other. He'd set his father up well, ensuring the man would never have to work again if he chose, but responsibility wasn't the same as availability and he knew that.

So why did he always find a reason to stay away?

Patrick Gallagher had long since given up running numbers, far more content to spend his evenings talking with his cronies at the pub or squiring a widow he'd been seeing for a few years now around town. His father had gone respectable, and he was glad for it.

Yet he still kept his distance.

"So what else are you hearing?"

"That's just it, son. I'm hearing a lot. No substance but a hell of a lot of chatter."

That same streak of unease that had dogged him after leaving Will's office flared high once more. "What sort of chatter?"

"I first heard it down at the pub when you got the job and didn't give much thought past how proud I was of you. But it's come up a few more times. From different folks 'n' all. Everybody seems to know something about this dig going down in Egypt. It makes me wonder why and I just thought you ought to know."

"Thanks."

Finn mentally batted around the idea of asking who had shared the news, but there was no need. Word spread so quickly among his father's friends, the likelihood of pinning whoever had originated the information was slim to none.

It was the very fact a group of men with suspicious

backgrounds should have any knowledge of his impending project at all that was the real question.

"Finn." His father stopped, the line suddenly quiet except for the subtle sound of Patrick Gallagher's breathing.

"Yes?"

"Be careful. Promise me that."

"I will."

"I know these are the fancies of an old man, but I need you to listen to me on this. I've got a bad feeling. Like the weeks leading up to your ma's passing."

The words hit with the force of a battering ram, the mere mention of his mother so foreign on his father's lips Finn almost wondered if he'd heard correctly.

"I see. Look, I've got a team of people with me. There's nothing to worry about."

"I couldn't sleep if I didn't warn you it's got my antenna quivering."

The line went quiet once more, and before he even realized it, the next words were spilling out. "So. Well. When I get back, we should get together."

"I'd like that."

"Me, too, Dad."

The heavy knock on her door pulled Rowan from her computer and she rubbed her eyes as she stared at the clock. She'd been reviewing various materials Kensington had dug up on the team assigned to Baxter Monroe's staff, trying to determine if any of them were vulnerable. She hadn't turned up anything yet, but her sister was mind-numbingly thorough. Rowan had only gotten through about half the materials and she'd been at it about four hours already.

She dragged open the door and let out a squeal when her brother Liam filled the door. With another small scream, she leaped into his arms. "What are you doing here?"

"Ro." Liam hugged her close and she was surprised to feel his thin form under her arms. Although both her brothers were on the leaner side of muscular, Liam had more heft to him than Campbell. Yet hugging him, she'd almost swear it was Campbell wrapped around her.

Rowan stepped back and gestured him into the room. "You've lost weight, Liam."

"It's great to see you, too." He shot her a wry smile before closing the door behind him. "What are you up to?"

"Prep for the job I'm working on. We leave for Egypt in two days."

"So I hear. Grandfather's got himself in a twist you didn't call the moment you landed."

"Campbell gave me up. He and Grandmother have been talking near daily on plans for the wedding, and I figured he let it slip."

"My money's usually on Kenzi but you're probably right. You know she and Grandfather are thick as thieves. I swear she has a call with him every morning as she eats her oatmeal and blueberries."

"No way."

"Yes, way. I finally put two and two together when all my calls from him seemed to follow a pattern. They talk at seven in New York, and by seven-thirty I'm getting a call."

"He watches out for us."

"Sometimes too closely."

Rowan wondered at her brother's cryptic message, combined with the clear loss of weight. "You sure everything's all right?"

"Of course. Just been busy."

She wasn't so easily brushed off, but her oldest brother

was known for his vaultlike ability to keep his mouth shut. She'd get it out of him eventually…when he was good and ready to share. In the meantime, she could enjoy his company or spend the time frustrated she wasn't getting anything out of him.

Following a pattern they'd set decades before, she opted for enjoying his company. "I didn't know you were in London."

Liam settled onto the couch. "I wasn't supposed to be but I'm working on a lead for Kensington and it was easier to do it in person."

"Seems awfully generous of you. And since when doesn't she like taking business trips?"

"Since she's decided she needs to single-handedly bring in all business for the House of Steele. She's bid on no fewer than eight projects in the last month and secured six of them."

"We've got to slow down or add to staff."

His eyebrows shot up at that one. "Would you trust anyone else inside our walls?"

"Hell no."

"Then who are we going to hire? We've got no one beyond T-Bone running point for Campbell, and Grandmother's been pushing Kenzi to talk to Great Aunt Marta's granddaughter, Fiona. Other than that, it's just us."

"Wasn't Fiona the one with braces who used to terrorize Grandpa's hounds?"

Liam's smile was quick and it was the first sign her brother might be inside somewhere. "Rumor has it she's grown up, Ro. And she's not that much younger than you."

"Yes, well, I suppose it does happen. And I think I do remember Kensington saying something about her. She's been in a master's program at Harvard?"

"That's the one." Liam leaned forward and dropped

his clasped hands between his knees. "You want to get some dinner?"

"Sure."

"Got anything to drink in the meantime?"

"Liam, what's going on?"

"Nothing."

"You can keep telling me that lie, or we can go get Indian food and I'll sweat it out of you with your chicken vindaloo."

Liam shook his head but he was already on his feet, clearly ready to leave. "You don't miss much."

"Neither do you. It's an annoying family trait."

"We all have it."

Rowan grabbed her coat and her purse. "And we all are annoyed about it, aren't we?"

Liam wrapped an arm around her shoulders, pulling her close. "I've missed you."

"I've missed you, too."

An hour later, Rowan was no closer to what was bothering Liam as they sat in the back corner of a small restaurant not far from the hotel. She had, however, spewed her guts on what had been happening in her life.

Damn it, but her big brother was crafty.

"Has Finn given you any reason not to think he's playing you straight?"

Rowan picked at a piece of naan bread, the soft, warm texture the exact comfort food she was looking for as she attempted to catch her brother up on all the ins and outs of her current situation.

Did she dare tell him what had happened all those years ago on the Warringtons' roof?

And did it really matter any longer anyway?

The bigger question, to her mind, was what did Liam really know?

"I got in some trouble when I was sixteen."

The glass of wine that was halfway to her brother's lips stopped, suspended for the briefest moment before he set it back down on the table. "In trouble how?"

"I attempted to steal a priceless bracelet from a friend's home. Halfway succeeded, too."

"Halfway?"

"You really don't know about this?"

"No, I don't." His voice grew deeper and his jaw tighter. "I know nothing about it."

If his tone hadn't been enough of a clue, the sheer lack of guile in his eyes—coupled with deep concern—satisfied her that the conversation she'd had with her grandfather had stayed between them.

So she started at the beginning and told him the entire story. The irony of the moment wasn't lost on her as she recounted the events of that night. She'd held her secrets for well over a decade, and in a day she'd shared them twice.

"Ro, why? It's not like you needed the money."

"I didn't do it for the money."

"Then why?"

She searched for the words, but they remained elusive. How did you explain to someone who didn't understand? Despite years of careful review of her behavior and the determination to make something more of her life, she'd never been able to fully explain those glorious feelings of completion. "I did it for the thrill. For the taking. That's all."

"I never knew. Never had any idea." The sadness she saw in that aqua-blue gaze hit home just how her behavior affected her loved ones. "And I'm still not entirely sure I understand why."

"It was different for me than the rest of you. I was the

youngest and my life changed the most. And stealing...
stealing was the one place I felt like I was in control."

He'd gripped her hand throughout the telling and it
was only at her words that he let go and reached once
more for his wine. "All our lives changed."

"I'm not saying you didn't suffer."

"What are you saying, then?" That vivid blue gaze
pinned her with its brilliance and in its depths she saw
something she'd missed for so very long.

Pain.

"I'm just saying it was different, Liam. That's all."

He nodded before his natural curiosity took over. "So
Finn was the guy who helped you escape?"

"Yes."

"Remind me to buy him a bottle of something really,
really nice."

"Grandfather's already summoned him to dinner. I
think he may beat you to the punch."

Liam sat back in his chair, a satisfied smile on his
face. "Grandfather's summoned you both to the house?"

"For dinner tomorrow."

"You know, I was going to head home in the morning,
but maybe I'll stick around."

"Great. You can run interference." Rowan sat back, the
rich scent of spices wafting between them, as their waiter
set their matched dishes of chicken vindaloo on the table.

Liam waited until their waiter had departed before he
shook his head. "No way am I helping. In fact, it's going
to be a joy to watch you both squirm."

"That's not nice."

"Not trying to be nice. You earned this summons fair
and square. I'm just glad it's not me for a change."

Rowan took a bite of her dish, wincing when the intense spice hit her tongue. She'd ordered her meal extra

hot, and the chef hadn't disappointed. "Don't worry. We all seem to rotate through the weight of all that good old-fashioned British scrutiny with shocking regularity."

"I'm not sure how the old man does it. We're grown adults and he still manages to instill fear and deference."

"I wish I knew. I might be able to fight it better if I did."

They ate in companionable silence for a few minutes, the clinking of their forks rivaled only by the sound of their water glasses hitting the table after every few bites.

"Why'd I let you talk me into this?" Liam muttered as he forked up more chicken.

"It was supposed to be part of my diabolical plot to get you to confess what you've been up to lately yet here I am running my mouth."

He reached for his glass, a small smile tilting the corner of his lips. "Score one for me, then."

"Seriously. What is going on?"

"Nothing other than running my ass off globe-trotting on behalf of our wealthy and often misguided clients."

"You'd tell me if you were having problems, wouldn't you?"

"No."

"Liam!"

"Oh, come on. It took you twelve years to let me know you were a thief and nearly got caught by thugs at the tender and vulnerable age of sixteen. I'm thinking of kettles and pots, little sister."

"You're impossible."

"And you've missed something because you're too busy pining over how hurt you are."

The combination of his words and the heat on her tongue had her coughing and it was several minutes later—her eyes still full of tears—that she was finally able to concentrate on his statement. "What have I missed?

"The thing I've been wondering since you started your story." He leaned forward, his voice quiet. "Where's the bracelet?"

Chapter 9

Jared Wright stabbed the answer button on his cell phone as he dropped behind the large desk in his office. A glass of vodka sat at his elbow and he reached for it as he grunted out a hello.

"Someone nibbled on the details on the message forum."

"And?"

"I dug into it. Seems the questions are coming from a professor at UCL."

Jared knew the program at UCL was one of the finest in the world, so it made sense an archaeology professor would be haunting Egyptian sites. "Were the questions scholarly?"

"Nope. He's looking for something."

"You think he's working alone?"

"Only way to know is to string him along with a few answers and then follow him."

The retort that sprang to his lips was quick and nasty,

but he held it back, taking a sip of his drink instead. Damn it, but it was nearly impossible to find people who could be proactive in a crisis. "Then do it. Don't let him know you're on him, and keep me informed."

"On it."

He disconnected the call and threw his phone on the desk. He finished off the glass of vodka and reached for the bottle. While the idiot was too quick to ask for approval of his actions, he *had* suggested the message board overall and obviously it had paid off.

Jared knew he'd come late to the internet game and he'd paid the price. Those who were more enterprising had found ways to use the web to their advantage, putting cryptic messages out and ensuring those in the know read between the lines.

The use of technology had put him behind and he was damned if he was going to lose any more ground.

His man would follow the professor and they'd get to the bottom of things. If the guy was as harmless as he seemed, a few hours of Teddy's time was a small price to pay. If not, someone else was looking to horn in on his territory.

Either way, he'd be ready for them.

He picked up the phone once more and dialed the woman he'd come to think of as his client. To think of her any other way left him a poor mixture of confused and seduced.

And he hated being either.

He'd worked too long to gain his place in the world to give it all away because he couldn't keep it in his pants.

"Hello, darling."

He tightened at the seductive purr from the other end of the phone, and Jared fought to keep his voice level. "Teddy got a hit on the forums."

"Did he, now? From where?"

"A professor with UCL."

"They're not engaged in the dig. This is so high profile all their students were denied because so many professionals want in on the project."

Her ready grasp of the excavation in the Valley of the Queens was absolute, and the comment only reinforced that. "Which is why it's likely idle curiosity."

"What forum thread got the nibble?"

"A few of them. The professor's nosing around anything having to do with the dig itself and also hit on that seed we planted on the curse."

"I knew it was only a matter of time until someone bit." Her husky laugh ran sensual fingers down his spine. "To think anyone believes in curses in this day and age. Aah, the wondrous powers of ancient Egypt. Even smart people lose their heads."

"Sucker born every minute."

The laughter ended abruptly as she kept the conversation on point. "You tell Teddy to be careful how he handles this. We're a week out from getting our hands on the jewelry. I don't want anything standing in the way and I don't want anyone tipped off."

Jared wasn't exactly sure how she did it, but she always ensured he understood she was ultimately in charge of the game. "He's always careful."

"See that he stays that way."

"Of course."

"Have you put the measures we discussed in place to keep our old friends off-balance?"

The change in topic was immediate and further proof that she had her finger on the pulse of everything.

"Everything we discussed is in place. They won't be in the Valley for the first extraction."

"Excellent." The spark of approval in that purr had him ridiculously pleased. "And, Jared…"

The tension in his body tightened another notch and he knew what came next, even without yet hearing the words. "Yes?"

"The back door's unlocked."

He wanted to tell her he was busy. Wanted to ignore the demands of his body and this shocking need to be with her as often as possible. Instead, he heard his voice, so heavy with need it echoed like a growl in his head. "I'll see you around ten."

The light tinkle of knowing laughter that greeted him before he disconnected the phone would keep him company, he knew, through the interminable minutes until he could see her again.

Liam's question hovered in her mind long after he'd deposited her back at her hotel, and Rowan couldn't shake off the restless need to find Finn and demand he tell her about the bracelet.

How had she missed something so important?

And if Finn did still have it, why had he kept the information from her?

She wanted to trust him and believe his past didn't define him, but what if he wasn't one of the good guys? Or worse, what if she'd allowed her attraction for him to color the purity of his motives?

Those questions and so many others had her bundling up a few minutes later and securing a taxi to take her across town to the Shard. The irony wasn't lost on her that she was in a cab instead of the Underground as she'd boldly proclaimed to Finn, but she needed speed, and the lighter evening traffic meant the cab was quicker.

Where she expected difficulty getting past security,

the process was anything but, and within moments the concierge was directing her to the elevator that ran to Finn's apartment.

"This is a pleasant surprise." Finn was waiting at the entrance to his apartment when she stepped off the elevator.

"Yes, well, we need to talk."

The rush of the past hour and the more-than-fascinating view of him dressed in jeans and a gray T-shirt that showed off his upper body to perfection had nerves leaping in her belly like a swarm of bees.

She was a woman who liked being in control—in her life, in her job, in her family—so the fact that she felt so distinctly off-kilter was more than a little unnerving. Especially when the curl of desire in her belly was doing a damn fine job of pushing all those angry bees out of the way.

"Come on in."

The heat of his body hit her like a brand when she brushed past him through the door and another lick of attraction hit her with all the power of an oncoming train.

Rowan fought to hang on to the tenuous threads of her anger as she walked into his large living room and stopped dead in her tracks. London spread out before her, the city's lights winking brightly through the windows. She could see the London Eye and Big Ben and Parliament across the banks. Could see the various walking bridges that joined each bank of the Thames. And when she turned, the central business district shone like a jewel, each distinct landmark bright with lights.

"These views are amazing. I realize I'm standing here, but this is really where you live?" She turned away from the windows, curious to what she'd see on his face. Pride? Ennui? Maybe both?

"We're both standing here, aren't we?"

"Yes, but I mean you live here. Like, every day."

He did laugh at that, his smile wide and his eyes full of the same wonder that tinged his words. "I'm still getting used to the views myself."

"How you doing with that?"

"Would I ruin your opinion of me if I told you I'm in awe every time I look out the window? I've been here about ten months and I still haven't stopped catching my breath at odd moments."

The ready evidence he wasn't wholly unaffected went a long way toward cooling her initial upset. "You say things like that and it's hard to stay mad at you."

"What did I do?"

"You don't know?"

"No, I don't."

He moved up behind her and settled his hands on her shoulders. He flicked the pad of his thumb along the base of her neck and she could have sworn she was in immediate danger of going up in flames. "Can I take your coat?"

She shrugged out of the thin jacket, not fully trusting there wouldn't be a quaver to her voice at the sensual play of his hands on her body. After he took her jacket, she turned on her heel, the windows beckoning her closer for a better look.

"What have I done, Rowan? I can't imagine this is a social call, especially since we have a meeting at seven tomorrow."

Her gaze alighted on Big Ben and she willed herself to take strength from it. The clock wasn't simply a landmark. It had stood watch over London for a century and a half, its bells ringing with hourly constancy.

It was up to her to do the same.

Long ago, she'd reformed her life, and while she knew

she dealt with many who lived in the shadows, she refused to out-and-out partner with someone who didn't feel the same way. With that vow in mind, she turned from the windows to face Finn.

And the uncertain reality that she might not hear something positive.

"This couldn't wait until tomorrow and it has nothing to do with Egypt."

"What is it, then?"

"Where's the Victoria bracelet?"

Finn exhaled on a heavy breath. He knew it was only a matter of time. Had thought as much when he'd replaced the bracelet in the safe earlier after his discussion with his father.

He simply hadn't calculated on the question coming so soon.

"Why the sudden curiosity?"

"So you do have it."

"Answer me first."

"It was my brother's idea, actually."

Finn wasn't sure how her brother got involved, so he gestured to the leather sectional that framed the living room. "Why don't you sit down and start from the beginning and please explain why your brother has anything to do with this?"

When he remained standing after she'd taken a seat, that cute little frown that meant she was thinking about something flashed across her face. "Aren't you going to sit down?"

"I'm going to get some wine first. For both of us, if that's all right with you?"

"Of course."

He kept a small bar stand on the one wall that wasn't

full of windows and he crossed to it now. "Why don't you start telling me while I open the wine? I have to admit I'm curious."

"Liam's in town and he met me for dinner. He managed to get the story of our late-night escapade at the Warringtons' out of me."

Surprise had him fumbling the corkscrew as he worked on opening a bottle of Cabernet. "He didn't know?"

"No one knew besides my grandfather. And, well, I've always suspected my grandmother knows as well because they don't keep secrets from each other, but that's it. The only other person who knew about my problem was my therapist, and even she didn't know about the objects I stole."

"Your grandfather didn't make you return what you stole?"

"Anonymously, yes."

The cork slid free and Finn set it next to the bottle as he reached for glasses. "How many did you pull before that night?"

"Big jobs?"

He turned around and couldn't hold back the smile. "Are there any other kind?"

"Fourteen."

The long, low whistle escaped his lips before he thought to hold it back. "Impressive."

"And stupid."

"I thought we already agreed to that." He poured the rich red into their glasses, then crossed back to the couch and handed her one. "To misguided choices."

"And mastering them." She took a sip, then set the wine down on his coffee table. "Delicious."

Like you. The words rose up so quickly his hand trembled as he lifted his own glass to his lips.

What was it about this small slip of a woman? She twisted him up in knots, and no matter how hard he fought to remain unaffected, every moment in her presence was like a drug.

"Now. Enough small talk. Where's the bracelet?"

"In my safe."

"What?" The word exploded from her lips as she leaped off the couch. "You cannot be serious."

"I'm absolutely serious."

"That's a priceless bracelet."

"And owned by the Royal Family."

A heavy sigh escaped her lips, the heft of his words sinking in. "It can't be."

"It's true. Lord Warrington bought it on the black market."

The words had their desired effect and she fell back onto the couch with a light thud. "He stole it?"

"Or had someone steal it for him. Either way, the provenance on that bracelet wasn't his."

"Well, it sure as hell isn't yours, either."

The lush wine turned sour on his tongue and he set his glass next to hers on the coffee table. "What did you want me to do with it?"

"Turn it in. Report it. Hell, send it off anonymously. You should have done what you needed to do to get it back to its rightful owner."

"And how would I have done that and not tipped those thugs off to who I was?"

"I don't know but you find a way."

An irrational shot of anger speared through him. "That's rich, Rowan, seeing as how you were the one who actually removed the piece from the Warringtons' safe."

She was back up off the couch, but instead of standing still, she skirted the coffee table to pace the room. The lights of the city glowed behind her and he couldn't hold back the deep-seated need that beat in his veins.

She was in his home. Here, among all he'd worked for.

"This isn't about me."

"Convenient time to get amnesia."

"I'm not the one who's held on to a priceless piece of jewelry for the last twelve years."

He couldn't sit still any longer, seated under her accusatory glare. With one solid motion, he was up and on his feet, ready to argue it out. "And where, exactly, was I going to send it? Last time I checked Buckingham Palace doesn't exactly accept unsolicited packages."

"A museum. A university. Hell, find some lawyers who handle royal business. Whatever, but you get it the hell back where it belongs."

"And what about that small little fact that I had a price on my head and was attempting to lie low? How was I supposed to handle that?"

"It's been twelve years, Finn. That's a long time for people to forget."

"And it's a short time in the world of poor choices."

She stopped her pacing and stood to face him, her blue gaze unwavering on his. "Is that the only reason?"

Somewhere in his soul, Finn recognized the moment for what it was.

Defining.

And he had to choose which way he was going to go with his answer.

The urge of the thief to never admit guilt rose up in his mind, but he tamped it down, his lover's heart hoping like hell she didn't walk away.

"No. It's not the only reason."

"Then why? Why do you still have it?"

"I kept it because of you."

* * *

The light from his desk lamp lit the corner of his home office in a strange glow as Will clicked his mouse through several screens, hunting for more information on the Nefertari tomb. The thread he'd followed after asking a few questions had seemed like a solid lead, but several hours later he couldn't find any further information.

"Bugger this."

"Doesn't sound very promising." Debbie stood in the doorway, her shoulder resting against the frame.

"Hey, babe." He couldn't hold back the smile when she came around his desk and he lifted his face for a kiss.

"Hey, yourself."

"I'm sorry. It's late." His gaze traveled to the clock on his computer screen and he winced. "I've been in here awhile."

"Yep."

"I'm sorry."

"Sadly, you're not. Or you aren't way deep down inside. You're lucky I love you anyway."

He wrapped his arms around her waist and pulled her onto his lap. "I'm *so* lucky."

Her lips opened under his and Will took the moment to savor his wife. He ran his hands over the hem of her nightgown before settling a hand on the soft skin of her inner thigh.

"Oh, no, you don't." The tease was offered with a smile, but her hands were firm on his as she stopped his fingers from traveling farther. "If we do this in here, you'll be back to your computer when the fun's over."

"You wound me, woman."

"And I want a bed." She hopped off his lap and moved around the desk. "That's my offer. Take it or leave it."

He couldn't hold back the smile. "Good thing I'm a

smart man. Let me shut down out of here and I'll be upstairs in five minutes."

"Promise?"

He didn't miss the skepticism in her beautiful gray
eyes or the small shot of embarrassment that his past behavior had put the doubt there.

Vowing tonight wouldn't be one of those nights, he
crossed his chest with his fingers. "Hope to die."

"See you soon."

He gave himself the sheer joy of watching her lush
backside sway as she disappeared from view, then hopped
back to the message board he was hunting through. He'd
post one more question, then head up to join her.

Until, of course, the words *Nefertari Tomb Curse*
caught his attention.

Chapter 10

"**Y**ou kept a priceless bracelet that belonged to one of England's most beloved monarchs because of me?" A series of tremors began coursing through her body as a wave of cold washed over her and Rowan wondered how she could feel so immediately bereft of her illusions about the man standing before her. "You can't be serious."

"That night changed my life."

"It changed mine, too. It doesn't mean you needed to hang on to the Victoria bracelet."

"You would have."

"No." She shook her head at the quiet accusation, her mind automatically racing back to those dark, reckless days. "No."

No?

If it hadn't been for her grandfather's insistence, she'd still possess the other pieces. Would she have kept the bracelet? And would she have changed her life in the ensuing years if that evening hadn't borne such harsh consequences?

Rowan wanted to believe she'd have made the required changes. Wanted to believe she'd see her way to healing from the brokenness inside of her.

She *had* to believe that.

"That night changed my life, too, Finn. Because I chose to change it. Thinking you died—hell, almost dying myself—went a long way toward ensuring I saw the light, but it was more than that. I *chose* to be different."

"I chose to be different, too."

"Did you? Can you honestly say you gave up your old ways? Because a man who feels no remorse for stealing is always able to steal again."

She knew it was unfair to throw his words back at him from earlier that day—and also knew she was the last person who deserved to sit in judgment of him—but she couldn't stop the horrible sense of disappointment that filled her.

Without warning, an image of Liam at dinner—his blue eyes awash in sadness over the story of her youthful choices—filled her mind's eye. Was this what Grandfather had felt like? Was this the staggering sense of disappointment that filled a person at the evidence of a betrayal?

She had no right to judge Finn Gallagher. None.

Yet so help her if she could hold back the torrent of words that seemed insistent on falling from her lips. "Can you stand there before me and tell me you've stolen nothing since that night?"

"Rowan—"

"No! I want an answer. I want the truth, Finn. Not some version of it you feel answers just enough of my questions to keep me dancing on the end of your leash."

"I haven't done that."

"Like hell you haven't."

His hands clenched and unclenched as he stared at her across the expanse of his living room, his large body set in hard lines. "What do you want me to tell you?"

"Everything."

"I can't do that."

His words stung like icy needles but they were the cold truth she needed to hear. "Then we have nothing else to say. I'll just gather my things. I'm afraid I need to withdraw from this project. I'll talk to my sister and see that you're reimbursed for your expenses so far."

"You don't need to leave. And you don't need to leave the project."

"Yes, I do."

He never moved from his place in the middle of the room, but she still felt his pain, radiating off him in hard, choppy waves. The lights of one of the world's greatest cities spread out behind him, yet all she saw was a lonely man, bereft of anything real.

She gathered her coat from the chair by the door and had her hand on the knob when he finally spoke. "I'll tell you everything."

The brass of the doorknob was cool to her touch, but she stopped and turned, oddly desperate to give him one more chance. "More promises of a thief?"

"No. The words of a man who has nothing left to lose."

"Tell me."

Finn had spent his life hearing the colloquialism that your past always catches up to you. On some level, he was glad to stop running.

And on the other hand, he'd never been so scared in his life. Not the night he snuck into an office building on his first big job and nicked a set of blueprints for a jewelry heist. Not the afternoon he signed his first deal for Gallagher International. And not the night he attempted to stanch the blood flow from a gunshot to his flesh as fear coursed through his veins that a young girl had possibly been captured by some of London's most depraved thieves.

"I told you how I got into the business."

"Yes." She'd crossed back to the couch and taken a seat, but she still held her coat in her hands, as if waiting for the opportune moment to run.

"Well, going straight doesn't mean everyone you did crooked business with wants you out of the game."

"And?"

"And I've kept up some side jobs along the way. Fewer and fewer as the years have gone by, but I still do the occasional job."

Where he expected some verdict in her gaze—or even some clue to what she was thinking—he saw nothing. Instead, she just sat there, quietly waiting for him to continue.

"It's no big deal. Or at least I keep telling myself it's no big deal, but it is."

He felt the words in a way he never had before. And in that moment he felt naked under Rowan Steele's steady gaze.

Through the years he'd felt very little remorse for his choices, but staring at the proof that you could make something more of your life, Finn knew a sense of shame.

"Why?"

He shrugged before taking a seat next to her. "Why not? You called it an addiction earlier and it's an apt term. I know what it is. What the beast that claws at your back feels like and thinks like and sounds like when it whispers in your ear."

"What sort of jobs do you take?"

"Ones that don't interfere with my legitimate work. I meant what I said. Gallagher International has been more successful than my wildest dreams, and the work I do keeps me incredibly busy. But every six months or so…the beast wants out."

"Do you have any interest in making different choices?"

"Hell yes. What do you think I'm trying to tell you?"

"What I want to hear, most likely."

"That's not fair."

She reached for her glass of wine, but paused before bringing it to her lips. "What is fair, then?"

"Let me prove to you I want to be different. That I can be different."

"But how can you be different if you keep the bracelet?"

"Because of you."

She shook her head. "I'm sorry, but that's not good enough."

"Why not?"

"You need to want it for yourself. You need to feel that, way down deep inside. Someone else can't do that for you."

The thought was so simple—profound, really—yet it wasn't the whole story. She made him want to make better choices. By her example and by the simple vibrancy that surrounded her like a bright cloak.

"I want to change my life. *You* make me want to change my life. Why is that so hard to believe? And what could possibly be wrong with that?" He reached for her, the need to touch her boiling over to the flash point.

Her coat still sat heavy in her lap, her hands folded neatly on top of it. He covered her hands with one of his own, entwining his fingers with hers, as he lifted his other hand to her cheek. "Rowan."

Her name hovered between them a fraction of a second before he leaned in and captured her lips with his. As a man used to taking what he wanted, the realization she wasn't a prize to be won struck him as the strangest sort of irony.

But when her mouth opened under his, he knew the sweetest victory.

Desire curled in his belly on swift wings as one kiss flowed into the next. The raw emotion of the past few days blended with the very real truth of the moment.

For the first time in his life, he was exposed. The years he'd spent thieving had finally been shared with another person. The lies he'd told himself and others had been confessed to another soul. The sins he carried had been unburdened on another.

Was it a fair burden to place on her?

He tried to concentrate on that—wanted to pull back and give her space—but the raging need for her simply wouldn't be sated. And then a light moan rose up in her throat as she tilted her head back, allowing him deeper access, and he was lost.

Finn took full advantage of the invitation, pulling her closer as she wrapped her arms around his waist. Their erotic play of tongues tortured his already-heated body, but he wouldn't stop.

Couldn't stop.

She tasted like the wine, only better. Lush and ripe, just like the nickname he'd teased her with.

"Peach." He whispered that single word against her lips. Felt hers smile against his before she pulled back.

"I didn't understand that at the time. Not fully. But I sensed it was just the slightest bit naughty."

"I meant it as a compliment."

Her eyebrows rose over that vivid blue. "Right."

"Yes, actually. I was nineteen at the time. Nineteen-year-old boys on the cusp of manhood aren't known for their romantic tongues. Thirty-one-year-old men, on the other hand…" He couldn't resist leaning forward and nipping her lips for another kiss.

"Sweet words, but they don't mean much."

Her statement was delivered in a breezy tone, but he refused to leave them lie. "They do mean something to me. You mean something to me, Rowan."

She laid a hand on his chest. "This will sound harsh, but despite my better judgment, you mean something to me, too."

"So we see where it goes."

"No, Finn. We can't do this."

"Why not?"

"Neither of us can afford distractions. I'm willing to give you the benefit of the doubt that you mean what you say, but it doesn't change our working relationship. The dig in Egypt requires our entire focus."

She struggled forward from the depths of the couch cushion, but stopped when he laid a gentle hand on her arm. "The trip's important. Incredibly important, but we can both do Egypt with our eyes closed. What else is this about?"

She didn't remove her arm, but neither did she sugarcoat her words. "Kissing you. Wanting to do even more. None of it changes the fact we're still on opposite sides of a very large disagreement, Finn."

"The bracelet?"

"Yes. You can't keep it. And as long as you have it in your possession, you can't have me."

The pronouncement was bold—he'd have expected no less from her—but it still stung. She was asking him to choose. And while he had no problem seeing his future on the up-and-up, he wasn't quite ready to let go of his past.

Nor was he crazy about an ultimatum.

"I've told you my reasons for retaining the bracelet."

"And I've told you mine for why you need to relinquish the piece."

"It's not that simple."

"Actually, it is." She stood once more, the coat in her hands. "I need to leave."

"I'll see you back to the hotel."

"I can take a cab back."

"I'll see you back. Just let me alert my driver."

Despite her protests, he did see her back to the hotel via the car he kept at the ready at all times. It was only a long while later, as he lay in his bed staring out the windows of his room, imagining the feel of her in his arms, that he understood why she'd left.

He hadn't put her first.

And no matter how much he wanted to make different choices for the future, he wasn't willing to atone for his past.

Rowan slugged down her second cup of coffee as she walked up the steps of the Underground station near the Shard. While the caffeine was a daily requirement for functionality, today her body needed it the same way she needed air.

She hadn't slept and couldn't get her mind to settle. She jumped from topic to topic like a deranged jackrabbit— Finn's desire to go straight, his reticence to give up the bracelet and the devastating reaction she had to him—almost as if the thoughts were on a loop. And each time she jumped to the next topic, she thought of new questions, all without answers.

At its core, though, was one simple question with no clear answer as to how she should proceed.

She was attracted to him.

Leaving his apartment the night before instead of curling up in his arms was one of the hardest things she'd ever had to do. And she now faced three weeks with him in the close confines of a dig site.

How was she going to keep this mindless attraction at bay? Especially when way down deep inside, she knew she didn't want to.

The demands of her body had begun to take over reasonable, rational thought, their only goal to be sated.

It was a humbling thought, really. Here she was, having spent years subjugating her irrational needs with an iron fist, and the same man who'd started her down that path was the one who made her want to leap off it.

The elevator ride to his office was quick, the breathtaking views of London as gorgeous as the day before. She nearly missed the buzzing of her mobile she was so enamored of her surroundings. She hit the answer button as a photo of Will flashed across the face of her phone.

"Hey there."

"Hey, yourself. I think I've got big news."

"You sound like you haven't slept."

"I haven't."

She let out a long, low whistle as the elevator doors swished open on the lobby of Gallagher International. "Debbie is going to hunt me down and kill me."

"Yeah, well, she's after me first. I blew off a late-night sex session after the kids fell asleep."

Finn's administrative assistant saw her from across the office and headed her way to let her through the door. "Will!"

"I caught a lead."

"You need to be getting caught on your wife."

"I know, I know."

Rowan shook her head, the irony of the moment not lost on her. She got all the archaeology she wanted and was fighting the urge to have what she was quite sure would be mind-blowing sex with Finn. Will got all the sex he wanted and all he seemed to focus on was archaeology.

As her grandmother had admonished her on more than one occasion, we always want what we can't have.

Celeste waved her through the glass doors, and Rowan pointed toward the phone and mouthed an *I'm sorry* before following her to Finn's office. An inconvenient shot of attraction wrapped around her as she caught sight of him leaning forward over his desk, his fingers flying over the keyboard of his laptop.

The opportunity was too sweet to resist—to look her fill without his knowing—and she stopped for the briefest moment to simply admire the view.

Finn Gallagher was an incredible specimen of a man. Strong, thick shoulders on a solid frame. A narrow waist that she could just see before the rest of his body disappeared behind the desk. A hard jaw that clenched and unclenched as he typed whatever it was he was working on.

He was devastating.

And the resistance she was working so diligently to maintain slipped another notch.

"Rowan? Are you there?"

"Of course I'm here."

"What did I just say?"

She tamped down on the grimace at being caught

twice. Will knew full well she hadn't been listening to him, and the sly grin that suffused Finn's features when he glanced up from his computer was proof that he'd known she was there. Drinking him in.

"Oh, repeat it for me. I just got off the elevator in Finn's office. In fact, hang on and I'll put you on speaker so we can both hear you."

"Good morning." Finn was up and around his desk, and since she knew his custom was to press a kiss to her cheek, she took a quick seat on one of his guest chairs and pointed toward the phone. "Will's on the phone and he's got news. I thought I'd put him on speaker so he could tell us both at once."

The small line that furrowed his brow and the quick hand he ran along his jaw confirmed her actions had struck a chord.

Good.

This was a new day and she *would* prove to herself she could resist the far-too-enticing package that was Finn Gallagher.

"Good morning, Finn." Will's voice echoed from the speaker on her phone where she'd placed it in the center of Finn's desk. After a quick recap of the information Will had provided in the elevator—minus the sex update—he launched into his findings.

"So I got several hits on those message boards."

Finn's gaze was focused on the desk, and again, Rowan found herself gazing at him longer than necessary, unable to look away. "Do you think the boards are secure?"

"You have to have a user name and password."

The frown was back, but this time Rowan knew she wasn't the cause. As Will talked through the types of people he usually met on the forums he visited, Finn scratched a note.

We should get your brother to take a quick look into these sites.

She nodded, recognizing the value of getting Campbell involved. Although all of them had a basic proficiency with technology, there wasn't a system in existence her brother couldn't get in or out of. He had the added benefit of understanding what something suspicious looked like in the digital world.

As her friend's voice droned on from the speakerphone, Rowan knew she'd better cut him off and get him to the point. "Will, what is it that got your feelers up?"

"The answers I'm getting from supposed experts make no sense."

Finn tapped a few keys on his computer before turning the laptop so they could both see it. "What did you ask them?"

"The basics we discussed. What they've heard about the dig in the Valley. What was the word on the expected cache. I even played around with the curse thread, curious to see what I'd fine."

"And?" Rowan leaned closer to the computer, intrigued by the list of threads on the site Will was most excited about.

"Anyone who comments on the thread says the curse is real. They've pointed to other ancient texts to prove their point, as well."

"You and I both know it's a bunch of bunk. There's no such thing as a curse."

Finn tapped a few more keys. "Doesn't mean someone doesn't feel it's not an awfully good deterrent to whatever's in that tomb."

"But how can it be a deterrent if no one really gives it any mind? I know the locals have been known for their superstitions, but not the professional archaeologists. I just find it hard to believe a team of research specialists are going to get spooked by something so silly."

Will's voice was tinny through the speakerphone, and the sounds of a class change were evident in the background. "One of the regular posters thinks the rumors of a curse are contributing to the red tape that the British Museum has been up against."

"How much do you trust this guy's input?" Finn tapped his finger to the screen, pointing on the link she needed to click next. "If I'm reading the thread you're referring to, the commenter is named Hampstead 84."

"That's him."

"And?" Finn pressed again. "How well do you know him?"

"I don't. That's part of why I hang out on these sites. It's a way to talk archaeology with others in the field."

"Have you seen this guy on the forums before?"

"A few times. He's been on around six months." Will's voice echoed from the speaker again, the noise growing in volume in the background.

"Will? You still there?" Since the sound coming out of the phone resembled the noise of a thundering herd on the African plains, she assumed it was his class.

"Yeah. Look, I've gotta go. My next group of undergrads are walking in. I'll follow up later."

"Thanks, Will." She ended the call and sat back to stare at Finn. "Something bothers you about this."

"A lot of things. Just add this one to the list of things that make me increasingly concerned about what we're going to find when we get to Luxor. It goes back to your original question to Will. Why the hell would a bunch of professionals give any credence to a curse?"

"You think it's more of a stall tactic?"

"Why not? We both know the museum's had a hell of a time getting all their permits. That's part of why they pulled me in on the job. I know the region and I've got my connections with the government and I was able to expedite a few things in exchange for giving my firm's services to the Egyptian government."

Not for the first time did Rowan see the depth of Finn's expertise and knowledge. He'd built a wildly successful global business and knew how to go toe-to-toe with the major players in their industry.

So why couldn't he see how he risked that by holding on to the Victoria bracelet?

An awkward silence descended between them and Rowan couldn't help but be sad for it. They'd had an easy, comfortable flow to their conversation, and the night before had obviously put a damper on that. And she had no one to blame but herself.

Perhaps it was for the best.

"I'm going to set myself up in a conference room, if that's okay. I'll email my brother and get him looking into the websites Will's been haunting."

"Stay here. I have some meetings I need to see to. Celeste can get you anything you need."

"You don't need to leave."

"Really. I was on my way out anyway."

She watched him go, regret like sludge in her veins. Whatever sexy moments they'd shared the night before had been effectively squashed by her lack of warmth this morning.

But instead of feeling as if she'd won the round, all she could muster up was the vague sense she'd lost the game.

Finn stepped out of the building and headed for a coffee shop around the corner. It was still early and the morning throng of people came alive as they rushed their way to work. He caught fragments of conversations as people passed, but it all swirled by in a blur, his own thoughts a whirling haze.

Damn it, the woman was infuriating.

He knew he hadn't done himself any favors the previous evening, but hell, she wouldn't even accept the most casual of greetings when he'd attempted to kiss her cheek.

The long line that snaked through the shop didn't help his raging irritation, but he'd be damned if he went back to the office so soon. So he stood in line and fumed as the rich scents of coffee, steamed milk and breakfast muffins assaulted his senses.

When he finally got to the counter, he'd calmed enough to put in his order and added a scone for good measure. The coffee would help the headache brewing behind his eyes, and the scone would hopefully go a long way toward sweetening his mood.

It was only after he'd picked up both and started back to the office that a frisson of awareness skated over his skin. He moved out of the throng of people to stand against the wall of a nearby office building, his gaze scanning the crowd for any indication of what might have set his radar off.

The same faceless crowd he'd walked with to the coffee shop streamed around him, their heads down or their phones glued to their ears as people raced wherever they needed to be.

So why couldn't he shake the feeling of being watched?

With casual movements, he leaned against the building and dug into his bag, breaking off a bite of scone. He worked the street in quadrants with his gaze, following the groups of people as he searched for anything out of the ordinary.

When several minutes of searching turned up nothing unexpected—no one loitering or standing up above the crowd—he balled up his now-empty paper bag full of crumbs and tossed it in the closest trash can.

Damn it, but he needed to calm the hell down. First the upset-lover routine over Rowan's cold greeting this morning. Now the weird reaction to a busy crowd.

The throng of people sucked him back in, and Finn considered how to play the morning with Rowan. While he wasn't immune to her, he wasn't a fifteen-year-old boy. He could control his feelings and be a professional.

And he'd take some solace that she wasn't as unaffected as she pretended, so they'd both be in hell on the trip to Egypt.

Images of her in a pair of shorts, work boots and a tank top filled his mind's eye as he rubbed at his forehead. It was going to be a long three weeks and—

His thoughts vanished as a hard shove came at his midsection out of nowhere, his coffee flying into the air at the heavy push. A quick, shooting pain hit his side before instinct had him pushing back at the threat.

Every instinct he'd attempted to squelch since leaving the coffee shop came roaring back to life as a heavy form, clad in a sweatshirt jacket with the hood up, took off, zigzagging through the crowd. People screamed and one woman even tossed her bag at the man but the guy was off and down the sidewalk, shoving people as he went, clearly bent on destruction this morning.

The man was well out of range, but Finn took off after him anyway. He'd sensed he was being watched and it was clear now he was the target. Finn followed the same zigzagging pattern down the sidewalk, but the heavy throng of people and the loss of breath had him slowing down. Why the hell did he get that scone? He never ate that crap.

And why the hell did his side hurt so bad?

On a heavy breath, he looked once more for the hooded figure, but saw nothing in the sea of morning commuters heading for the building.

On a resigned sigh, he turned and headed for his office, the entire experience nagging at him in the deepest corners of his mind.

Was that intended for him? And to what end?

He beelined for the elevators as soon as he was back in the building, his mood even fouler than when he'd walked in. The coffee had been a bust, his head was throbbing and he needed to check his damn side. The dull ache hadn't subsided, but was growing progressively worse.

The walls wavered as he stepped off the elevator, the glass shimmering as he saw clear through each of the panes, all the way through to the windows on the far side of the floor. With stubborn determination, he focused his gaze on Rowan, still perched at her desk right where he'd left her.

Colors added themselves to the wavering walls as he marched toward her, keying himself in to the office through the secured door in the lobby. His feet felt as if they were encased in lead, and each step was agony as he walked down the hall.

His foot caught on the carpet and he stumbled, slamming into the glass wall that made up the conference room next to his office. The impact must have been enough to draw attention because Rowan looked up from her computer, her gaze going dark before she leaped out of her chair.

She must be mad about something else....

The thought tumbled through his mind as the image of her running toward him wavered, just like the glass.

"Finn!"

His name echoed through his head, but the sound came from far away, as if he was underwater, and he laid an arm on the glass wall for support. It took her forever to run the distance from his office to where he stood in the hallway, and then she was there, her arms wrapping around his waist.

"What's wrong with you?"

"What?"

Side. Tell her about your side.

The voice in his head thought the words but he wasn't sure if they made it to his lips. And then he fell on top of her, his arms wrapping hard around her shoulders as he stumbled on his feet. Why didn't his feet work anymore?

"What happened to you?"

Words floated to his mind—did they float to his lips?—when she shifted, her hand coming down hard on his ribs. He screamed, the sound an embarrassment to his ears, before the soft, crooning tone of her voice broke through the agonizing pain to calm him.

"Shhh. Shhh, Finn. Come on. A little farther to the couch in your office."

Those strange colors continued to fill behind his eyes and he vaguely realized people had come out of another conference room when he saw Rich and Mark race toward them.

"Okay, Finn. Take it easy."

Large hands grabbed him on each arm, lifting his weight from Rowan's shoulders, and before he knew it the soft leather of his office couch cushioned his body.

Rowan leaned over him, dragging at his suit jacket before she took a sharp intake of breath. "You've been stabbed."

Chapter 11

Rowan took a deep breath and tried to remember what she'd been taught in all those stupid classes Kensington was always foisting on them. She snagged the scarf she'd worn that morning and bunched it up to stem the bleeding before she barked out orders to the two men who'd helped Finn into his office.

"Is there a doctor in the building?"

"I don't know," one said as the other shrugged.

Celeste barreled into the office, her face set in efficient—and worried—lines. "There is one. Rich, call the concierge and tell them we need a doctor. They'll know what to do."

"Do I tell them why?"

"Of course." Celeste shot him a dark glare. "Why wouldn't you?"

"He's got a knife wound."

"Which means the doctor needs to come prepared." Celeste barked out the order and Rowan mentally gave the woman points for stoic British efficiency. She gave her even more points when the woman came near Finn, her voice gentle as she gave instructions. "Hold that against his side and don't let up on the pressure."

"Thanks."

"I'm going to wait by the elevators for the doctor. I'll leave you to it. You'll be fine." Celeste patted Rowan's arm, the move going a long way toward stemming the trembling that had started in her legs when she caught sight of the red stain expanding on Finn's white dress shirt.

"Finn, can you hear me?" She tried to keep her voice level but the same quivering in her legs seemed to have migrated to her throat. "Finn!"

His lashes fluttered briefly before his eyes opened to small slits. "Rowan? What happened?"

"That's what we're trying to figure out. You were stabbed."

"Side. Hurts." His eyes closed again as a shiver racked his body.

"Yeah, I know." She turned, looking for something to cover him with, and saw her jacket hanging off the back of the guest chair. "Finn! Come on, stay with me."

"What?" He mumbled the word, but his voice was stronger.

"Hold your hand right here." She pressed his hand to the scarf and fought the hard, choppy waves of fear that buffeted her as her gaze landed on the bloody material. "I want to get something to cover you."

His eyes blinked open once more. "I'm cold."

"I know. I'm going to get my coat but I need you to keep the wound covered."

"What wound?" His eyes opened wider and she saw

the dawning of understanding in his gaze. "What happened to me?"

"It looks like you got stabbed."

"What?" He struggled to sit up and she pressed on his shoulders to keep him prone on the couch. "Outside?"

"Oh, no, you don't. And yes, presumably outside, since I've yet to see any knife-wielding lunatics in your offices." She laid her hand over his until she was satisfied he'd keep the scarf in place over the wound, before she jumped up and raced to get her coat. Within moments she was back, wrapping the coat around his body.

"There's a doctor in the building. Did someone call for them?"

"Celeste's waiting for the doctor at the elevator."

"Can you wrap me tighter?"

A quick glance at the coat and Rowan knew it wasn't going to do much to keep him warm, until she hit on an idea. "Do you have the wound covered?"

"Yes."

"I'm going to do my best not to put pressure but you need more heat." She climbed up next to him, the deep plush of the leather couch ensuring she had enough room to stretch out next to his large body.

"Can you get closer?"

"Am I hurting you?"

"No."

"Are you keeping up the pressure on the wound?"

"Yes."

She stretched farther, avoiding any contact with his arm that held the scarf in place, and entangled her limbs with his. Her chest pressed against his unharmed side and her legs wrapped around his. "Are you feeling anything?"

"I think so."

"Does it hurt?"

"Not with you here."

She glanced up, the slightest edge of teasing in his voice tipping her off. "Are you getting off on this?"

"Kind of."

"Finn Gallagher!" She wanted to leap off the couch but another shiver racked his body and she was afraid to move. "What is wrong with you?"

"Nothing worth worrying about." He wrapped his free arm around her, that smile still firmly in place.

"But you were passed out. And you're cold, which I think means shock."

"I'm fine."

"Then let me up."

"I need your warmth."

"You need your head examined." Rowan muttered the words and kept up a good front, but she was inordinately pleased to see him responding so well. His skin had lost some of its earlier pallor and his gaze was clearer. "I can't believe this happened. Did you see who it was? And where were you?"

"I went to get some coffee and was walking back. I got a weird feeling and stopped, pretended to loiter for a few minutes but didn't see anything. Figured it was my mind playing tricks."

"Only no tricks."

"Evidently not." He shifted and grit his teeth, and she didn't miss the raw agony that flashed across his face. "Bastard pushed into me like he was stumbling and then shivved my side."

"Who do you think's doing this?"

Finn was prevented from saying anything by the arrival of the doctor, a genteel-looking woman who marched into his office with stiff, efficient movements that would give Celeste a run for her money. "So what have you done now, Mr. Gallagher?"

"I swear it wasn't me."

Doctor Efficient's tone stayed firm but a small smile lit her mouth. "You always say that."

Rowan shifted off him to give the doctor room. "It's a knife wound, doctor."

The older woman shook her head before she kneeled in front of the couch and removed the coat. "When I took this job I expected I'd hand out aspirin for headaches and take a look at the occasional person who tripped running too fast. And then Gallagher International moved into the building and my work has been far more interesting."

"I've only seen you twice before."

She ripped open a sterile pair of rubber gloves dug out of her medical bag and snapped them on. "Yes, and seeing as how you've only been in this building for ten months, I would hardly say that's a good track record. Especially since the first time was for stitches when you thought it'd be fun to rappel between floors and the second was to make sure you didn't have a concussion from a small and still unnamed accident on your way to work."

Rowan tried her best to pick her mouth up off the floor at the litany of Finn's injuries. "You can't be serious."

"Oh, not only am I serious, I was told by building management Mr. Gallagher over here was going to need to get an incremental rider on his insurance premiums if he didn't shape up." The woman lifted the bloody scarf and let out a heavy exhale. "Looks like they were smart to cover their bets."

"I'm not suing the building." He grit his teeth once more as she probed the wound. "Especially since it's my own bloody fault this stuff keeps happening."

The doctor pulled a syringe out of her bag. "*Bloody* is certainly the operative word."

She worked in silence for a few minutes, the same efficient movements she'd exhibited when she walked into the office the bedrock of her treatment. "You're awfully lucky. The wound is clean and not all that deep."

"I don't need stitches?" Finn's gaze drifted to where the doctor applied a liquid bandage to his wound before he shifted his focus. "Hear that, Rowan? I'm not quite the menace I seem."

The doctor finished up and wrote a prescription Celeste offered to go fill. Finn was sitting up and joking, and Rowan knew she needed to calm down and just be happy he was alive.

The doctor pointed to the now-discarded scarf on the floor. "Is this yours?"

"Yes."

"I hope you weren't all that attached to it." The woman dropped it into a small plastic bag she'd used for the other medical waste. "I need to take it with me."

"I'll live." Rowan heard the distance in her tone and wondered at the letdown from her own adrenaline rush. "And apparently he will, too."

"His hide is surprisingly stubborn and resilient. I would ask that you keep an eye on him. See that he takes it easy for a few days."

"We're leaving tomorrow night for Egypt."

The doctor appeared to weigh her words before she finally spoke. "I prescribed sleeping pills along with the antibiotic. See that he takes both."

Rowan wasn't sure when she'd become Finn's caregiver, yet she couldn't say she was all that upset with the role. "I will."

"Excellent." The doctor nodded as she gathered up her medical bag and the waste. "I've got one last question."

Finn edged to a sitting position on the couch. "Of course. What is it?"

"How exactly did you end up with a stab wound?"

Finn stood from the couch, unwilling to sit in a less-than-advantageous position for the discussion. "*Stab* implies internal organs. I had a small brush with the sharp end of a knife. Bad commute this morning."

"You want to try another one, Mr. Gallagher?"

The good doctor's patience was clearly at an end and he quickly hunted for something a little less cheeky. "I'm only half joking. I ran to get some coffee and breakfast. Ms. Steele was using my office and I wanted to clear my head for a bit. We've had some late nights prepping for our business trip."

"Go on."

"Someone was stumbling through the crowd. He ran into several people and I can only think I was in the wrong place at the wrong time."

"Seems like a habit with you." The doctor dragged a phone from her pocket. "I need to report this."

"You're welcome to, but I hardly think there's anything to report. I didn't even need stitches."

A play of emotions whipped across her face and he held his breath for the briefest of moments.

Would she buy it?

Or was he about to spend a good portion of his day with the police?

"And you truly don't think you were the intended victim?"

"Hardly." The lie tripped out with ease and Finn deliberately avoided Rowan's gaze. He was already in her personal doghouse. Deceiving a medical professional likely wasn't doing him any favors.

"As you so aptly put it, the wound hasn't punctured anything, nor did it require anything resembling major medical attention."

"No, ma'am."

"I am, however, going to write it up. And if anything else suspicious happens, I reserve the right to rescind my generosity."

"Of course."

"And could you please *try* to stay out of trouble?"

The wry tone of her voice suggested she had no faith he'd even make the attempt, but Finn couldn't resist one last assurance. "Of course, Doctor."

He had to give Rowan credit. She waited until the doctor had not only cleared his office but until the elevator doors closed on her watchful form before she exploded. "What in the hell happened to you? And why are you lying to a doctor?"

"She didn't believe me."

"That doesn't change anything."

"Actually, it does. The small flesh wound I have can hardly be considered an actual stab wound—"

"Even though we both know that's what it is."

He held up a hand. "She can't prove there was anything malicious behind it, nor did it require all that much attention. And do you really want to spend the day with a team of police nosing around our business?"

"Why does everyone suppose we're a team on this? Any time spent with the cops is all about you, buddy."

"Oh, really?" He couldn't resist moving closer, pleased when she held her ground. "And don't you suppose they'd want to talk to you, since you were with me during our attempted mugging the other night? Two hits in almost as many days raises suspicions."

Whatever she was about to say faded from her lips. "What the hell is this about, Finn? And who wants to keep us from going to Egypt?"

"I wish I knew."

"You've done other work for the museum and so have I. We both know the players involved. Why does it feel like there's something just out of reach? Like someone's pulling the strings?"

"I don't know."

He might not know, but he couldn't argue with Rowan's assessment. From the very start, the entire project had the strangest feel to it. And the imagery of a puppet master, dragging the strings offstage, was an apt one.

"I got lucky and spoke to my brother earlier. He's pulling one of his all-nighters. He's looking into the web forum. I can have him do some more nosing around."

"Nosing in what? From what Will's said, there's a small online community tied to these forums."

"Campbell can get into Baxter Monroe's email, if you want him to."

Finn was used to taking every advantage he could find, but even he had to admit Rowan's brother had some serious skills. "He can do that?"

"He'd kill me if I said yes, but yes, he can do it. And if I give him a good reason why we need to know, he'll do it without getting all uppity and moral about it."

While he was the last person who should be pointing a finger in judgment, he couldn't quite ignore the irony of her statement. "Isn't the ability to do that sort of the opposite?"

She leaned in, her voice low. "Would you steal for just anyone?"

"No." As an afterthought, he added, "And it's not nearly that sordid."

"Go with me for a minute." When he only nodded, she continued, "You don't do jobs for the hell of it. You do them to some personal code that only you know and understand. Despite my recent reaction, I do understand that." Her gaze dropped. "I never had that. My personal code wasn't nearly as refined. Or discriminating. It was a sickness."

Whatever direction he'd expected their conversation to take, Rowan's sudden admission wasn't it. "That may be the case, but you weren't entirely wrong last night, either. Our choices do define us. Who we are. The jobs we take."

Jobs.

Something stopped him and flipped the entire problem on its ear. "Wait a minute."

"What?"

"You've got a point on taking jobs."

"In what way?"

"Who stands to gain from the dig in Egypt?"

"Monroe's certainly lining his pockets. He'll make a fortune in speaking engagements for the rest of his life, not to mention book deals and whatever salary increase he can command at the museum."

"Right, but he's got that no matter what. He might be a little toady, but he's a well-positioned toady."

"Yeah, right." Her indelicate snort let him know exactly what she thought about that.

"Come on, you have to agree. Not liking him isn't reason enough to assume he's hiring thugs to shiv me in broad daylight."

Her gaze drifted to the red stain that colored his shirt before she looked away. "Fair point."

"There's also the museum brass. They stand to gain

from this, as does the auction house who ultimately gets some of the lesser pieces."

Her somber gaze sharpened. "This is going to auction?"

"Yep. The scholarly committees involved have all agreed some select pieces can go out to collectors. After the auction house gets their cut for handling the auction, all proceeds will be split between the Egyptian government, a UN coalition on preserving antiquities and future grants in the region."

"Who's competing for the prize?"

"All the major houses. I spoke to the head of Hamilton's a few days ago and they're well positioned to secure the project."

"Yet we haven't been looking at them. This is big money, Finn. Nothing like the artifacts on this dig have seen the light of day, and no respectable collector has ever been able to get their hands on something like this. The bids are going to be enormous."

"So's every major collection the auction houses touch. They don't need to resort to criminal activity to get projects. Hell, I know all of these people because of the work we do. There's no way Hamilton's or anyone else is going to risk their reputation like that. The ramifications are too great."

She didn't appear convinced, but obviously decided not to argue the point for the moment. "Who else?"

"No one else stands to gain other than the black market."

"And since when does the black market show up attacking people assigned to the dig? To anyone involved, you're there to authenticate the cache, nothing more."

"True."

"So why is someone trying to take you out?"

* * *

Rowan's words were still rattling around his head a half hour later when he walked into his apartment. He needed to clean up before going to dinner with the Steeles. If the few extra minutes in his apartment would help him calm down, well, that would be even better.

Damn it, why couldn't he stop shaking?

He headed for the bathroom, stripping the soiled shirt off as he went. He tossed it in the kitchen garbage, then kept on to his room. Another wave of shivers racked his chest and he cursed the betrayal of his body as he snatched a washcloth from the closet and wet it with hot water.

He'd tried to hide the shivers from Rowan, but no matter how hard he'd willed himself to calm, he couldn't stop the post-adrenaline letdown that wouldn't let go of him.

He was more shaken than he'd normally want to admit.

Was there something bigger at stake?

In his line of work, he knew better than most that the antiquities culture was fraught with wealthy players who often attempted to play outside the rules. It was the sole reason he'd maintained an outlet for his less-than-reputable work over the years.

And while he hadn't lied to Rowan—that portion of his activities *had* diminished over time—it was still a part of his life.

So who could possibly be playing in the game, and if they were, why was he a target?

You don't kill the golden goose.

He stared at his reflection in his bathroom mirror, the wound on his side and the flesh around it bright pink. His motions were limited, but they were a hell of a lot less limited than if he'd had stitches. He could only thank his lucky stars the thug with the knife hadn't met with success.

The wound was a scratch and it wasn't likely to give him too many problems.

The wound was a scratch....

"Damn it!" He threw the washcloth on the counter, the wet cotton landing with a thud.

You didn't kill the golden goose, but you sure as hell could slow it down.

And someone clearly didn't want him and Rowan to get to Egypt on time.

The heavy knocking on his door drew his attention and he stomped from the bathroom, his senses on high alert. No one had called up to notify him he had a visitor. He flung open the door, surprised when Rowan stood on the other side. "How'd you get up here?"

The briefest hesitation tinged her voice, but it was gone so fast he had to wonder if he'd even heard it. "I nicked the extra elevator pass you had in your desk. It's dangerous to keep it there, you know. You live in one of the most secure buildings in the world, yet anyone who comes into your office can get up here."

"Situational ethics, Rowan?" He couldn't resist pointing out the obvious. "The office is secure, too. And I have a guard dog outside my office nonstop."

"I earned that jab fair and square."

"Yes, you did."

"You still shouldn't leave this lying around." She waved a small key fob at him and he took it. She wasn't entirely wrong, but it galled him to think he'd grown lax in the past few months, the convenience of living where he worked obviously getting to him.

"That looks pretty bad." Her gaze drifted to his waist,

and again, he had the sense the sands were shifting under his feet.

He heard the genuine concern in her voice, yet her gaze held something else entirely as it roved over his skin. *Hunger.*

And suddenly, whatever pain he felt vanished at the very real evidence of her interest. "It's not so bad."

Her eyes narrowed and any hint of sensuality vanished from her gaze as she moved forward, her hand on his stomach. The muscles there quivered involuntarily at her touch. "What's this?"

"It's a liquid bandage."

"No, this!" She closed the remaining distance between them and placed her fingers on his skin.

The heat was immediate—electric—and he could only imagine this was what it felt like to be branded. His skin was hot, yet all sensation seemed centered in the flesh underneath the pads of her fingers.

But it was only when he looked down at her hands that her reaction registered.

Tears shimmered over the clear blue of her eyes. "That's where you got shot, isn't it?"

"Yes."

"Oh, Finn. I'm so sorry." Why hadn't she thought about a scar?

The admonition rang over and over again in her mind as her gaze returned once more to that puckered flesh underneath the last rib on his right side. The knife wound a few inches below it had colored the skin on that side of his body pink with the fresh injury, but the outlines of his scar were unmistakable.

"How many times do we have to go over this, Rowan?

My injuries that night weren't your fault. I was in that house of my own free will."

"And you stayed behind to help me. A stranger."

"I couldn't leave you there to fend for yourself. And none of it changes that I earned this fair and square."

His words filled her with a subtle heartache she didn't know how to assuage. She'd spent so many years living with a combination of guilt and anger that it was more challenging than she'd ever have expected to learn to let go.

"I've had dreams. Nightmares about that night ever since it happened."

"Often?"

"Often enough. At first I had them almost every night." She shrugged, the sheer terror of those first days filling her mind's eye. "It faded over time until they only came when I was stressed or tired."

"I'm sorry."

She couldn't resist throwing his words right back at him. "It wasn't your fault. Besides, I considered them penance."

"Consider yourself atoned." His voice was husky and he moved a fraction closer, his hand reaching up to cover hers where it still pressed to his flesh.

The memories faded as his touch pulled her back to the here and now and the magnificent specimen of a man standing before her. The hard planes of his body filled her vision, and she lifted her other hand to touch him. A light dusting of hair covered his chest, tapering to a thin line over the ridges of his abdomen. She traced the path, fascinated when his stomach muscles tensed under her touch.

"Rowan." He leaned forward and pressed his forehead to hers. "I think you need to stop."

She rested her hands on his shoulders, the thick ropes

of muscles under her fingers so enticing she couldn't resist dragging her palms over his skin in a hard caress. His skin vibrated at the contact and she felt the subtle beat of his blood pumping under her touch.

"What if I don't want to?"

He never lifted his head, but his words held a world of regret. "Nothing's changed since last night."

"No, it hasn't." She dropped her hands and stepped back, the sudden realization her behavior bordered on that of a tease if she didn't get out of there quick. "I'm sorry. I should leave you to get dressed."

The overpowering desire that curled under her skin like a living, breathing thing nearly had her going back into his arms, but she held off.

Because no matter how badly she wished things were different, they were still on opposite sides of a very large chasm.

Chapter 12

Finn knew Alexander and Penelope Steele missed little, but it had been many years since he'd felt himself sized up in quite this way. Add Rowan's brother Liam to the mix and he'd basically run the triumvirate of Rowan's overprotective family.

The dinner they'd shared earlier in the formal dining room had given way to coffee and dessert in a small parlor off the main hallway. Despite the less formal environment, the scrutiny was as unyielding as dinner.

And no matter how he tried to gauge his performance, he could only think he'd come up lacking.

Whether it was from genuine interest or a desire to break the awkward silence, Penelope smiled at him as she added sugar to her coffee. "Finn, dear. Where in Ireland is your family from?"

"Dublin, ma'am. And you? I can hear the hints of the Emerald Isle in your voice."

Her smile grew bright at that and he thought perhaps he'd finally hit on a topic that wasn't controversial. The talk thus far—of his business, the impending trip to Egypt or his new office space—had resulted in stilted conversation and subtle disapproval.

"County Cork."

"And don't think she doesn't have the gift of blarney to prove it." Alexander piped up over his coffee and his open smile was the first time since they'd arrived Finn thought he might be on more stable ground.

"Oh, I don't know." Penelope's face maintained its serene lines but he didn't miss the mischief that alighted in her green gaze. "You've kissed that stone on more than one occasion, my dear. It's yet to sweeten your tongue."

Rowan rolled her eyes from her perch across the room and Finn wasn't sure if he should take heart or make up some medical emergency and duck out. He'd even momentarily thought about rubbing at his wound in hopes he could get it to start bleeding again.

And how far gone was that?

He'd dealt with stickier situations in his life—ones that actually involved life-and-death decisions—so why was he sweating one evening with a pair of octogenarians?

"How do you like living in the Shard, Finn?" Liam took up the conversation ball and Finn latched on to it like a drowning man. "Rowan's been raving about your work space but I'm curious what you think of it as a residence."

"You thinking of buying a space?" Finn eased into the conversation, the change another welcome diversion from Alexander's scrutiny.

Liam shrugged lightly, the casual gesture at odds with the intense man Finn knew him to be. "I've considered it. The floor plans are gorgeous but I'm sort of attached to New York as my home base."

"You should see the views from Finn's place. You can see all of London." Rowan's voice floated over the room, effectively stopping all conversation.

Finn fought a wince, but just barely. What was she thinking? And why did she bring up the fact she'd been inside his apartment?

If a cow had walked into the room and died on the carpet, it would have made less of an impact than her statement.

As it were, Alexander's already stoic visage darkened. In that age-old way of older men intimidating the younger ones who came calling, Finn didn't doubt the man knew where and how to hide bodies.

What was even more shocking was that the dark gaze was still mighty effective and he was long out of the classroom.

"Finn, I'd like to talk to you."

He recognized the summons for what it was and rose at Alexander's words. "Of course, sir."

"Grandfather." Rowan rose to follow. "We're having a nice evening. Why do you need to talk to Finn?"

"It's nothing to worry about, just a quick conversation. Go join your grandmother in the library. She wants you to get some pictures for her in Egypt. She's made you a list."

"Grandfather—"

"Go on, Ro." Liam smiled as he lifted his after-dinner cognac. "I'll run interference."

"That's what I'm afraid of." Rowan took her grandmother's hand in hers and helped the woman from her seat.

It didn't take long for the women to depart, the ritual old-fashioned and borderline archaic. Finn was about to say as much—what the hell did he have to lose at this point?—when a broad grin split Alexander's face. "I'd say he passed rather well, wouldn't you, Liam?"

"Like a champ."

"Excuse me?" Finn had the distinct sensation of swimming underwater as he dropped back into his seat. "Passed what?"

Alexander slapped his knee. "The gauntlet."

"I wasn't aware that was part of the evening's entertainment." Finn glanced at the cognac Liam laid at his elbow. "What's this for?"

"A peace offering."

"You have feelings for my girl, now, don't you, Gallagher?" Alexander's direct stare bored into him with all the subtlety of a thousand volts of electricity.

"She's a special woman."

"Damn straight she is. She's also headstrong, impulsive and often reckless, and you'd be stupid not to have feelings for her." The old man leaned forward. "Something makes me think you're far from stupid."

"I like to think so." Finn couldn't hold back the grin at that. "And she is pretty headstrong. A trait from your wife's family?"

Alexander did laugh at that, and Finn thought they perhaps had moved another step further. "I think both branches of the family tree contributed. And from what I know of her mother's parents, those branches were likely ripe for climbing, as well. But I'm getting off topic."

What *was* the topic?

"Look, Mr. Steele. I'm quite sure you didn't bring me here to size me up as a possible date for your granddaughter. She's more than capable of making those decisions for herself."

When both men remained silent, Finn continued on. "So why am I really here?"

Alexander leaned forward, his sturdy frame and vivid blue eyes an older match for his grandson. "We need you to protect her."

"What did you say to him?" Rowan pulled on her coat as she stood with her grandfather in the foyer. Liam had dragged Finn off to look at something, and Grandmother was in the kitchen wrapping up leftovers, despite Rowan's protests she wasn't going to be eating chicken cordon bleu for breakfast tomorrow.

"Nothing."

She quirked a single eyebrow, the gesture one he'd taught her. "You said nothing at all?"

"Beyond casual conversation?"

"Grandfather, come on. Spill it. What did you say to the man?"

"I asked him to keep you safe."

"Oh." The realization that he worried for her safety quickly dulled the ire that had flooded her veins since she and Grandmother were not so subtly asked to leave the room. "I'm capable of taking care of myself."

"I know that."

"Really capable. I take classes in self-defense. And I research the projects I'm working on. And I have a set of contacts in place around the world that I can call on for assistance. I'm not helpless, Grandfather."

The congenial smile he'd worn since the evening had ended vanished, replaced with the quick spark of anger. "I never said you were helpless and don't suggest I did."

"What did you mean, then?"

"I like the idea there's someone else watching out for you. You spend too much time alone. I got to look some-one in the eye and ask him to take care of you. To watch out for you. Don't deny me that."

She took his arm and gestured him back into the small parlor off the front hall where they'd had dessert. "You know the House of Steele isn't without some danger. We minimize risks, but it's not a desk job. I thought you were okay with that."

"I am okay with that. And I'm damn proud of what my grandchildren have built. None of it changes how I worry."

As she stared into his bright blue eyes—eyes that had seen so much of the world, both good and bad—she knew she owed him better than simply dismissing his words. "I know you're proud of me. Of all of us."

"Every damn day."

The events of her younger days were on her mind—her time with Finn had ensured that—but she couldn't deny the focus on events from her youth had churned up emotions that went well beyond her interactions with Finn. "How can you say that you're proud of me? I haven't always done good things."

He gripped her hand with his and she marveled at the strength still to be found in him. "You overcame those things. That's not only something to be proud of, it's something to celebrate."

"But you stood by me. Even after…" She swallowed around the lump in her throat. "Even after you found out."

"*Especially* after, my dear."

"I betrayed the values I was raised with."

"And then you proved you had them in spades when you changed your life." He patted her hand. "Sometimes our pain is so great, we can't see anything else."

"It's still there sometimes." She hesitated, then continued what she started, her voice a whisper. "The urge to steal."

"Do you give in to it?"

"No." Unless she counted key fobs into the apartments of men she couldn't stop thinking about.

"Do you let it control you?"

"No."

"Then why worry about it?"

She laid a hand over his. "It's not that easy."

"Oh, my darling. It's not that hard, either. Life is full of joy and sorrow. You must take the joy when you find it."

Memories of that morning in Finn's apartment filled her mind's eye. The image was entirely inappropriate to have when talking with one's grandfather, yet it was oddly apropos to his comment.

Take joy when you find it.

But how did she take that leap when the person on the other side of the canyon represented all the demons she fought each and every day?

Will flipped off the light on his desk and gathered up his papers. Debbie was still pissed off from the night before, and he figured he should put his hours suffering the silent treatment to good use.

Besides, grading sixty essays had a strange sense of penance to them.

The self-imposed exile had gone a long way toward making a dent in the papers and he'd finish up the rest tomorrow during his free period. Now it was time to head home and face the rest of his punishment. Not that he could blame Debbie. Last night he'd taken absentminded and obsessed to new heights.

And while he *knew* he should feel remorse, damn it if it didn't feel as if Rowan and her friend were onto something. Additional comments had been added to the forum by the poster he kept questioning, but something in the wording had caught him off guard. The poster had used the name Nefertiti instead of Nefertari, and it had his instincts firing.

While the two Egyptian wives were often interchanged by the general public, they were two distinctly different women who'd lived a half century apart. Someone who truly understood the period would have known better. He'd said as much on the forum, disgusted by the lack of scholarly vision before he'd thought better of it and erased the post. He was supposed to be an unobtrusive visitor, and he needed to leave the damn professor hat in the office.

Even with that knowledge, the post had bothered him and he'd shot a note to a former colleague who now lived in Cairo. Briggs would have an ear to the ground and could be counted on to get the latest gossip on key projects in the region.

Because whatever suspicions Rowan had, Will was rapidly coming to agree with her.

Something smelled rotten in this equation. Of course, if anyone could get to the bottom of it, it was Rowan Steele. Nothing fazed her and she was tireless in the pursuit of her goals.

His mind was still whirling with the possibilities when he climbed the steps from the Underground a half hour later. October would soon be giving way to November and he could feel the bite in the air. Wind whipped around him and he huddled deeper into his jacket as he walked the last few blocks toward home. He passed the park he and Debbie loved to take Eli and June to on the weekends, memories of his children's peals of laughter rising up over the playground equipment, and another shot of remorse filled him at his asinine behavior the night before.

He loved his family to distraction. They were the lights of his life, so—

Pain washed through his skull as something heavy hit him from behind. A deep scream welled in his throat at the assault as everything happened at once.

He whirled, but the movements felt clumsy, as if his limbs were too large for his body.

And the pain. The crazy, screaming pain behind his eyes was almost too much to bear.

He lifted his hands to clutch his head, the messenger bag he carried on his arm so very heavy. That weight almost pulled him down and he nearly gave in to the urge to drop to his knees until he stared into the eyes of his assailant. Dark eyes, filled to the brim with menace as the man lifted the cricket bat once more.

Will swung out, his significant height advantage giving him a greater reach, and the bat connected with his forearm. The sickening thud of bone and the cracking of the bat met his ears but he ignored it.

He had to get away.

His feet felt too big and he stumbled a few steps before he caught his balance and willed himself forward.

Toward home.

Rowan watched the city pass by through the windows of Finn's car. The evening with her grandparents didn't quite deserve the moniker "unqualified disaster" but it was close, and Finn had borne the brunt of it. Her phone buzzed from the depths of her coat pocket, and she ignored it as she tried to figure out a way to make the evening up to Finn.

I'm sorry was far too tame and terribly inadequate.

"They love you."

She pulled her attention from the view outside the windows and her maudlin thoughts.

"Even if they are a bit ham-handed in how they show it."

"Oh, I don't know." Finn rubbed his side in the same area she recalled seeing his gunshot scar and she wondered if he even recognized the gesture. "There's something touching about it."

"They grilled you like we were headed to the prom instead of on a work trip."

"Yet I repeat my original point. They love you."

"It's overwhelming sometimes."

"How so?"

"Forget it." She already regretted the harsh words. As he said, her family loved her. They looked out for her, as she did for them. It was just how it worked.

"Come on, Rowan. You said it for a reason."

"It's a lot of things, really."

"So tell me about it." His grin was broad and altogether cheeky. "You know I know how to keep secrets."

It was only because he had a good point that she started talking. Or that was what she told herself. And then she didn't care what the reason was because it just felt good to get it out.

"My whole life, I've always felt I've needed to prove myself. Work harder or try harder because I'm the baby. Everyone wants to take care of me. And because I'm the peacemaker of our family, I let them."

"I thought older children were the peacemakers."

"You did meet my brother, right?"

"Liam's not so bad."

A vision of her brother ordering them around the park when they were kids came to mind. "He's great. But keeping the peace is not his strong suit. Unless, of course, it suits whatever objective he has at the moment."

"All right. There are two more siblings between the two of you. How'd you get to be peacemaker?"

"I don't know exactly. It's just who I am. I want happiness and harmony and—"

"And your family's been a source of little of it."

"Exactly."

"Did it change after your parents died?"

"Their deaths changed every dynamic of our family. The way we interacted with each other. Our relationships with our grandparents, both my father's and mother's side. One day we were one group of people and the next day something new entirely."

He reached out and linked his hand with hers. "And you had to deal with it at a time when so many other aspects of life are changing, as well."

How did he understand?

All the pent-up anger and frustration she'd carried for far too long seemed to fade in the face of his understanding. "You get it."

"I'm an observer, Rowan. You are, too. In order to steal from a place, you have to know how to case it. How to really see it and how it works. The comings and goings. The noisy moments and the quiet."

Like a punctuation mark to her comment about noisy moments, the buzzing of her phone started again and she fumbled in her pocket with her free hand, silencing the ringer.

"I suppose that's true. I've always seen too much. My youthful choices simply gave that trait an outlet." She stared down at their linked hands, the gentle support enough to make her keep going. "I had words with Liam last night at dinner. When I told him about my, um, activities as a teenager."

She gave Finn a quick recap of the conversation before admitting what was truly upsetting her. "He always seems like the one who's got it all together, and I think I hurt him when I suggested my pain was harder to bear."

"You probably did."

"What?"

"You both lost your parents. That's a hardship for anyone."

"I wasn't trying to insult him. I was just trying to explain my actions."

"And he responded on a visceral level, from deep inside his own pain."

Rowan wanted to sink inside herself when faced with such obvious truth, but she knew that was the coward's way out. Instead of trying to make her feel better, Finn wasn't afraid to point out the truth. Other than her grandparents, she'd had little of that in her life.

That honesty mattered. A lot. "Damn, but you do see a lot."

"That's my job."

The darkened interior cocooned them, and the problems they faced seemed far away. Egypt. The Victoria bracelet. Even their shared past.

Instead, all she saw was the two of them. And all she knew was the moment that wrapped around them.

"My grandmother took a shine to you."

"It's my heritage. We Irish stick together." He laughed, a hard, coarse sound. "I suspect she wouldn't be quite so welcoming if she knew about my less-than-stellar career choices."

Rowan heard the raw notes in his voice and turned. Half his face was in shadow, the other half illuminated by the lights outside the car windows. The moment was oddly poetic, summing up the reality of his life.

"It's hard to live two lives."

His hand tightened around hers before he broke the contact. "Is that how you saw it?"

"Always. There was the person people saw every day and then there was the person on the inside I hid from everyone.

"It's a lonely place."

"Then leave it. You don't need it anymore, Finn."

Something raw and elemental framed the half of his face she could see. His struggles were stamped there in the harsh lines of his profile and the corded veins that stood out on his neck. "It's not that easy."

It's not that hard, either. Life is full of joy and sorrow. You must take the joy when you find it.

Grandfather's words from the front hall echoed in her mind and she marveled how closely the conversation with Finn mirrored the one she'd had a short while ago.

"I don't know who I am if I'm not a thief."

Finn's quiet voice floated around her, the words a reminder of what she'd believed for far too many years.

She focused her gaze on him once more, watching the play of light over his face as their driver turned onto the Strand. The shadows faded and she could see all of him.

And the bleak chill that colored his eyes a pale green.

"I know who you are. You're Finn Gallagher. You're a businessman and an historian. You believe the things from our past have value. You know the benefits of hard work. And you're far too smart to think you can be defined in such simple and misguided terms."

"It's not misguided when it's true."

Her phone rang again, the heavy tone of the ringer intruding on the moment. "I'm sorry this keeps going off." She dragged the phone out of her pocket, intent on turning it off when she saw Will's name stamped across the screen.

"Answer it." His tone was implacable.

"Will?"

"Rowan! It's Debbie." Frantic crying greeted her, heavy sobs punctuating her sentences. "Will. It's Will. He's been hurt. Beaten."

"Debbie? Where are you?"

"House." More sobs echoed from the phone. "We're on the front steps. Will said it's urgent."

"Did you call for help?"

"Where is she?" Finn's voice intruded.

"Their home in Bayswater."

Finn was already disengaging the privacy glass and barking orders to their driver.

"Call for help." Rowan fought the rush of fear that filled her veins like a dark, putrid sludge and focused on helping Debbie. "I can't hang up and I can't get a straight answer through her crying."

Finn nodded and Rowan focused on Debbie. "We're on our way and Finn's calling for an ambulance."

Rowan grabbed her tablet from her purse and tapped through her address book to give Finn a destination.

Debbie sobbed in her ear, her words increasingly fragmented as she switched between sobbing at Will to stay awake and giving Rowan updates.

"Are his eyes open?"

"Sometimes. He called your name."

"Debbie." Rowan punched up the command in her voice, willing Debbie to calm down and fervently praying for Will to hang on. "I need you to listen to me. Did he say anything about what happened to him?"

"No! No." More sobs filled her ear. "What?"

Rowan fought to keep track of the thread of the conversation and knew her job was more to keep Debbie sane than anything else. The car flew around corners and they even went briefly airborne as their driver hit a curb. The streets passed in a blur, but every so often Rowan caught a familiar landmark. "We're almost there."

Another loud sob filled her ears before Debbie went quiet. A hard crash echoed and Rowan could only assume the phone was dropped.

And then she heard Will's voice.

"Egypt, Rowan. It's the thread. Nefertiti."

"Will." The tears she'd held at bay welled up and spilled over and she didn't care. "You need to save your strength. The doctors are on their way."

"Should…be…Nefertari."

"Shhh, Will."

"Rowan!" Will's voice shook with the command. "Listen. Con…contacted Briggs. He can help you."

"Briggs from college?"

"He's in…Cairo."

Sirens echoed through the phone and Debbie's quiet, helpless sobs competed with the noise. "Bye, Rowan."

"Will—" She wanted to keep him there—wanted to say something else—but she knew he needed his family.

And as her own tears fell, she kept hearing one word over and over.

Bye.

Chapter 13

The street in front of Will's home was chaos as they pulled up. Lights flashed from all the emergency vehicles, washing the scene in a garish display of color that was far too cheerful for what had happened.

Finn fought his instinctive fear of cops and followed Rowan's retreating form. She'd raced from the car the moment it came to a stop, and even now he could see her weaving in and around the throng of people on scene.

And he was there to pull her into his arms when the dam broke over her sobs the moment she saw the large body sprawled over the sidewalk.

"Shhh." He pressed his lips to her ear, crooning nonsense as he cradled her tiny form against his chest.

"Will. Oh, Will. It's my fault."

He said nothing beyond the nonsense words, but did allow his gaze to roam the scene. Emergency workers still hovered over Will's body, and several cops surrounded

Debbie. One had draped her in a heavy wool blanket and Finn didn't miss the streaks of blood that covered her face and neck.

The last few minutes in the car were tense and he didn't get much from Rowan except the confirmation of Will's last words. He was attacked because of the trip to Egypt.

More specifically, Finn knew, Will was attacked because they'd called him in to help on the assignment.

Which only reinforced the question he'd asked himself all week. What the hell was going on? He'd spent his life on jobs and on occasion one did go sideways, but never like this. And never to someone so peripheral to the job as Will was to theirs.

Anger coursed through him with the force of a tsunami at the senseless loss of life. And fear was its counterpoint as he desperately tried to make sense of it all.

How could he even think of taking Rowan into this situation if the danger was so high?

Rowan slipped from his arms, dragging her hands over her cheeks. "I need to see Debbie."

"Of course."

He kept a hand on her arm and escorted her around the throng of professionals hard at work. Debbie sat on a small brick ledge that ran the perimeter of their property, her face red with tears as she sat huddled in a blanket. Rowan sat next to her and pulled her close, and Finn tried again to sort through the events of the past days.

All Will had done was nose around a message board. People didn't get killed over digital forum threads on the internet.

His gaze drifted to Will's form on the sidewalk, taunting his beliefs. The cops had covered the body, but it didn't change the stark wash of grief that gripped the scene.

Or Finn, when he calculated his own role in Will's death.

Rowan waved him over and he positioned himself so the body wasn't visible if their gazes traveled as his had.

"Debbie. This is Finn. He's helping us."

Shock painted the young widow's gaze, and her eyes were red with tears when she looked up at him. "I need your help."

"Of course."

The woman shook her head and grabbed his hand. Her grip was strong and her voice was desperate when she finally spoke. "Not like that. I *need* your help."

"Of course."

"Rowan said you'd find the people who did this."

Could he do that? He'd skirted a lot of lines in his life, but hunting down individuals with the intent to garner payback had never been at the top of his agenda.

"Please, Finn. For my husband. For his children that have been left behind. You have to find them." Debbie's voice dropped. "And you have to make them pay."

Jared paced the warehouse—his first real-estate purchase years before—a waterfall of obscenities streaming from his lips. The urge to throw something was strong, but nothing was handy, so he had settled for pacing and screaming, then screaming and pacing. "When the hell did this go so off the buggered rails?"

He'd worked his way up from London street thug to small-time crime leader to the position he enjoyed now as one of the city's top crime bosses. Very little in the city went down without him knowing it, and in the past few years, his empire had expanded to much of Europe.

He was a man with a plan, and bludgeoning a university professor to death wasn't on the agenda.

"He's a damn teacher. What sort of threat is a teacher?"

Although Teddy had walked in with a cocky swagger, a half hour of getting the piss verbally beat out of him had knocked him down a few pegs. He now sat on a folding chair in sullen silence, only answering questions when asked. "He's working with Gallagher."

"So? He posted a few messages on a damn board. You were supposed to watch him. We set those threads up to deter attention, not create it."

"Something was off with the professor. He's too sharp. And he was sending messages all night long. I'm telling you, he's onto us. I read the code analytics and someone hacked into the back end of the system."

Jared lifted a hand, the discussion veering into territory he knew nothing about. "You had no authorization to do this."

"I acted as I saw fit."

"With a cricket bat?"

"It's easy to burn and remove all traces of it ever existing. Just the way I like my murder weapons."

"There should never have been a damn murder in the first place." The reassuring metal of his gun sat in his waistband, and Jared toyed briefly with idea of taking Teddy out.

Could he do it? Despite the boneheaded move, the man had been in his employ for a long time. Long before the Victoria bracelet. Hell, they'd grown up together.

So why was it lately all he wanted to do was get rid of Teddy and see his lifeless body dropped into the Thames?

Was it her?

She'd whispered in his ear more than once that he needed to cut his deadweight. Poor performers didn't belong on a high-performance team; they only dragged everyone else down.

You're a businessman, Jared. Learn to act like one.

Then she'd given him a book on management tactics and told him to read chapter six on how to fire people, before she stripped down to a thin nightgown that left nothing to the imagination.

Jared refocused his attention on Teddy's huddled form. "And you don't think anyone saw you?"

"Street was dark and no one was around."

"Let me repeat the question. Do you think anyone saw you?"

"Hell no, mate. It's a quiet street in a quiet neighborhood. It was nothing like sticking Gallagher this morning."

"Like doing what?" The words dripped from his lips, nearly in slow motion. "When?"

"It was nothing, mate. Just a little shake-up."

Rage—pure as a fresh snow—rose up from the very depths of his being. "On whose orders?"

"I've got initiative."

"I've known you a long time, *mate.*" He stressed the word for effect. "And in all that time, I've yet to see a lick of initiative in you. Who told you to touch Gallagher?"

When Teddy said nothing, Jared let the anger pour forth in a river of vengeance. "Who?"

He kicked the legs out from Teddy's chair at the same time he screamed, the effect of simultaneous noise and motion sending the man into a disorienting fall. Before he could scrabble to his feet or reach for whatever weapon he had on his person, Jared was on top of him, his gun already in hand.

"Who told you to attack Gallagher? Who's pulling your strings?"

"I got nothing to say, mate."

Sweat poured from his forehead as he looked into the flat green eyes of one of his oldest friends.

He'd miss Teddy. Would miss him terribly, but he couldn't tolerate someone who didn't follow orders.

Jared leaped up, the move casual as he extended a hand to Teddy to help him stand. The man took it, relief washing his face in a shaky smile. "Thanks, mate."

Years flashed before his eyes as Jared lifted his pistol, but he ignored them in favor of what needed to be done.

The gun exploded before Teddy even registered the shot was directed at his head.

Rowan heard Finn's voice but couldn't seem to focus on anything he was saying. Everything sounded as if it was coming from a distance, like she was underwater, struggling to surface.

"Rowan."

She turned to look at Finn, the tone of his voice extra sharp. "Yes?"

"We're here. At your hotel. Let me walk you up."

He helped her from the car, then followed her to her room. Had it only been two days since he'd last walked her up?

So much had happened, much of it bad. The attack the other night after the museum party. Finn's knife wound this morning. And now Will.

Another sob racked her frame as the image of Will's prone body laid out on the sidewalk resurrected itself in her brain.

"Shh."

"It can't be real. I keep thinking it's a dream and then I see Will's body and Debbie crying and I know that it is."

"I'm sorry it's real. So sorry." Finn kept his arm around

her as they walked toward her door. "Why don't you give me your key?"

She dug it out of her purse and handed him the plastic card, his gentle compassion going a long way toward pulling her from her thoughts. "Thank you."

"Do you want me to get you anything? Something from room service? Do you want me to call anyone? I can call your grandparents."

A hard stab of guilt lodged under her skin but she ruthlessly tamped it down. Instead, she forced bravado into her tone and turned to face him across her hotel suite. "I'd prefer they don't know. They'll only worry."

"And they'd be right to."

"I can't put them through that."

His gentle tone vanished, replaced with one that was hard and implacable. "Rowan, you can't do that to them. They're going to hear about it. They deserve to hear about it from you."

"And let them spend the next three weeks thinking I'm in Egypt at risk?"

"You are at risk. We both are."

She wanted to ignore his swift response but knew an omission to her grandparents was the same as a lie. And she'd stopped lying to them a long time ago.

She thrived on the risks in her job—enjoyed doing the things that few could or even wanted to—but she'd never faced a situation quite like this one.

"It's three in the morning. I can't call them now. But I will. In fact, I'll go see them in the morning and tell them in person."

"That's fair."

"It's about the only fair thing about this situation." She wiped at the tears that didn't want to stop and dropped onto the couch. "I can't stop picturing his body. And when I get a few moments of reprieve, Debbie's words run through my head. She's a widow with two small children. Because of me."

He was back at her side, his arms wrapped around her. "You didn't do this, Rowan."

"But Will would still be alive if it weren't for me." A hard laugh welled up in her throat. "It's ironic, isn't it? I spent the last twelve years convinced I'd gotten someone killed and was all wrong. I find that out and two days later I actually *am* responsible for someone's death."

"You didn't do this." He pressed his lips to her forehead. "You aren't responsible."

She took comfort in his words, but couldn't erase the guilt that wouldn't go away. Like a brand on her skin, she'd carried it for over a decade. "I'm sorry I left you to die."

Finn lifted his head and stared down at her. "What's that supposed to mean?"

"At the Warringtons'. I left you there to die and I just kept going."

"What would have been better? Getting shot at, too? You were in survival mode, nothing more."

"But I left you."

"And I wanted you to."

His hazel gaze had darkened in the dim light of the room, the irises a tawny gold. No matter how hard she searched, she didn't see judgment or anger or any lingering hostility. But how could that be? "I left you."

"And if you hadn't, you wouldn't be here today."

Another protest formed on her tongue but faded when he pressed his mouth to hers.

"I couldn't bear it if you weren't here, Rowan." The words were a whisper against her lips before he gathered her up and dragged her onto his lap.

The cold that had settled deep inside of her the moment she heard Debbie's cries on the other end of the phone faded as Finn cocooned her with his body. The external heat matched the rising heat inside of her and she wrapped herself around him, desperate to give in to the attraction that consumed them both.

"Finn." She whispered his name. Only his name.

And then reached for the life-affirming opportunity to be with him. "Please stay with me."

He did lift his head at that, his eyes hazy with the demanding strains of arousal. "Are you sure?"

His hard body stiffened beneath hers and she smoothed her palms over his shoulders. "I've never been more sure about anything. Stay. Please."

He leaned forward to press his lips to hers. "I'd like that."

His arms wrapped around her and he dragged her the short distance to the bed, landing on his back and cushioning her as she fell over him. She marveled at his strength and scrambled up to a sitting positing so she could explore him properly. "You're wearing too much."

His smile was lazy, but she still saw the edges of wariness in his eyes. "Just taking it slow."

"Maybe I don't want it slow." The tease rose up and she realized it was the truth. She wanted mind-numbing pleasure and she didn't want to have to think any longer.

"Then what are you going to do about it?"

She quirked an eyebrow at him, rewarded with the rumble of his laughter before she reached for the long column of buttons on his shirt. His heart thudded underneath her shaking fingers as she pulled the first button loose and it was the encouragement she wasn't even aware of needing.

Finn was as aroused as she was.

The thought was exhilarating and so very sexy. His fingers ran lazy circles over her thigh where she knelt next to him, and Rowan struggled to keep her mind on the task at hand. Moment by agonizing moment each button popped free until she was able to lean forward and drag the shirt off his thick frame. Hard muscles flexed under her fingertips and she gazed on the perfect ridges of muscles that sculpted his arms.

"This T-shirt is in the way." She dragged the white cotton up his torso, stopping abruptly when she caught sight of the bandage that covered his side.

"Oh, Finn. I'm sorry. Does it hurt?"

"If I say yes, are you going to stop?" His smile was broad despite his terse words.

She traced the edges of the bandage before lifting her fingers to trace the puckered scar from the gunshot. "Are you sure?"

His hand was tight over hers, stilling her movements. "Positive."

While she suspected the wound had to be giving him some trouble, the doctor's assessment that morning had been more than encouraging and the damage had been minimal. With that in mind, she sat back and allowed her gaze to roam over his torso, feasting on the hard planes of his body.

He was like one of the sculptures she loved to look on at the museum. As hard and unyielding as the *Younger Memnon* statue, yet so vibrantly alive.

Real.

And gloriously touchable.

"You're beautiful." She leaned forward and pressed her lips to his chest, kissing a trail from one nipple to the next before shifting to lick a path along the thin line of hair that disappeared into his slacks. He exhaled on a heavy breath when she came to the waistband of his pants and she took a moment to stop and look at him.

The arousal she'd seen earlier was nothing compared to the eager desire that lit the depths of his gaze. Tension bracketed his mouth and his entire body practically hummed with sexual tension.

She swallowed hard, the intensity of the moment catching her off guard. She wanted Finn, of course, but never had she made love with a man when it felt so *necessary*.

"Rowan?"

"Hmmm?"

The tension never left his body, but when he spoke there was nothing but a gentle tenderness in his tone. "Is everything all right?"

"Everything is more than all right. It's perfect."

Rowan's words echoed in his ears and he couldn't hold back the primal burst of satisfaction that flooded his body. They'd danced around their attraction the past several days—hell, there'd been seeds of it all the way back to their youth—but they were on opposite sides of a large chasm he'd thought them unable to cross.

And it was with that realization that he knew he needed to stop what was rapidly heading out of control.

Finn reached for her hands, drawing them together in his. "Maybe we shouldn't do this."

"What?" The sexy smile that hovered about her lips faded and Rowan sat back on her heels, disengaging her hands and dropping them on her lap. "Why not?"

"For starters, it's not because I don't want to." The stiff lines of his body added their protest and he fought the urge to scream when she shifted next to him, her hand brushing his thigh.

"What is it, then?"

"Nothing's changed since last night, Rowan." He was honor-bound to say the words and wouldn't have it any other way, but even as he said them he couldn't help wondering if his personal choices really were ruining his life.

Oh, he'd always thought himself in control, but was he? And even if he attempted to stop stealing, could he give it up?

His gaze roamed over Rowan's slim form. The slender shoulders and small frame. The tender lines of her jaw and the bright, vivid blue gaze that drew him in and made him want more.

He'd spent his life as a thief and had carried very little remorse for that fact. But could he really take this from her, especially when he doubted his ability to change?

She was hurting over the death of her friend and here he was taking advantage of her vulnerability.

"Everything's changed since last night, Finn."

"Externally, yes. But not what's between us. I can't take advantage of your pain."

He watched a world of emotion flit across her gaze before something very much like acceptance settled her face in serene lines. "We are in different places and I won't pretend I approve of what you continue to do. But I don't want to postpone the joy of being with you. Don't want to miss out on something I want so very desperately."

She reached for his hand and lifted it to her chest. "The attraction between us? It was there at the start."

"I know."

"And I'm done running from it. From us."

"And in the morning?"

"That's tomorrow. I want right now with you."

The gentleman that did live inside of him kept arguing he needed to walk away. But the man who had feelings for her simply couldn't do it. "I want you so badly."

"Then share this with me, Finn. On this, please believe we're agreed."

He'd spent years mentally enslaved by the next big deal. Whether legal or illegal, he'd made a life built on the acquisition of things.

How humbling, then, to have something so special—and infinitely more valuable—be given freely. He pulled her close once more. "Yes."

Their need already heightened, it didn't take either of them long to strip the other of their clothes. Finn shifted their positions to settle himself on top of her. He ranged kisses over her face and neck before dipping his head to capture a nipple in his mouth.

Her harsh intake of breath followed by a light moan was his reward, and he cupped her breast with his other hand, his fingers plying her sensitive flesh. His body screamed for release, but he was so desperate to brand every inch of her, he ignored his body and pressed on.

Her figure was so small and firm, the body of an athlete. He continued to follow her curves, kissing a path from her nipple to the underside of her breast, then down the quivering muscles of her stomach.

He ran his tongue over those ridges, then blew lightly on her flesh. Those muscles that fascinated him to distraction rippled once more under the sensual assault and he smiled to himself before he continued his carnal march over her flesh.

The slim line of her panties—the only article of clothing he'd yet to remove—acted as a barrier to his lips and he stopped, slipping his fingers underneath the thin material. The wet heat of her flesh had his body clenching hard in response as he slid his fingers over the smooth seam before slipping a finger inside. He was rewarded with the hard lift of her hips. "Finn!"

"Yeah, baby."

Her hands danced over his shoulders before grasping his arms to pull him closer. "I can't wait."

"That's what I'm counting on." He pressed his lips once more to her flesh before dragging her panties off, then moved to position himself over her body. He snatched the condom he'd pulled from his wallet when they removed their clothes, and ripped it free of its packaging.

Rowan accepted him once more as he resettled himself between her thighs, the heat of her flesh a torment. She reached down and gripped him—another torment—before guiding him into her body.

The rhythmic lift of her hips as he buried himself inside of her, again and again, had the tension in his body rapidly spiraling out of control. Sweat slicked them both and he fought desperately to hold on. To make the moments last.

Despite every effort to hold back his release, the demands of his body quickly overtook his intentions and he held out a few moments longer until he felt her inner muscles around him.

With one final thrust, he buried himself inside of her and took solace in the warmest welcome he'd ever known.

Chapter 14

Rowan watched the early-morning rays of dawn edge the curtains and thought about the past forty-eight hours. She'd slept briefly after she and Finn had made love a second time, but woke less than an hour later and had been staring at the walls ever since.

At least she wasn't cold anymore. The warmth of his body, pressed to her back, had allowed her to feel physically safe, even as her mind ran through the risks they were both facing.

Risks that she'd never anticipated when she agreed to the job.

Someone was watching them. The incidents that had piled up over the past two days were far from random, but it was the personal aspect of the violence that had her puzzled.

Finn was assigned to the dig and he'd subcontracted with her to join him. He was authenticating the dig. It was standard protocol in the management of artifacts and antiquities, and his presence on the excavation team was far from unique.

So who would want to keep them away?

Which was why, no matter how she turned it over in her mind, she kept coming back to the same place.

It was personal.

As if she and Finn were the targets of a puppet master neither could quite define.

Finn shifted, tightening his arms around her before pressing a kiss to the back of her neck. His voice was husky with sleep when he finally spoke. "You taste delicious."

She smiled and bent her head to give him better access to that warm, sensitive spot he'd honed in on. "Aren't you a sweet-talker in the morning."

"I've got the sweetest subject." He pressed another kiss before gently tugging on her arm to get her to roll over. "A sweet subject who didn't sleep very well."

"You knew that?"

His gaze was open and direct, but she saw the concern, as well. "Yes. Is it Will?"

"Will. Your incident yesterday morning. The attempted mugging after the museum. All of it points to something personal and I can't understand why."

Those large, sturdy shoulders that made her feel so safe and secure stiffened before he lifted up onto an elbow. "You think we're the targets?"

"Don't you?"

"I've been so busy associating this with the dig itself I hadn't thought about it."

She ran a hand along the whiskers that lined his jaw. "But when you frame it up in that light, you start to see what I see."

"Yes."

"Who do you think's responsible? I thought about Baxter but he's too focused on himself to run something this complex."

"And I never took him for a killer, just a conniving climber of the corporate ladder."

"Anyone else?"

"No one comes readily to mind." He rubbed the bandage that still covered his side. "The thing that hasn't made a lot of sense is that this wound wasn't that big."

"And you're complaining?"

"Hardly. I just mean it wasn't lethal. A deterrent, yes, but actually harmful? Not in the least."

She couldn't be more grateful for that fact, even as she knew Debbie sat across town, unable to escape the same fate. "It was lethal to Will."

"Yes." He leaned in and pressed his lips to hers in a gentle kiss. "Yes, it was and I'm sorry."

She wrapped her arms around his waist and pulled him close. He had escaped a bad fate—they both had—and she needed to focus on that miracle.

They'd get to the bottom of it. They had to.

Her grandmother greeted her at the door of the townhome. "Good morning, sweetheart. This is a pleasant surprise."

Rowan threw herself into her grandmother's arms without conscious thought and didn't even try to hold back the tears.

"Rowan!" Her grandmother patted her back in large, soothing circles before stepping back and pulling her into the foyer. "Come inside, sweetie, and tell me what's wrong."

Her grandmother led them into the same parlor they'd

had dessert in the night before. It had long since been cleaned of the previous night's entertainment, but she could still smell the light scents of coffee and brandy as she walked into the room.

Maybe they'd always been there, a subtle reminder of the people who lived and loved in the house, and she'd simply never noticed.

Or maybe they were there to remind her how quickly life could change.

Either way, as she stared into her grandmother's concerned eyes, Rowan knew Finn had been right to suggest she come this morning.

"It's about my friend Will. The one I talked about last night."

"That tall, lanky man you've known since college."

Again, the tears clogged her throat and her grandmother's warm smile faded. "He died last night."

Penelope led them to a small settee. "What happened?"

Rowan avoided some of the more gruesome specifics and focused on as factual an accounting of the story as she knew. It was only when she came to the end that she whispered the same words she'd told Finn the night before. "I can't help but feel responsible."

"You didn't do this, Rowan."

"I know, but if I hadn't asked him…"

"Stop. Just stop." Her grandmother's tone was firm before she pulled her close in a hug. "We all make our own choices and he chose to help you. I understand why you're upset, but you do him no good wallowing in guilt."

"I'm not wallowing."

"Yes, you are." Penelope Steele pulled back but kept a firm grip on her shoulders. "I know you well enough to know the signs."

"I asked for his help."

"And he gave it freely. Remember that."

"He's a professor, Grandma. A college professor with two small kids. That doesn't just happen."

"Then you need to find out why it happened."

"That's just it. There's no rational reason for it. He was nosing around on some message boards for us, nothing more."

"Has Campbell checked into it?"

A quick lick of embarrassment hit her that she'd forgotten she'd pulled her brother into the project. "He's been looking, yes."

"What did he find?"

"I don't know. I forgot I'd asked him. I've been so wrapped up in losing Will."

"If there's something deeper there, your brother will find it. In fact, we'll call him when we're done. Together."

"Thanks." She gripped her grandmother's hand, willing some small part of the woman's stoic strength and wisdom to impart itself to her. "For everything."

Her grandmother took a heavy breath. "There's something I need to say. Your grandfather and I have gone several rounds on this, and to say we're on opposite sides is an understatement."

Her grandparents were normally in tune and in sync with each other, so the fact they weren't spiked her curiosity. "Opposite sides of what?"

"He's afraid for you. He's been worried about this trip from the get-go and would like nothing better than for you to stay home."

"And you?"

"You need to go. There's something in Egypt and you need to find it."

"What something?"

Her grandmother ran a finger down her cheek, the

move warm and so reminiscent of their long-ago bed-time ritual. Her grandmother always hugged, then ran that lone finger over a part of her face, as if memorizing the visage of the ones she loved. "The key to your happiness, darling."

Finn glanced up from the maps he'd spread out on the small meeting table and couldn't hold back the smile. Rowan had been quietly mumbling under her breath since they took off a half hour before, and the grumbling had grown louder.

"Are you okay?"

"Fine." She closed the paperback she was holding and tossed it on the chair next to her.

"Problem with your reading selection?"

"Don't get me started." She unbuckled her seat belt and crossed the cabin, those frown lines still marring her forehead.

Try as he might, he couldn't resist poking her a bit more. "What was so bad about it? Awful writing? Poor characters?"

"Not exactly."

He eyed the pale pink book across the aisle before looking at her once more. "Then what is it?"

"I'm sick to death of reading stories where the man has to swoop in to save the woman."

"Maybe you're reading the wrong kind of books. That cover is awfully pink."

"I actually like that author quite a bit, so don't be dissing her pink cover. And I read fiction across all genres and it's the same across the board. In each and every one it's always the hero rescuing the heroine. Swooping in to save the day."

He puffed up his chest and pointed toward it with his

thumb. "Us heroes need to rescue someone roughly once a month in order to keep our hero status."

Her smile was small, but it was there all the same. "You're a funny guy. All I'm saying is why can't it be both of them? Or why can't the heroine rescue the hero every once in a while?"

Without question, her annoyance wasn't about scenes in a book, no matter how prevalent. "Why does this bother you?"

"Do you really want my rant on this?"

"Bring it on, postfeminist angst and all."

"It's not postfeminist angst. It's real-world experience."

Finn knew without her saying anything what came next. "And what did that experience tell you?"

"Being rescued isn't all it's cracked up to be. Especially when the person who rescues you doesn't make it."

He reached for her hand, wrapping it in his own. "You need to get past this, Rowan. I didn't die that day."

"I *can't* get past it. And I've spent my life trying to make up for it."

"But I'm fine." He stopped, anxious to find the words that would finally calm her mind. He *hadn't* died. Hadn't even come close, yet she carried this irrational guilt that she could have done something. "I understand you've only had a few days to get used to that, but the facts are the facts."

"I didn't act very heroically when I had the chance. That's not a character trait I'm proud of."

They'd gone a few rounds on this already and nothing he said seemed to make a dent, so he opted for a new tack. One he thought her logical mind might be better able to take in. "Do you know I've used that night to help me get better?"

"Better how?"

"The body heals quickly at nineteen but I was still down for several days. And I went over that night in my head. Over and over what I could have done to get us both out of there."

"There was nothing to be done."

"That's where you're wrong. I didn't prep properly for the job. That was my first and most significant mistake."

The set of her shoulders changed, relaxing as his words sunk in. "Me, too."

"And I didn't cut and run when I had the chance, which was my second mistake."

"You were helping me."

"I was flirting with you and I shouldn't have bothered. We needed to move, and instead I wasted precious minutes in that closet." Unbidden, a smile sprang to his lips. "You smelled so good. And you looked so damn sexy in that black outfit you wore."

A light blush suffused her cheeks and she ducked her head. "You weren't so bad yourself. I kept asking myself why I wasn't afraid of you, mask and all, but I kept getting distracted by your broad shoulders and come-hither eyes."

He batted his eyelashes and got a small laugh. "Our opponents didn't feel the same, which brings me to my last point. I didn't expect company and wasn't prepared for it."

"There were a lot of us in that town house that night."

"It's always bothered me. Why were we all there? The house was conveniently empty, maybe too conveniently, yet there were three sets of thieves casing it? On a bracelet no one was supposed to know about."

"I never thought about that aspect."

"Because you've been too busy feeling guilty. Negative emotions distract our focus and make us lose sight of the bigger picture."

She hesitated for the briefest moment before she spoke. "Is that why you don't feel remorse for what you do?"

"One of the reasons."

"What are the others?"

The night before filled his thoughts. The open and easy way they made love and the physical intimacy between them that left no room to hide. He needed to do the same with his words.

"I've always thought it was hypocritical to do something and then feel guilty about it afterward. Especially when you keep going back and doing it again."

"I see."

From what she'd shared of her youthful escapades, it was clear Rowan had done exactly that, but he forged on. They stole for different reasons, and sugarcoating his truth wasn't helpful to either of them.

"I stole for a lot of reasons, but the primary reason I stole was for the age-old reason people take things."

"What's that?"

"I needed them. My father and I had nothing, and the kids I went to school with never let me forget it. So I stole to buy the things."

"And the other reasons?"

"Pride and prestige. The personal confidence that said I could do it. The thrill and adrenaline rush. All of it's a part of the whole."

"You have those things now. Your business is wildly successful and you're a respected leader in our industry. You can buy anything you want ten times over. Why keep doing it?"

Did he dare tell her?

Even as he wanted to remain silent, Finn knew he owed her better than that. Making love had changed everything between them and not just because sex always did.

For all the guilt she carried and the remorse that had shaped her as an adult, she wasn't the only one with baggage. Wasn't the only one who saw less of a person when she soul-searched for her own personal meaning.

When he looked inside, he saw the emptiness that had shaped him. Saw the shortcomings of his parents that had brought him to his choices in the first place.

And knew that they'd long since stopped being a part of the decision.

"Because, Rowan, when you do it too long, it becomes your identity. And I don't know who I am without it."

Bright, unyielding sunshine greeted them when they arrived in Cairo. Rowan dragged on her sunglasses and reveled in the warmth for a brief moment before descending the steps of their private plane.

They'd made the decision the day before to fly into Cairo instead of Luxor to meet Will's contact, and she couldn't hold back the very real concern they were putting someone else into danger. Despite the concern, she had to trust her brother's skills on that front.

She'd used a good portion of the flight over connecting with Campbell via a phone chat and nearly nonstop email over the plane's Wi-Fi. He'd filled her in on all the things he'd discovered when hacking into the computer forum Will had used. The most suspicious part was the presence of a lot of behind-the-scenes traffic from a London IP address that had been rerouted around the globe several times over.

Finn stepped off the last step of the plane and came to stand next to her. "You look upset."

"I'm concerned whether Campbell and I made the right decision about not contacting Briggs yet."

"Campbell hid the man's back-end information from the site forum so he can't be traced."

"Yes, but is it enough?"

The confirmation that the forum site had seen higher-than-usual traffic and suspicious activity was concerning. But it was the fact the signal had been deliberately rerouted that had put Campbell in a geek-induced rant. When she finally got to the bottom of what he was talking about, he'd confirmed he was hiding the data from Briggs's computer so his presence on the forums couldn't be traced.

Finn laid a hand on her arm. "If the people behind this are using data to control the situation, there's no one I'd trust more than your brother to handle things."

There was no one she trusted more, either, but it was the faceless threat that she couldn't get past. "They're out there, Finn. And I hate that we still have no clue who they are."

"We'll find them. And if Campbell can trace the signature of that London IP address, we'll have more to work with."

She was still worrying about the decision to include Briggs a few hours later as she and Finn set off from the hotel. "I told you I could get us a car."

"I don't want to draw attention to ourselves."

"This is a cosmopolitan city. A car isn't going to attract attention."

"It will if someone's watching out for us. Besides, we've got a lot more flexibility on foot."

The early-morning sun that had greeted them when they'd arrived had given way to an even sunnier day, and the heat surrounded them as they traversed through Old Cairo. Rowan adjusted her large bag before Finn reached out and grabbed it. "I can carry that."

"It's no big deal."

He grunted as he hefted the strap over his arm. "You carry rocks in here?"

"It's my bag. I carry everything in there." She tried to take it back but he sidestepped her reach. "You really don't need to carry it."

"Consider it my fall fashion statement."

She shook her head but kept walking. Her grandfather's worry the other night had been sweet, but she'd felt his sentiments were misguided. Now, with Finn's heavy footfalls keeping pace with her own, she couldn't deny how wonderful it was to have someone along for the journey.

A partner.

And when had she begun seeing him that way?

"I don't know why I'd ever doubted you would know where you're going." Finn's voice interrupted her thoughts. "I don't think you've missed a turn once."

"I spent a lot of time here during college."

"Was that the Hanging Church we passed a few blocks back?"

"Yep. I wish we had more time and I'd take you through it."

"I've been through it once myself, but it's been a long time." He linked his hand with hers, entwining their fingers. "We should come back after this is all over. I'd love to see Egypt through your eyes. I thought I knew it, but it's nothing compared to what you've seen and done here."

The tender words were spoken so casually, Rowan suspected he didn't even know what he implied under his words.

To come back meant they'd be together after their work on the Valley of the Queens ended. It meant permanence and a relationship and time spent together that wasn't framed by a project they both worked on.

To come back meant they were a couple, sharing their lives with each other.

"I'd like that."

She couldn't see his eyes behind his dark shades but his broad shoulders—shown off to perfection by the black T-shirt he wore—relaxed ever so slightly. The motion was so insignificant she'd have missed it if she weren't looking, but it spoke volumes.

Maybe he did know what he was saying after all.

"Is that it?" Finn pointed toward a hanging sign that proclaimed the word *books* in English and Arabic.

"That's him." She shook off the curious question of what might happen to them once they got home and focused on the task at hand. "Look. We can't just blurt it out about Will. Briggs and I emailed earlier and I could tell he still doesn't know."

"We're not blurting anything. But we do need to know what he knows. We also need to know if Will trusted the right person."

"I know him, Finn. Briggs is not a bad guy."

"Probably not, but do you want to risk it?"

"No."

"Then we have to figure out what he knows first."

They stepped into the store, the scent of old books heavy in the air. She took a deep breath, the comforting smell going a long way toward calming her nerves.

She hoped Finn was being overly cautious about Briggs, but also knew he was right. With a deep breath, she pasted on a smile and walked toward the counter at the back of the store.

Delighted surprise lit Briggs's face as he caught sight

of her the moment she and Finn emerged from the floor-to-ceiling bookcases.

"Rowan!" He slipped from around the desk and pulled her into a tight hug. "It's been so long."

The sweet archaeology student she remembered filled her mind's eye as she hugged him back. "Too long."

She introduced Finn and Briggs and couldn't quite hide her amusement at how the two men sized each other up. Although Briggs hadn't been in the field in a long time, he hadn't gone soft, either. Briggs's impressive frame and dark good looks had clearly put Finn's back up, and Finn's movements were stiff and stilted.

A small wave of happiness broke through the tension that rode her body at the silly display of machismo. She'd been around her brothers long enough to recognize the signs, but it was funny to be the subject of that testosterone battle.

When Rowan settled a hand on Finn's arm, Briggs relaxed. Whether it was her overt body language that she trusted the man she was with or something else, she didn't know, but it was enough to change her old friend's attitude. "I have some of the books and papers Will asked me to pull together for you."

Finn's arm muscles flexed under hers at the mention of Will's name but she kept up the pleasant facade. "He said you had information that might help us on the dig."

"Come on back. I've laid everything out in the reading room."

The clutter of the main store gave way to a small, comfortable room full of overstuffed chairs and a few study tables. Just as Briggs promised, the table was full of several old books, a few maps and what looked like an oversize piece of papyrus preserved in glass.

"You've got an incredible collection."

Finn's comment seemed to be the last piece to defuse the tension, and Briggs's features relaxed completely. "Some of it was my father's and the rest I've acquired over the years. He was part of a British archaeology team stationed here for several years. He and my mum eventually moved back home to settle in Wales but Cairo got its hooks in me. Unlike our Rowan here, my love is in the recording of history, not the discovery of it."

The truth of his words had her throat tightening and Rowan swallowed hard around the lump. She, Will and Briggs had been part of the same program in college, and while all three had started in excavation, convinced it was their great love, the men had both found other avenues to live their passion.

Finn picked up a book and flipped through it, his gaze never leaving the pages. When he did speak, his tone was casual. "Will mentioned you and he were communicating on a chat board, too."

"It's a bad habit of mine. A true waste of time."

Rowan smiled. "It's something you enjoy."

"It still doesn't mean it's not a waste of time. But despite that, it's a fun way to keep my finger on the pulse of what's happening. The dig you're going on is big news here."

"There's little still left to discover in the Valleys. Everyone loves a good Egyptian dig story." Rowan ran her hands over the glass-enclosed papyrus. "It fascinates all of us."

"Will seemed a bit concerned in his emails, especially around the curse nonsense, and I have a few ideas there."

Her gaze locked with Finn's over Briggs's bent head as he shuffled through a few books, opening to pages he'd clearly tabbed in preparation for their visit. He flipped through several before landing on the piece he was searching for. "Here it is."

Rowan scanned the passage Briggs had earmarked. "This says the curse is a deterrent, nothing more."

"Exactly." Briggs nodded. "Another technique Ramesses II used to keep his world ordered and controlled."

"But scholars know this." Finn took the book from her to read the passage. "Right here, it says as much and this book is clearly rather old. Why would a forum that modern day scholars use to communicate believe any of this?"

"Good question." Briggs snagged a small laptop off the edge of the desk and moved the mouse. The screen came to life, the site they'd all focused on filling the screen. "This forum has been a source of community and conversation for well over a decade. But I got curious, so I went back through the archives."

Although it pained her to think Briggs's curiosity could put him in the same danger as Will, she also couldn't hold back her own ready curiosity. "What'd you find?"

"Every time there's been something suspicious in the last few years, the same sort of rumors surface. It's always from a new poster who hasn't been on before."

Finn tapped the screen. "People must come on and off these things pretty regularly."

"The community is small, Finn. You know that in your authentication work. It's a highly competitive field and only the truly determined survive." Briggs's wry smile only reinforced his point. "Everyone knows everyone or knows of everyone."

"And these people who keep coming off and on aren't known." Rowan thought about some of the posts she'd read over the years and had simply ignored, passing over the hobbyist to get to real information.

"And it's an easy place to hide." Briggs snagged a

small notebook off the table. "Here's what's also interesting. There's a strange similarity to the user names."

"Knightsbridge 21. Kensington 42. Hampstead 84." Finn read them off. "They're all London neighborhoods."

"And he just doubled the number, whether consciously or as a way to keep track of something." Rowan let her gaze drift over the books, then to Finn.

He must have read the question in her eyes because his subtle nod encouraged her to continue.

"Briggs, there's something I need to tell you." She took his hand and pointed to the chairs. "Let's sit."

"What is it?"

"Will was murdered the other night in London."

Briggs's features clouded immediately and he cried freely as she told him about Will's attack and what they believed.

Long minutes later, he wiped his eyes. "We must find the ones who did this. Tell me what I need to do and I'll do it. Anything."

Panic swelled in her throat and turned the light breakfast she'd had at the hotel over in her stomach. "I can't put you in this danger, too. I can't lose another friend over this."

"Will was my friend, too."

"I know, but we can't leave you unprotected, and Finn and I can't stay in Cairo. We're needed in Luxor tomorrow to begin the excavation." She debated telling him about what Campbell had done to his computer account—knew Briggs deserved to know the truth—but also knew his grief was fresh and his ideas were more about avenging Will's death than any real sense of malice. "I need to know you're safe."

"I'd like to arrange for security detail." Finn's tone was somber, but any traces of the machismo she'd seen earlier had vanished. In its place was the man she'd come to care for more than she ever could have imagined. "I've already secured a firm that I trust, and I can have them here within the hour on your okay."

"I don't understand." Briggs shook his head. "It's a website, nothing more. It can't be dangerous."

Rowan reached for his hand, wrapping it in her own. "That's what we thought. What Will thought."

A range of emotions flitted across her friend's face, but that same determination to find who was responsible wouldn't leave. "We still must find who did this."

"And we will." The lethal tone of Finn's voice laced his words. "We will find who did this."

The store's electronic alarm dinged when the front door opened, and Briggs nodded. "Let me go greet this customer and then we'll determine next steps."

The bell rang again, the innocuous sound punctuating Briggs's comments. It was only when he neared the doorway of the reading room that Finn leaped into action.

"Briggs, no!" Finn tackled him to the ground before the man cleared the door frame.

Rowan watched in horror as a wave of fire blew through the outer room, followed by the devastating, earsplitting ring of an explosion.

Chapter 15

Finn rolled off Briggs, desperate to find Rowan. The walls shook around them and the fire's flames were already consuming the bookshelves outside the door frame with shocking speed.

"Rowan!"

"I'm here!" She got to her feet on the other side of the reading room, where she'd been thrown by the force of the blast. Her movements were shaky, but she was in one piece and he offered up a quick prayer of thanks.

Briggs lifted his head, rising horror filling his face. "What is this?"

"We need to get out of here. Now."

Finn's harsh tone was clearly what the man needed to focus and he was on his feet, despite several glances toward the outer portion of his store.

"Back door, Briggs! Come on."

They both waved Rowan toward the door in front of

them, but she raced back to the table where they'd set everything up.

"Rowan! Come on!" Finn knew the old building had little structural integrity to begin with, but the fact it was filled with ready kindling ensured it would go quickly.

"I'm coming." She snagged her oversize bag and Briggs's computer before running back to grab the glass-enclosed papyrus and the book they'd left open next to it.

"Rowan!" Finn grabbed her arm and pulled her in front of his body, and they both followed Briggs out the back of the store. A small alley consumed them and it was Briggs who led them through the narrow space.

"Why the hell did you go back?" Finn muttered the words as they wove through the restrictive alley, veering around potholes and various other things he had no interest stepping in.

She kept a brisk pace but was busy trying to stuff the computer and book into her bag all while juggling the glass.

With a groan, he reached out for the bag and dragged it open. "Here, give me the computer."

She did as he asked, then followed with the glass when he had the computer settled in the seemingly bottomless bag. There was no room for the book, so he held it. The urge to ditch it was strong, but she hadn't been entirely wrong to grab it.

"That's an ancient papyrus. I couldn't leave it behind."

"It's not worth getting killed." He dragged the bag back onto his arm.

"I wasn't killed." She shot him a cheeky smile. "And I have the papyrus."

He shook his head. Damn, but how did she do this to him? Even in the midst of her own personal danger, she was focused on other things. "Crazy woman."

Briggs came to a halt at the edge of the alleyway. "Wait for a moment."

"What is it?" Rowan leaned forward to look around the man's shoulder but Finn snagged her arm and pulled her back.

"I heard footsteps."

They both waited, holding their breath as they listened to the quiet air that swirled around them. Finn pressed against Rowan's arm, dragging her a few steps farther back into the alley.

When did Briggs suddenly realize they were being followed? And shouldn't he be more shell-shocked over his store instead of leading them down the alley?

"Rowan." Finn whispered her name and she turned, her gaze preternaturally sharp.

She gave him the briefest nod as she took another small step back.

But it was when Briggs turned, a sad smile on his face, that they both knew he wasn't their friend. "I'm sorry, Rowan. Really, I am. It was just a job, you know."

Finn didn't wait for the man to confess his sins, but instead swung out with the heavy book in his hands, the thick weight connecting dead center of Briggs's face. A huge howl went up as Briggs dropped to the ground, but Finn's only thought was to get them as far away as possible.

He grabbed Rowan's hand and dragged her along with him as they raced back the same way they came.

"There was a store door open." She pointed down the alley in the direction of a line of trash cans.

"Where?"

Footfalls echoed behind them, and the heavy shot of a gun firing had them both instinctively ducking as they moved.

"The next door, Finn!"

He caught sight of a screen door with open access to the space inside and rushed them toward it, dragging her in front of him as another bullet echoed down the alley.

They barreled through the door, Rowan screaming the entire time for the people in the store to stay back in a mixture of English and Arabic, over and over, as they ran pell-mell through racks of clothing, shelves laden with canned goods and several revolving racks that held bags of chips.

Rowan grabbed at the cans as she ran, tossing them onto the floor as a deterrent, and he shoved at the racks, their tottering crash behind them giving him hope they might have slowed their pursuers down.

They burst through the front of the store onto the street. The narrow lane seemed far more menacing than when they'd walked up the street not even an hour before, and Finn kept moving despite having no idea where he was going.

"The church. Come on!" Rowan pointed toward the twin towers of the Coptic church in the distance as she kept pace beside him.

"We'll be stuck there."

"Not if we find the right place to hide."

A loud shout echoed behind them and Finn wasn't about to argue; he just followed her as they wove in a zigzagging pattern down the street, avoiding the occasional car or group of pedestrians, the honking or screaming of either echoing in their wake.

They raced up the front steps, bumping past throngs of tourists as they went. Hanging on to each other would slow them down, so he kept Rowan in his sights but let her run as fast as she could. Once they cleared the entrance, the interior of the church spread out in front of them.

He followed her as she moved quickly to the edge of the gathering space, searching for any small alcove they could hide in. The loud shout of a guard went up, and Finn hesitated the briefest moment to turn and gaze toward the front door.

One of their pursuers stood at the door, arguing with the guard in a mix of Arabic and English, and Finn caught enough to know the man was passing himself off as police.

"Wanker," Rowan muttered as he followed her into a small alcove. "Thinks he can pretend to be undercover."

"It may work. And his second friend appears to have taken a different direction."

Rowan pointed to a long row of candles atop an oversize table. "Under there. The tablecloth will hide us and we can figure out next steps."

It wasn't an ideal hiding place, since it meant they were still trapped inside the church, but it would give them the time they needed to regroup. He followed her small frame under the cloth, grateful she'd selected an empty alcove away from the prying eyes of the tourists taking in the church as he attempted to fold his large body into the small space.

He didn't miss her broad smile when he struggled to drag his feet fully under the cloth covering. "I don't think this was quite what you had in mind when you said you wanted to take me through the church."

"Probably not." She leaned forward and pressed a hard kiss to his lips. "But we'll make do."

They sat in tense silence for a few minutes, waiting for discovery. When the immediate threat passed, he pointed toward her bag, his voice a low whisper. "Do you have anything in this bottomless monstrosity we can use as a weapon if it comes to that?"

"You mean aside from its lethal heft?"

"Tell me about it." He made a show of rubbing his shoulder. "I carried it."

"I carry it every day."

"Glutton for punishment."

The teasing seemed out of place for the situation they found themselves in, yet Finn couldn't deny it felt good to sit still and catch their breath.

Rowan dug through her purse, intent on her goal, but he still didn't miss the notes of pain layered underneath her soft-spoken words. "I can't believe Briggs sold us out."

"Maybe we'll find out why on his computer."

"He's still out there."

"Unless they don't need him any longer."

Her head snapped up. "You think they're going to kill him?"

"It depends on how useful they think he is. How entrenched he is in their organization. A lot of things."

"And here it is again. Another personal connection."

"Look, Rowan. Briggs made his choice."

She waved a hand. "I know that and unfortunately I also understand he's the one responsible for that. It doesn't change the fact I've known him a long time, and whatever his eventual outcome, it hurts to think about it."

They sat in silence awhile longer, her quiet digging through her purse the only sound in their small hiding space until she stopped abruptly.

The distant sound of footsteps grew louder and he dropped a hand over hers as they waited. Noise floated around them, then quieted when several people stopped and stood inches away from them, lighting prayer candles.

Through it all, they remained in place, their hands locked tight.

The moment the footsteps from the other side of the curtain faded from their hearing, Rowan whipped out a small, cloth-wrapped package. "What about my lock picks?"

"Aren't they a little small?"

"We can stuff them between our fingers. A swipe like that wouldn't feel all that great. And—" she whipped a second packet out of her bag "—I carry two sets."

The moment struck him as so silly and strange, yet he couldn't have held back if he'd tried. "You're amazing, you know that?"

"Nah, I'm just resource—"

He didn't let her finish her statement. Instead, he leaned forward and wrapped a hand around the back of her neck, pulling her close, the soft, short wisps of her hair tickling his fingers. "Amazing."

He pressed his lips to hers, the taste of her the sweetest rush on his tongue. The reverent environment wasn't lost on him; instead, it lent an air of importance to the simple act of giving comfort and sharing their feelings for each other.

Her hands trailed over his face, tracing his jaw, before she lifted her head. "We should probably go."

"Are you sure?"

"There's an entrance on the opposite side of where we came in. If we leave separately, we should be able to get back outside." She pressed her lips to his once more. "And this time I promise we can call a taxi."

"I'll go first. Stay here and when it's clear I'll let out a sharp whistle."

"Here. Take these." She shoved one of the pick sets into his hand. "Hold them like I said."

She helped him lodge the sharp tools between his fingers, even as the thought of using them wasn't high on his list of activities for the day. "Now you."

Rowan followed suit, positioning the picks in her dominant hand.

He listened for any noise, then lifted the curtain on the back side of the table for a look at the room. Sunlight still streamed in through the windows, dust motes curling in the beams, but the alcove was empty. He slid out, about as gracefully as when he slid in, and winced when the picks scraped against the floor. A muffled "shhh" echoed from under the table and he couldn't hold back a smile at the bossy rejoinder.

The majority of people were in the interior of the church, and his quick scan of the area didn't turn up anything unusual. He let out a short, sharp whistle and waited, his back pressed to the wall.

Within moments, Rowan sauntered out of the small alcove. She'd positioned her hand around the edge of her heavy bag so the picks weren't visible.

At the evidence he wasn't comparably covered, he tossed a pointed glance to his exposed hand. She placed her empty hand over the picks and he hoped it would be enough to get them out of the church unnoticed. "Let's go."

"Walk slower."

"We need to get out of here."

She dropped his hand and snagged the back of his T-shirt, effectively slowing his movement. "There's a guard across the way and he's looking at us. Slow down."

Finn appreciated her quick read of the situation and slowed, waiting until she'd once again wrapped her left hand around his pick-filled right. "Are they hidden?"

"Yep. Now stroll."

The seconds crawled and the distance to the front

of the church and the other exit Rowan had identified seemed endless, but he kept his pace moderate. They'd come this far; it would all be for naught if they ended up in a police station under interrogation.

When they finally saw daylight, Finn exhaled on a heavy breath. The area was still crowded with people, but the cloying sense of confinement that came with being trapped inside began to fade. "That was close."

"Or maybe not."

The heavy press of a gun hit the center of his back and Finn stopped moving. "What do you want?"

"You really don't know?" The man kept his voice at a low register so as not to be overheard but his accent was British.

"I'm afraid I don't."

"Maybe I can do something about that."

Rowan squeezed his hand once before she moved, her actions as graceful as a cat's. The hand shielding his lifted and shoved him off balance at the same time she swung her other hand, wrapped tight around the picks. Finn briefly registered the man attempting to capture them—medium build, sandy hair, goatee—before he lost his footing and stumbled, just as Rowan had obviously intended.

Her hand continued its deadly arc and connected with the side of the man's face. He let out a howl of pain as he reached for his cheek, the action reflexive enough for Rowan to knock into him with the bag, dislodging the gun.

The heavy piece clattered to the ground but Rowan ignored it and was already grabbing Finn's hand as they ran for the street. They both shouted and waved their hands for a cab hovering down the street. Finn pushed her on ahead of him, shielding her from the lumbering, screaming man who chased after them.

She flung the door open and scrambled in, turning toward him the moment she had a seat. "Finn! Come on."

The open door beckoned and he dived in, unable to fold his large form into the small space as quickly as she did. The thug chasing them leaped toward his feet and snagged his shoe but didn't get a firm grip. Rowan was already barking out orders at the cab driver. "Drive. Now. Go!"

Whether the driver spoke English or not didn't seem to matter, especially when Rowan began tossing money onto the front seat. Finn struggled to right himself and nearly fell back out the car door as the driver took a sharp curve.

Rowan's hands were tight on his and she dragged at his shoulders, one hand fisted in the material of his shirt while the other dragged at him from under his arm.

He finally managed to get his body fully inside the taxi and slammed the door closed. On a heavy breath, he reached for her and pulled her close. "That was fun."

"Are you okay?" Her hands were already roaming over his body, checking for any damage, when he caught sight of the blood that covered her fingers.

"Me? You're bleeding."

"It's not mine." When he reached for her hand, she lifted them out of reach. "Don't touch me. There are wet wipes in my purse. Would you grab them?"

He dug out the small packet after she directed him to a side pocket, and pulled out several sterile, wet sheets. "Here. Get that blood off you."

"With pleasure."

It was only as she was scrubbing the blood off her hands, the thin bones of her wrists flexing with the motions, that the thug's words struck a chord.

You really don't know?

With startling clarity, Finn did know. And he had a rising sense of panic the people after them knew, too.

None of this was about the Nefertari tomb. Or Egypt. Or even discrediting a made-up curse.

Someone wanted the Victoria bracelet. And he'd walked straight into their trap.

Rowan tried desperately to wash the stench off her body, but no amount of soap seemed to make her feel clean. Hot water sluiced over her head and neck, then down over her breasts and stomach, but it didn't seem to matter. The physical traces of blood and smoke were long gone, but the water still couldn't erase the brand both had made on her skin.

"Rowan." Finn's voice echoed from the doorway. "You've been in there for a while. Are you okay?"

Her lack of a response had him across the bathroom in seconds, and before she could think to protest, he was inside the stall. "What's wrong?"

"I'm fine."

"You're pale and shivering and it's a billion degrees in here."

He reached over her shoulder to adjust the steaming water before his gaze swung back around to her face. "Tell me."

A hard sob caught her square in the throat, the harsh events of the past several days finally overwhelming her. "I thought I was okay with it. Really. And then I got in here. And all the dirt started streaming down the drain and I wasn't okay with it anymore."

He pulled her against his chest, the wet cotton of his T-shirt warm against her cheek. "It's a lot to take in."

His heart thudded strong and solid beneath her ear

and she tried to focus on that, taking comfort in the sure, steady beat. "I'm glad you're here, Finn. So glad."

The water continued to sluice over them both, and as his clothes got soaked, her thoughts shifted and grew more urgent. She *needed* him. Needed the comfort and the mindless pleasure to be found in his arms.

He'd already changed out of his clothes from earlier, replacing both with the fresh T-shirt and shorts he now had on. His erection pressed against her stomach through the thin material and she focused all her attention on his body. With quick movements, she slipped her hand beneath the waistband of his shorts and gripped his full length.

"Rowan—" Her name came out on a clipped groan. "I already feel like enough of a lecher for getting a hard-on while trying to comfort you."

"We'll comfort each other."

He gripped her wrist, holding her still. "I'm serious. Just let me hold you."

"I want more." She reached up and nipped his jawline with her teeth and lips. "So much more."

"We can't."

"Yes, we can." She captured his lips once more with hers, desperate to show him with her mouth and her hands how badly she wanted him.

So why did she get the vague sense he was holding back, even as his body betrayed him with the urge to give in?

And then there was no time to question or argue because his hands were on her, sliding over her skin and pulling the most exquisite pleasure from her body.

She dragged at the wet T-shirt, lifting it over the hard planes of his stomach and chest. When the wet material caught on his chin, he smiled. "Let me."

The wet cloth hit the floor of the shower with a heavy *thwack,* followed almost immediately by his shorts, and then he was back against her, his body hard and demanding as he pressed her into the shower tiles.

Rowan celebrated the moment, so much ugliness fading away as he made her clean with his body. The play of his hands over her skin, the drag of his lips over her flesh and the brand of his body as he filled her—all of them combined together to chase away the ugliness of what they'd both survived over the past days.

She traced the slim line of the knife wound, now free of its bandage, and was pleased to see the flesh already knitting together.

Her warrior.

Hers.

The thought was so swift and immediate, she stilled, her fingers hovering over the cut.

"What is it?"

"Nothing." She whispered it on a shake of the head before she placed her fingers back on his body and traced the hard lines of his stomach. At the thick, heavy pace of his breathing, she reached for the condom he'd had enough sense to snag from his shorts and leave on a small ledge, tearing the foil in quick movements.

Finn's question faded away under the pounding spray and he returned to her body. With his mouth and hands, he pleasured her. With his quietly whispered words, he seduced her. And with deep, soulful gazes, he worshipped her body.

And when he lifted her leg and wrapped it around his waist, she took him in, welcoming him fully into her body. His thrusts were sure and deep, and with each movement Rowan could have sworn she heard her soul shatter into a million tiny pieces, right along with her body as her release exploded from the depths of her being.

She took him and they rode the pleasure together.

Her warrior.

The man she loved.

Rowan turned off the bathroom lights and stepped into the bedroom. Although she'd originally worried sharing a room would be awkward, it was the opposite. She felt safe knowing Finn was with her, and the moments between them were slow and easy, full of lazy, knowing glances and gentle caresses.

And the very real knowledge that she was in love.

Whatever she'd expected it to feel like, the simple, easy slide that had consumed her over the past few days was more powerful than she'd ever imagined.

And while she knew they still had things to work out, she was confident they'd find a way.

She'd finished up her time in the bathroom and had changed into capri pants and a thin blouse. They'd opted not to go out to dinner, not knowing what still might await them out in the open. Instead, Finn had ordered a lavish dinner from the hotel restaurant, and even now the room-service attendant was setting up their feast at the small table that dominated the far side of their room.

The man added the final flourish of a bottle of wine while Finn dealt with the bill, then gathered up his things to leave with a kind smile. He navigated the small space with his delivery cart and misjudged when he passed the bed.

Their bags lay in a small pile on the floor, and the delivery cart struck her purse and an old leather backpack of Finn's as their attendant attempted to pass by. His profuse apologies had Rowan smiling and she quickly assured him in Arabic there wasn't anything to worry about. She let him safely out the door, locking up behind him, then turned, already anticipating the dinner they were about to share.

Her gaze focused on Finn, Rowan made the same mistake as the waiter and stumbled over the thick strap of Finn's bag.

And then everything happened at once.

The force of her foot pulled his bag loose, dragging it several feet from where it lay on the floor. The contents that filled the bag spilled from the top, and a small velvet pouch, no larger than the width of a baseball, tumbled onto the top of the heap.

Whether it was simple memory or something more, she didn't know, but as she stared down at the velvet pouch, Rowan knew.

And when she lifted the small bag and untied the drawstring, she could only let out a cry of dismay when the Victoria bracelet fell into her hands.

Chapter 16

Rowan's shock registered from clear across the room and Finn knew his moment of reckoning had arrived. The warm, rosy glow on her cheeks faded, replaced with something he'd never thought he'd see.

Despair.

"Why is this here?"

"Because I travel with it."

Her eyes widened but the exaggerated motion did nothing to bring any color or warmth into her pale face. "I'm sorry?"

"I carry it with me."

"It's a stolen object of priceless value. What do you mean, you travel with it?"

How did he explain this to her? And why did every excuse springing to his lips feel wholly inadequate?

"I can't leave it among my personal things in my home. There's danger in what I do, and I can't risk dying and having the bracelet discovered."

"So carrying it in your things is better?"

"I can dispose of it more easily if it's with me and things get sticky."

"You don't worry about customs?"

"I have provenance papers that usually let me pass without question. You know our profession helps on that front."

"You had it today? In Old Cairo."

"Yes."

Her fingers trembled around the edges of the cuff. "And you carry it so you can easily dispose of it? So this priceless object that isn't even rightfully yours could be tossed away in a jungle or buried in a tomb somewhere if you get into a jam?"

"Yes."

"But it's priceless. How could you see it thrown away instead of simply given back to its rightful owner?"

He swallowed hard at the disappointment that rode her face in harsh, tired lines. "It's mine."

"No, it's not yours!"

The shout carried across the room and he moved quickly to stand beside her. "Shh. We don't know who's nearby."

"Fine. Because there's really nothing more to say."

"Rowan—" He broke off as she snatched her hand away from his.

"I trusted you. Believed in what could be possible between us. And this is the proof that there can't be anything between us."

"An hour ago in the shower you felt differently."

"An hour ago I thought I was sharing my body with the man I loved. But this?" She tossed the bracelet onto the bed. "I don't know who you are."

She loved him?

The knowledge slammed into him with the force of an avalanche.

Rowan loved him.

Before he could say anything, she ran back to the bathroom and he heard the lock click from the inside.

"Rowan, come back. We need to talk."

Her voice was muffled from the other side of the door. "I can't leave our hotel room and I can't be near you right now. Please go away."

When she said nothing further, he sat down hard on the bed and picked up the bracelet she'd tossed down. He'd always believed the bracelet brought him luck. And now? When faced with the evidence of her shattered feelings for him, Finn knew the bracelet had been nothing but a pile of fool's gold.

Bethany Warrington sat back and took in the man sprawled across the cabin from her. For all his cutthroat business practices, Jared Wright was a surprisingly huge rube and she was counting the minutes until she could get rid of him.

He'd grown up on the streets and had never fully eliminated his street-rat tendencies. Or the naïveté of the uncultured masses.

Their flight attendant sauntered out from the back galley of the private plane with a full bottle of champagne and leaned over his sprawled form. "More champagne, Mr. Wright?"

"Yes." He eagerly lifted his empty glass, and even from a distance, Bethany could tell he'd spent a long, leering minute eyeing the attendant's cleavage.

Boorish behavior that only reinforced her thoughts.

With a throaty purr she'd perfected before she was

even out of her teens, she called to him across the cabin. "Enjoying yourself, darling?"

He lifted his refilled flute. "Quite." He patted the seat next to him. "Come sit by me."

"I'm working."

"I'm working, too, but it's a long flight. Doesn't mean we can't enjoy ourselves a bit before we get down to all that hard work."

Her smile never dropped, but the press of her fingernails into her palm nearly drew blood. "We'd be working a lot less if your men in Cairo hadn't bungled the kidnapping."

"Tomorrow, my love. We'll get them tomorrow. For now, come join me." He patted the seat next to him once more.

She fought a huge sigh and crossed the cabin. She was at no one's beck and call, but it wouldn't do to get him overly suspicious. They still had several pieces that now needed to fall into place in Luxor, and she couldn't afford for him to grow a brain at this late hour.

"What did you have in mind, darling?"

"Let me show you."

She fought an eye roll and let him have his moment, groping her breasts and moaning in her ear all the ways he wanted to take her. Whispering "oh, yes" a few times, she succumbed to his ministrations before taking the upper hand.

Literally.

As his eyes practically crossed in his head, she counted off all she needed to do upon their arrival in Luxor. She'd waited so long for this moment, and her own arousal spiked at the proof that she'd finally have what she'd wanted all these years.

"That was amazing, baby."

"That's exactly what I was going to say about you." She pressed a quick kiss to his cheek and hid her amusement behind the toss of her long mane of hair. She'd avoided his attentions for a long time, but it had become necessary a few years before to give in to his interests in order to meet her own.

Damn sod had grown a fat head, convinced his successes in London's seamier activities were all his own doing instead of her careful work behind the scenes. It still amused her how quickly sex rebalanced the scales in her favor.

Thankfully, their moments together were blessedly short, and it never failed to entertain her that he was so easily fooled by a few complimentary words and some light panting.

Men.

They were so quickly distracted by the lure of sex.

In her experience, the quick score of physical pleasure beat out their ability to think rationally each and every time. They believed what flashed on the surface, and if they could taste and touch it, that only made it better. Men held little imagination and even less ability to work toward a goal. Which was why they made the perfect partners for her work.

She'd learned young she had to reach out and take what she wanted. Sitting around waiting for it got her nothing but waiting. Action, however, got results. And if that action was outside the bounds of what was considered right and proper, that was just too bad.

As she envisioned the way the next forty-eight hours would unfold, Bethany had to admire how neatly everything had come full circle.

After all, it was Rowan Steele who had set her on the road to her future.

Oh, her dear childhood friend had thought herself so clever, but Bethany had seen through it all. The girl had a chip on her shoulder the size of Russia and had moped through high school like a zombie. Bethany had steered clear of her until that one day.

That one fateful day.

Rowan nicked a wallet out of Serena MacAlister's brand-new purse, and that lone action had been enough to give Bethany an idea.

The rest had simply fallen into place.

She'd set the wheels in motion within days, easily luring Rowan's unknowing cooperation through the promise of information and a few airheaded moves with the alarm code and the safe combination. It had been so easy. So simple.

She'd watched her mother play the fool for years and had mimicked sixteen years' worth of teaching.

And the anticipation of seeing Rowan thinking things through had been thrilling, even if Bethany had found the waiting game tedious at times.

In the end, despite the fact she didn't get the bracelet that evening, things had worked out strangely for the best. Her father's acquisition wasn't exactly a secret and others had paid attention to the annual holiday departure of one of London's wealthiest households.

Three separate parties had descended on the house that night, and two came up empty-handed. It had taken years of digging and she'd never discovered the identity of the third until a bit of news came to her attention.

A priceless bracelet Finn Gallagher secretly kept on his person when he traveled.

And just like that day outside Serena's locker, all the pieces had once again fallen into place.

* * *

Rowan traced the edge of the bath towel in her hands, the pattern likely committed to memory for the rest of her life she'd followed it so many times. Up, down, over, around.

Over and over and over again.

No matter how many ways she tried to see Finn's point of view—what little he'd actually shared—she couldn't understand his motivations. Or the crazy, idiotic reason the man chose to carry the bracelet with him.

But as long minutes had stretched into even longer hours, she'd been forced to look inside herself and acknowledge the one area that was her sole responsibility.

The two of them hadn't resolved their differences of opinion or the disparate ways they chose to live their lives. She'd fallen into a physical relationship with him and he'd never once said he'd changed his mind on keeping the bracelet. He'd even gone so far as to try to stop their first night together because they were still on opposite sides.

Yet she'd blithely believed they'd figure it out and work through their differences. Which, if she were honest with herself, meant she'd convince him to give the bracelet back, stop any extracurricular thieving and settle into the life she wanted him to lead.

While she refused to fault herself for wanting something better for him, she knew full well she'd been narrow-minded in her approach.

And none of it changed the fact that she was still madly in love with the man.

Be bold, Rowan Steele.

Her father's long-ago words rose up in her mind, stilling her hands on the towel. She hadn't thought them in years, the warm, encouraging gaze that accompanied his inspiration too difficult to bear thinking about.

But she thought about them now.

Be bold.

Even now, so many years after he was gone, she could hear her father say the words. The deep timbre of his voice filled with equal parts encouragement, excitement and pride.

Be bold.

She'd spent her adult life equating boldness with risk taking. But it was something more.

What if being bold meant you loved with all your heart? What if it meant you had to take a leap with the one you loved, even when all the pieces didn't add up? Or what if it meant you had to walk away when the values you held dear weren't the same as those you cared about?

Rowan leaned her head back against the counter and closed her eyes, her father's voice echoing in her head, encouraging yet providing no answers to her questions.

Be bold.

The drive to the airport and the short flight to Luxor were uneventful. All signs of the previous day's danger had vanished as if it had never been. If only the anger she couldn't let go of could do the same.

She and Finn had kept to opposite sides of the cabin the entire way and it was only now, as they stood before their side-by-side hotel doors, that Rowan knew things were really at an end for them personally.

They'd each do their portion of the excavation—cool, calm, professional—and get the hell out of Dodge. She was committed to preserving whatever came out of the tomb, just as she'd signed on for, but that was it. She'd also mapped out just how she'd get her hands on the wall that outlined Nefertari's heritage, but she needed to get a feel for the dig team before she could finalize those plans.

"Would you like dinner?"

His quiet words pierced her heart, but she shook her head. "I'm going to order something in my room."

"We should probably get to the site around seven tomorrow."

Her cell phone buzzed from where she juggled it in her hands and she absently glanced down at the face. And saw the message from Campbell.

Call me. Nearly rerouted the London internet signature.

"What is it?"

"It's Campbell. He's got something."

Finn was at her side in a moment. "We're calling him back together."

"Of course." She made quick work of the door lock before tossing her things in the corner of the room, with Finn following suit. In moments, she had her phone on speaker and Campbell's voice greeting them.

"Hey there, Dora the Explorer. How's Egypt?"

"Eventful."

As soon as the words were out, she wished she could pull them back as Campbell went into overprotective-big-brother mode. "What's that supposed to mean?"

"Nothing. Look. I've got Finn here with me. Tell us what's going on."

"Only if you promise me you'll be careful."

"I'm always careful." She tossed the words back at her brother, so similar to the conversation she'd had with Kensington before leaving New York.

"No, you're not. That's what always worries us."

Finn's knowing gaze only added to the wedge of guilt

that lodged in her chest. "Come on, Campbell. I will be. I promise."

As if sensing that was all he'd get, Campbell's somber tone faded, replaced with his trademark geek speak. "I traced the internet signature on the forums. The one coming from London but bouncing around the globe."

"Yes?"

"So if bouncing the signal wasn't the first clue something was going on, the significant encryption on it is great big clue number two."

"You get to the bottom of it?" Finn's absolute focus on the call and Campbell's intel had a small wave of regret washing through her. Finn was good at what he did and he knew how to work with others. He'd be a great partner.

They'd be such great partners.

Only they couldn't be.

"All I have so far is that it's centered around Knightsbridge."

Her gaze collided with Finn's at the mention of their long-ago meeting place. Raw emotion clouded his eyes and Rowan was pretty sure she saw the same in hers.

On a light cough, she refocused on Campbell. "You get an address?"

"That's my problem. No matter how I try to go into the system, I'm hitting a wall."

"You can't scale it?" Rowan couldn't hide the surprise in her voice, and the hard grunt that echoed through the phone ensured she didn't want to. Although she and her siblings all carried the trait in spades, Campbell was the one who most loved to figure out puzzles.

And one he couldn't solve only got him more focused.

"I didn't say that." The sound of keys tapping echoed through the phone and she could picture her brother in front of his laptop, his blue-eyed gaze locked on the screen. "But I need a bit more time. T-Bone's working it with me, so we should have it by midmorning your time."

"Text me as soon as you do."

They disconnected and Rowan stared at her now-silent phone, willing her brother to find the address.

"Rowan, there's something I need to tell you."

Finn's serious tone caught her attention.

"There's more? You keep other things locked up in your safe?"

"No, not things. It's been a feeling up to now but I think it's something more."

"Like what?"

He stood to pace the area between the table and the bed, his large frame filling up the small space. Even with the slight panic that there was even more he wasn't telling her, she couldn't hold back the lick of attraction that sparked wild and hot in her veins.

Nor could she ignore how his black T-shirt and black slacks lent an aura of casual power to his already impressive frame.

And she certainly couldn't ignore how she still wanted to reach out and touch him, using the physical to hide from the reality of their situation.

"Yesterday, in Cairo, when that man chased us out of the church. Do you remember what he said when he held the gun to my back?"

"I know he threatened you."

"He asked me how I didn't know why we were being followed."

She tried to conjure up the conversation but the adrenaline of the moment and her focus on using her lock picks as weapons had her attention admittedly diverted. "He didn't give you reasons, though. I don't remember it fully, but I think I'd have remembered that."

"No reasons, but he was British. And there was something in the taunt that I've not been able to get past. I think he was talking about the bracelet."

While the Victoria bracelet hadn't been out of her thoughts for more than a few minutes at a stretch, Rowan still didn't understand how it could have anything to do with the danger they were facing in Egypt. "That doesn't make any sense. We're not here because of the bracelet. We're here for an excavation in the Valley."

"I can't define it, but that's what I feel. Add on the personal overtones to everything that's happened. And the computer signal generating from Knightsbridge. It's too neat and too connected to what happened twelve years ago."

She didn't want to dismiss him—years of trusting her gut had taught her that ignoring internal red flags was a bigger mistake than thinking your ideas might be off base—but it still didn't change the fact that they were on a job that had nothing to do with the Victoria bracelet.

"I don't want to dismiss it out of hand, especially because you're nothing if not coolly rational under fire. But I'm struggling to connect our personal folly with a project for the British Museum."

"Personal folly?" He quirked one eyebrow and she saw the first smile cross his face since those tense moments yesterday in the hotel.

Her own smile expanded quickly. "It seemed to fit."

"Folly. Not a word you hear every day."

"Nothing about this is ordinary or everyday."

"No, it's not." Indecision briefly lit his features before he had his hand over hers and pulled her out of the chair. "Nothing about us is ordinary, either."

"Finn."

"Or this need for you I can't sate, no matter how much I tell myself I have to walk away."

Where indecision clouded their conversations, it was bold, decisive action that ruled the physical. He dragged her into his arms and she went willingly.

Hot, greedy need flared between them, rising high like a bonfire as his lips pressed to hers, demanding a response. His tongue sought entrance to her mouth, and when she opened for him, the shockingly carnal sweep of power only grew and expanded when she met him thrust for thrust.

They pressed each other on, with their mouths, with their hands, with wicked, whispered words of need.

And it was only when the physical threatened to over-power her that Rowan dragged herself from his arms. "We can't do this."

Hunger filled his gaze and the air around him filled with a pulsing tension that was nearly visible as it radi-ated from his body. "I want you."

"I want you, too." She fought the urge to wipe her lips, still wet and warm from his. "That's the whole damn problem."

Finn stared up at Nefertari's tomb and shaded his eyes from the bright sunlight. He'd been here before, but the site never failed to take his breath away. Just like the woman at his side.

He'd spent a frustrated and sleepless night tossing for the sheer want of her. His body ached for release in her arms even as his mind urgently sought a way out of the trap he'd made for himself. But by the time dawn lit the edges of his window, he knew what he needed to do.

Even if Rowan refused to stay with him, it didn't mat-ter. He needed to give the bracelet back. The answer was so simple, but the path to the decision had been fraught with mental land mines he preferred to keep deep under the surface.

He was more than his actions, yet he knew his actions spoke volumes about his character. He was more than the impoverished childhood that had shaped him, and it was time he not only acted that way but understood it in his skin.

He'd crafted a business that he loved and a life that was the product of hard work. And if he worked at reforming his life, maybe he'd finally convince the woman he loved that he was worth a second chance.

He turned to face Rowan once more, hope boldly dancing in his chest. She stood beside him, dressed exactly as he'd pictured in his mind's eye when he'd first proposed she join him on the dig. That slender frame was clad in a tank top and khaki shorts with a pair of work boots. Her vast array of excavation tools hung around her waist to complete the ensemble.

He'd seen her in several different outfits so far, but nothing compared to the rugged nature girl who stood next to him, ready to dive headlong into three weeks of grueling work.

"You ready?"

She turned to face him, resignation wiping away the excitement that had filled her face. "Sure."

"There's something you need to know."

Her features remained impassive, but something sparked in those gorgeous blue eyes that still gave him hope. "What?"

"When this is over, I'm giving it back."

"You are?"

"Yes. The object as well as whatever else I can quietly restore. I don't need them any longer. I just need you."

"Let me know how I can help."

"You already did." He extended his hand and knew the greatest joy when she took it, threading her fingers with his.

They descended into the tomb, hand in hand, down into the antechamber. Four large pillars supported the ceiling in the wide-open chamber, painted in a representation of the night sky. The entire room was covered with depictions of passages from the Book of the Dead, and well over two thousand years later, the paintings were still bold with color.

Egyptian gods surrounded them, Osiris and Anubis, Hathor and Ra, and so many others.

"So few get to see this." Rowan dropped his hand and moved to the middle of the room. Her voice was reverent as she stood in one place and turned in a slow circle, examining each wall before turning another quarter to look at the next side of the tomb. "So few will ever look at this and feel the weight of history surround them in vivid color."

"The government restricts visitation to the tomb in order to preserve the paintings."

"Yet here we are." Her gaze drifted toward the last wall before returning to capture his. "We're lucky, aren't we?"

"Very lucky." *Lucky to have found each other.*

"Our work allows us to see things many can only dream of. World historic sites. Ancient artifacts. Even museums after closing hours. It's easy to take it all for granted. To stop realizing just how special that sort of access is. We're the lucky ones, Finn."

When he only continued to stare at her, the gravity of the moment imprinting itself on his soul, Rowan smiled, the light of her filling up the dim room. She pressed her hand against her chest. "We own this. Possess it. In our hearts."

"Yes, we do." He moved forward and pressed his palm to her cheek, that beautiful smile still filling her face with bright light. "And it's enough."

A heavy thud echoed behind them and they broke apart, a raised voice invading their private moment. Baxter Monroe marched into the chamber a few moments later.

"So you made it." Baxter's oily voice echoed around them. "We were beginning to worry."

"We were only delayed by a day." Rowan spoke first. "And from the rumors I heard this morning, the government's still wrapping the site up in a lot of red tape."

Baxter snorted before shifting the heavy pack he carried on one shoulder to the other. "I swear these people don't know their heads from their asses. We're spending a lot of money to be here. You'd think the government could get their acts together. They're more than happy to let us excavate, but we can't take anything out of the chamber yet for examination."

Finn gestured Baxter toward the burial chamber. "Take us down so we see how far you got yesterday."

"We got nowhere yesterday."

"Nothing at all?" Rowan moved toward the corridor entrance, her voice ripe with excitement.

"No."

"Well, let's get down there, then." She patted Baxter on the back. "And prepare for a better day."

Baxter moved into the lead as they descended farther into the burial chamber, and Finn expected no less. The man loved being in control like a toddler loved throwing tantrums, and he gloried in the role of tour director.

Finn knew damn well Rowan's knowledge of the tomb

would make Baxter look like an amateur, and he admired her restraint as she asked simple questions the museum director would be able to answer.

The burial chamber opened before them and Finn exhaled a reverent breath. The weight of history filled the chamber and Baxter's voice faded as Rowan's rose up in his mind.

We own this. Possess it. In our hearts.

Rowan had come so far in her life and had been forced to deal with her demons. She'd not only battled them, but she'd conquered them, too.

Now he would do the same.

He drank in the beauty of the room, and as he stared at the wondrous space, Finn understood what Rowan had tried to make him see for the past week. The things in their lives didn't define them. Nor could things bring back the ones they loved.

He believed it now.

Which was his only excuse for missing all the clear signs of a trap.

The empty chamber, bereft of excavation equipment.

The very few people that occupied the room when there should have been an entire team.

And the woman standing in the center who held a gun pointed directly at Rowan.

Chapter 17

Rowan stared into the familiar face of Bethany Warrington and finally understood. She'd spent years—endless years full of questions that seemed to hold no answers—and now she'd finally know.

With as flat a voice as she could muster, Rowan stared her old friend in the eyes. "This is all rather elaborate, don't you think?"

The features she'd thought dim were anything but as Bethany's sharp gaze flicked around the chamber. "I'd say it's fitting. You came into my home and took something of mine. Now we're on your turf and I want something of yours."

"I don't have it. I never did."

"But he does." Bethany sauntered over to Finn, her smile warm and seductive as she ran a finger down his chest. "On his body, I'd wager."

With another flat laugh, Rowan tried to figure out the game. "You can't be serious."

Bethany leaned forward and pressed a kiss to Finn's neck before she traced a path over his chest and down his stomach. "Rumor has it you never leave home without it. And since I couldn't exactly get inside that destroyer of the London skyline that you live in, I thought I'd change the playing field."

Tension bracketed Finn's body in hard lines, but he didn't move a muscle under the misplaced seduction. "Now, why would I do that?"

"You tell me."

Finn shrugged. "You're the one with all the answers. I'm just the poor sot who walked into the wrong place with my girl."

"I love a man who tries to sweet-talk his way out of a situation. It's such a magnificent waste of time. And I love it even more that he called you his girl." Bethany's husky laugh echoed off the walls. "If it's a ploy for sympathy, you can save it."

Bethany's eyes narrowed and Rowan sensed the woman was anxious to move their little reunion along. "Why are you doing this?"

"Because you have what I want."

"So you waited twelve years to go after it? Doesn't feel like a rock-solid plan, Bethany."

"Oh, don't worry about that. My plans are far better thought out than yours. Hiding on the roof of my house?" Her old friend tsked lightly. "That's so old school."

"How'd you know that?"

"I know all of it."

Rowan shook her head. "You were on vacation."

"I was with my grandparents. Do you honestly think my parents wanted me along on their holiday?" The seductive voice gave way to something harsh and infinitely more dangerous.

And now the cracks were starting to show, Rowan thought.

"I was a burden, according to my mother. Always underfoot. Here you were, so lucky to have escaped that, and you didn't even realize it."

Lucky? Rowan balled her hands into fists, the urge to leap out and attack Bethany so intense she could actually see red. It was only when she looked at Finn, the compassion and understanding telegraphed from his gaze across the chamber, that she finally began to calm.

Focus.

Keep her talking.

Be bold, Rowan Steele.

With her father's words ringing in her ears, Rowan forced a bored calm into her voice she didn't feel. "So you set me up?"

"*Set up* is much too simple a term. I manipulated you. Teased you with the glow of gold. All I had to do was sit back and let you have at it."

The friend Rowan remembered from childhood was a mirage and it surprised her how badly that simple fact hurt. Although their friendship had dissolved as both had grown up and gone their separate ways, she had carried fond memories of Bethany.

Although they hadn't stayed close, at that time in her life, Rowan had enjoyed having a friend who was easy to be with. Where others always wanted to probe if she was "doing okay" and how she was feeling, Bethany had offered her simple friendship with no strings attached.

How disappointing, then, to realize Bethany's string was actually a noose.

"Oh, don't look so sad, Rowan. We all get bested from time to time."

Which was exactly what she was afraid of.

Rowan took in the rest of the room. There were three men in the chamber besides Baxter. One still sported a line of scratches down his face, courtesy of her lock picks. The other was the man who'd followed them down the alley in Cairo.

But it was the third that rang all Rowan's bells. The man from the Warrington job.

"So let me guess. You hired these guys all those years ago?" Bethany's gaze flicked to the line of thugs, and Rowan kept up her questions, desperate to get as many answers as she could. "But you were only sixteen. How'd you do it?"

Bethany stood next to the man from the closet. "They were at my house all on their own, rumors of my father's acquisition broader than dear old dad even knew. But Jared here's an ambitious fellow. He was more than happy to listen to my tales of woe when I discovered him after the theft gone bad. I told him my plans, and imagine his excitement to right a heist gone wrong."

"It's about damn time." The man's smile was as menacing as she remembered and it was focused on Finn. "Imagine my surprise when years later we get a report someone spotted the bracelet on a job. Right there in your things, just as pretty as you please."

Rowan's gaze collided with Finn's.

So now that they knew the reasons, they needed to figure out how to get out alive.

Finn cursed his sheer idiocy. He knew the job Jared spoke of. Remembered the distinct unease that a member of his crew was watching him, even though he couldn't prove anything was amiss. Now he knew what had set his internal radar humming.

He'd carried that damn bracelet for years and never

had a mishap; the one time he did, it was all over the London underworld in a matter of minutes.

Folly.

Although he'd joked about it at the time, the word had haunted him since Rowan had used it the day before. And now not only would he pay for his, but Rowan would, too.

Bethany's gaze swung toward him. "Take them off."

"Take what off?"

"Your clothes, darling. I want the bracelet."

He'd left the bracelet in his bag at the hotel for the first time in years. But would Bethany believe he didn't have it on his person? "I don't have it."

"I don't believe you."

He shrugged. "I don't care what you believe. It doesn't make it any less true."

Finn knew he only had a few minutes, and he had some questions of his own. He'd also sized up the room and he had an idea. Although he and Rowan didn't have guns, Baxter carried a huge load of excavation equipment on his back and Rowan had her tools on her belt.

A snippet of conversation from Baxter's launch party kept playing over and over in his mind, Rowan's taunt to the incapable dolt giving him an idea.

And here I thought this incredible discovery was all because you got your panties in a twist and tossed a small, pointed archaeology trowel across a priceless burial chamber.

They needed a diversion.

But first he needed answers.

He caught Rowan's gaze before flicking his toward her belt. The light trail of her fingers over her tools ensured she understood the message.

They'd both been blessed with quick fingers. He could

only hope the talent they'd both put to misguided use would be the thing that would save them.

He turned his gaze toward the museum's prize idiot. *Let the diversion begin.*

"How'd you get in the middle of this, Baxter? I always knew you were a little wanker toady, but this is bad even for you."

"I make a pittance at the museum. I decided to up my game."

"And the answer to that was to partner with these guys? Do you have any idea how far over your head you are?"

"Hardly. I decided to put my talents to better use. Something you know an awful lot about." Bravado dripped from his lips, but it couldn't hide the sweat that pooled over his brow and ran down the sides of his face.

Baxter still carried the excavation tools and had continued shifting the heavy bag from side to side. If he could catch him off guard, Finn estimated he could get some momentum off the sheer heft of the bag.

But that strategy still didn't change the fact the men on the other side of the narrow chamber had guns pointed at Rowan. Nor did it change the wild card that was Bethany.

And her gun was the steadiest of the bunch.

Rowan kept her hands off her tools—no use tipping off Jared and his thugs to her intentions. And she could only thank their supreme lack of intelligence that they didn't see the variety of sharp picks and pointed trowels on her belt as weapons.

Little did they know.

The real trick would be escaping the chamber without any gunfire ricocheting through the small, enclosed room. No matter how horrible the situation—and this one was pretty damn bad—she was a scholar, and the thought of losing something so precious had her seeing stars.

If they could only get outside…

"He doesn't have it." The words were out before she could stop them, and at Bethany's narrow-eyed gaze, Rowan knew she needed to see the con through to the end.

"And you do?"

"It's in safekeeping."

"Likely story."

Rowan shrugged. She had no idea if it was working, but she pressed on. "Think what you want. I've given him a hard time since I found out he had the bracelet. I mean, who the hell traipses the world with priceless jewels in their carry-on?"

Bethany's face remained set in hard lines, but Rowan didn't miss the calculation in her gaze.

"Since he can't take proper care of his things, I took it." Rowan shot Bethany a triumphant sneer. "Despite what you may think, Bethany, I'm rather good at stealing."

"Oh, darling, no need to get uppity. I never said you weren't good at it."

Rowan tossed another sneer at Finn. "Men. So concerned about what's in their hands they never look at what's around them."

The agreement in Bethany's gaze was telegraphed loud and clear. "Fine. He stays here and you come with me."

"Nope."

Bethany waved the gun. "I don't think you've got a choice."

"Actually, I do. Since I won't give up the location and Finn has no idea where I put it, you're out of luck."

"Oh, so small-minded, Rowan. You think I won't torture it out of you?"

The thought sent chills down her spine, but Rowan pressed on. "Do you really think that would work? I've honed keeping my mouth shut since a tender age."

Bethany's laugh ran shivers down her spine. "And I've honed my persuasion techniques nearly as long and I've got a whole box full. Don't screw with me."

"Then we all leave the chamber."

Rowan held her breath and waited to see who'd out-bluff the other. Under normal circumstances, she'd never have thought she'd talk her way out of the chamber, but there was something personal in Bethany's insistence on getting the bracelet.

And the fact it was personal made Bethany the weaker party in the negotiation.

"Where is it?"

"Out of the chamber. I won't risk a bullet going wild and ruining something this old and precious."

"If you're dead, why would you care?"

Bethany's soft-spoken words ran another layer of chills down her spine. "Let's just say that's the difference between you and me. This will stand long after we're gone."

"Oh, save me the pompous speech. The people who built this place are long since gone, too. Long past ever caring it existed."

Rowan knew Bethany spoke the truth. The grief of the living far surpassed the peace of the dead. But faced with the possibility of not making it out of the chamber—of not living her life with Finn—Rowan suddenly knew the most desperate desire to *live*.

"Let's go." Bethany tossed orders to the thugs, sending the victim of Rowan's lock picks first up the corridor to the outer chamber, followed by Baxter and Finn. Rowan and Bethany fell in line behind the second thug, and Jared brought up the rear.

Rowan could see the back of Finn's broad shoulders and took solace in their strength. They could do this, and the small, sloping hallway was their best chance. The ascent was slow and Rowan waited on some signal from Finn. She didn't have to wait long.

"Rowan, I love you. No matter what happens, I need you to know that."

"I love you, too."

"How sweet and touching." Bethany was quick to intrude on the moment, and her companions added their laughter to her snide words.

The cocky laughter provided the slightest advantage and Finn didn't disappoint.

"Always, *Rowan*." The extra emphasis on her name had her hands moving to her tool belt.

But it was his final word that unleashed chaos. "Now!"

Finn shoved hard at Baxter and his thick pack of tools, pushing him into the lead thug with a gun and sending them both to the ground.

Rowan had her sharp, pointed trowel in one hand and a heavy pick in the other. With unwavering focus, she slammed the pointed edge of the trowel into the hand of the man in front of her, slicing through the skin of his gun hand. He howled in pain and dropped the gun immediately.

She maintained her momentum, swinging the pick behind her before launching herself backward into Bethany, the two of them falling into Jared like dominoes. The heavy sound of gunfire echoed around them in deafening waves, but the corresponding pain of a gunshot wound never came.

Instead, all she saw was Finn, striding toward her like a conquering hero, his hand outstretched. She reached for him like a lifeline, and they scrambled over and around a struggling Baxter and the first thug, who still lay in a heap.

They cleared the large antechamber in a run and kept on moving toward the corridor that would get them outside the tomb to safety. Her ears still rang with the heavy blast of gunshots and she could barely hear anything beyond the thud of her heart. Instead, she focused on the rays of light, visible in the distance, beckoning them forward.

Finn's hand never left hers, and he pushed her in front of him as they reached the narrow hallway that lead to the exit. With trembling legs, she pushed herself harder up the sloping stairway, frantic to get them outside once more before any further gunfire rang out.

And it was only when they reached the bright sunlight of the desert that Rowan allowed herself to hope they'd escaped the nightmare.

Finn pointed toward a small building about five hundred yards away. "The security station. We need to get there."

She nodded and kept moving, her strength and stamina absolute as they raced toward the small building that was their final hope of ending this. He waved his arms and shouted as they ran, quickly catching the attention of two security guards.

"Hands up, Finn! They need to know we're not going to hurt them."

Rowan's instructions came just before he saw the guards wrap their hands wrapped firmly around their guns.

Rowan shouted for help over and over in Arabic, then English, and the guards ran faster toward them.

She ran through a quick overview of what had happened and got the ready assurance additional help was being called in. The police set them up in the small guard-house with specific instructions to wait.

Finn dragged her into his arms immediately. "It killed me to see you with those guns trained on you."

"Right back at ya, Gallagher. I've always hated guns but never more than at that moment."

"You were amazing. And you knew exactly what I meant about the tools on your belt. You saved us."

"We saved each other."

He pressed his lips to hers for a quick, hard kiss. "I'm still giving you the edge, sweetheart."

"I told you I was sick of women sitting back and waiting to be rescued."

His bark of laughter was loud and immediate as he pressed another kiss to her lips. "So you did."

She clung to his waist, and Finn couldn't stop running his hands over her shoulders and back, as if reassuring himself she was all right. "Did you have any idea it was Bethany?"

"None. I always thought she was a dim bulb." Rowan's shaky laugh tugged at his heart. "How wrong was I?"

"Oh, baby, we both were."

He'd spent so much of his life focused on possessions it was humbling to realize just how misguided he'd been. There was no possession on earth that matched the beauty of being with her. Nothing he could ever acquire that meant more than the gift of her love, given freely.

"I love you, Rowan."

She lifted her head, and in the gorgeous blue depths of her eyes he saw his future. "I love you, Finn."

"I want to make a life with you. And I want to do it in the light. No sneaking around and no more shady jobs."

"We are a pretty good team."

"The best."

She took a deep breath, her words urgent when she finally spoke. "Before that night at the Warringtons', I was empty. And it took me a lot of years to fill those holes, but I did okay. I had my family and my work. And I know I was lucky. But there were still holes. Still gaps of darkness that I never seemed able to fill."

"And now?"

"You fill the emptiness, Finn. And I have no reason to hide in the dark places anymore, either."

He dragged her against him once more and pressed his lips to hers. Love—fierce and tender, wild and warm—flowed between them.

And in her arms, Finn found his forever.

Epilogue

Rowan marveled at what a difference a day made. Or, in her and Finn's case, a few weeks.

They were once again gathered in her grandparents' townhome, but this time Alexander Steele was more than intent on treating Finn as a member of the family. The awkward glares were gone, along with the stilted conversation, and her grandfather had been his most charming self. "That business of yours is booming, Finn. And the work you did to return that long-lost bracelet to the Royal Family certainly has tongues wagging. Rumor has it they may hire you for a few more jobs."

"Yes, sir, they have contacted me about some work."

Rowan didn't miss the quick light that filled her grandfather's eyes, and from Finn's wry smile, she sensed he didn't, either, but she was too happy to care.

They were together and safe and she'd never anticipated her future more than right this moment.

Happy laughter floated around them, and the conversation only grew louder as the evening wore on. Campbell and Abby exchanged adoring glances. Kensington and her grandmother sat in deep conversation about who knew what. Liam and Finn were, last she'd heard, exchanging war stories about adventure travel in New Zealand.

She took it all in, unable to hold back the simple joy of being with those she loved.

The joy faded slightly as her thoughts shifted to Will's family, as they did so often. She'd spent time with Debbie and knew the woman's grief would never fully go away. She could only hope in time the smile would return to the woman's eyes. Finn had already helped her set up a college fund for their children and had seen to their financial needs, as well.

Will wasn't the only one to pay a price. Bethany's crimes had gone far deeper than anyone knew, and the British government hadn't taken long to extradite her from Egypt. Although her latest focus had been on the bracelet, she'd been involved in several high-level thefts along with an impressive résumé of corporate espionage and blackmail.

Her accounts had been buried deep, but Campbell's skills had done wonders for the case against her. Once he'd dug past the Knightsbridge connection on the internet forum, it hadn't taken him long to tug on a few strings. Bethany's house of cards had depended on a deep network of interlaced accounts, and Campbell had discovered them all.

The warm hand covering hers pulled her from the whirlwind of her thoughts, and she smiled up at her grandfather, his blue eyes twinkling with merriment. "I got that joke before, Grandpa. About the Royal Family."

Her grandfather pressed a hard kiss to her forehead

before settling in the seat next to her and taking her hand.
"'Course you did. Finn did, too. That's why I told it."

"You're incorrigible."

"And you wouldn't have it any other way."

She couldn't resist giving him a big hug. "No, I wouldn't."

"You're happy."

"I am."

His gaze stayed warm on hers. "You deserve it, my girl. All my grandchildren do, but I'm happy to see the shadows have disappeared from your eyes. More than I can say."

"Thank you for standing by me. And thank you for seeing that I came out the other side."

A light sheen of tears filled those blue eyes so like her own. "We're family. That's what we do."

She thought of Finn and the life he'd had to create, practically on his own. She then thought of his recent outreach to his father and hoped some of the years could be repaired. Or, if not fixed, at least replaced with some new, happy memories.

But she knew that not all families had what she had. And not all children were lucky to grow up with the support of people like Alexander and Penelope Steele.

"No. We're the *Steele* family. And that's what we do."

"Well said, my girl. Well said." He patted her knee. "Which brings me to my next point. Do you have to head back to Egypt so quickly? The holidays are nearly here."

"I told you Finn and I aren't going back until the first of the year."

"That tomb's not going anywhere."

She lifted one lone eyebrow, unwilling to let him bait her. "Now that Baxter's spending his life in prison stripes, the British Museum's allowing me to lead the dig to expose the Nefertari Wall. Do you know how huge that is?"

"So's planning a wedding."

As if sensing the brewing family debate, Liam's voice rose up over the din as he called everyone to order. He held a bottle of champagne in his hand. "It's time for a toast."

Kensington and Abby helped Liam line up the crystal flutes her grandmother had brought from Ireland decades before. Campbell gave their grandmother his arm to escort her to a seat next to Alexander, and no one missed Penelope's not-quite-whispered, "I told you not to nag our girl."

For her part, Rowan found Finn and sighed in contentment when his arm wrapped around her shoulders. He nodded in the direction of her grandparents. "They're an incredible pair."

"Yes, they are."

Rowan knew in her heart just how true that was. They'd given her roots and wings—the deepest sense of security and the encouragement to leave the nest.

But it was when her grandfather lifted his flute, ordering everyone else to do the same, that Rowan knew the greatest gift.

His love.

"To my granddaughter Rowan. The most stubborn soul I've ever known. Ever since she was a wee babe, that gritty perseverance has been matched by only one thing. The size of her heart." They all drank before her grandfather lifted his glass once more. "And to Finn."

Finn's arm tightened around her shoulders and she couldn't help but smile at the show of nerves.

"You stole my granddaughter's heart."

A hard bark of laughter welled up in her throat, matched only by the one currently shaking Finn's shoulders. "Yes, sir, I did."

"See that you take the very best care of it."

Finn turned toward her and took her champagne glass, setting hers and his down on a nearby table. He then reached for her and pulled her fully into his arms. "I intend to, sir. Every day of my life."

* * * * *

Look out for another HOUSE OF STEELE *adventure!*
Kensington Steele is about to meet her match
in the form of a sexy and formidable security expert in
THE ROME SEDUCTION.

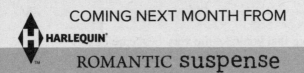

REQUEST YOUR FREE BOOKS!
2 FREE NOVELS PLUS 2 FREE GIFTS!

ROMANTIC suspense

Sparked by danger, fueled by passion

YES! Please send me 2 FREE Harlequin® Romantic Suspense novels and my 2 FREE gifts (gifts are worth about $10). After receiving them, if I don't wish to receive any more books, I can return the shipping statement marked "cancel." If I don't cancel, I will receive 4 brand-new novels every month and be billed just $4.74 per book in the U.S. or $5.24 per book in Canada. That's a savings of at least 14% off the cover price! It's quite a bargain! Shipping and handling is just 50¢ per book in the U.S. and 75¢ per book in Canada.* I understand that accepting the 2 free books and gifts places me under no obligation to buy anything. I can always return a shipment and cancel at any time. Even if I never buy another book, the two free books and gifts are mine to keep forever.

240/340 HDN F45N

Name	(PLEASE PRINT)

Address	Apt. #

City	State/Prov.	Zip/Postal Code

Signature (if under 18, a parent or guardian must sign)

Mail to the **Harlequin® Reader Service:**
IN U.S.A.: P.O. Box 1867, Buffalo, NY 14240-1867
IN CANADA: P.O. Box 609, Fort Erie, Ontario L2A 5X3

Want to try two free books from another line?
Call 1-800-873-8635 or visit www.ReaderService.com.

* Terms and prices subject to change without notice. Prices do not include applicable taxes. Sales tax applicable in N.Y. Canadian residents will be charged applicable taxes. Offer not valid in Quebec. This offer is limited to one order per household. Not valid for current subscribers to Harlequin Romantic Suspense books. All orders subject to credit approval. Credit or debit balances in a customer's account(s) may be offset by any other outstanding balance owed by or to the customer. Please allow 4 to 6 weeks for delivery. Offer available while quantities last.

Your Privacy—The Harlequin® Reader Service is committed to protecting your privacy. Our Privacy Policy is available online at www.ReaderService.com or upon request from the Harlequin Reader Service.

We make a portion of our mailing list available to reputable third parties that offer products we believe may interest you. If you prefer that we not exchange your name with third parties, or if you wish to clarify or modify your communication preferences, please visit us at www.ReaderService.com/consumerschoice or write to us at Harlequin Reader Service Preference Service, P.O. Box 9062, Buffalo, NY 14269. Include your complete name and address.

HRS13R

SPECIAL EXCERPT FROM

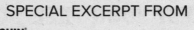 HARLEQUIN®

ROMANTIC suspense

When Arabian princess Laila agrees to help stop a
terrorist group within her country's borders, she never
expects to find love with the distrusting FBI agent who
will do anything to keep her safe.

Read on for a sneak peek of

PROTECTING HIS PRINCESS

by C.J. Miller, available November 2013 from
Harlequin® Romantic Suspense.

"What are you doing?" Laila asked, taking his arm.

Harris stared at her. "Why didn't you go with your family?"

"And leave you here alone?" Laila asked.

He didn't want Laila in the thick of this. An attempt had
been made on her life in America and he didn't know if she
had been one of the targets of the bombing here. "You need
to be somewhere safe."

She gripped his arm harder. "I am safest with you."

Another explosion boomed through the air. Harris grabbed
Laila and shielded her with his body, pulling them to the
ground. Was the sound a building collapsing from the damage
or another bomb? Harris guessed another bomb. Laila was
shaking in his arms. Harris waited for the noise around him to
quiet and concentrated on listening for the rat-tat-tat of gun
shots or another bomb.

His protective instincts roared louder. He wouldn't let anything happen to Laila. "I'm going to help where I can."

Her eyes widened with fear. "What if there is another bomb—"

He had some basic first-aid training and he'd been a marine. Dealing with difficult situations had been part of his training. "There might be another one. There's no time to wait for help."

"I can help, too," Laila said, lifting her chin.

"You aren't trained for this," he said.

"No, but I'm capable and smart. I will be useful. Don't treat me like a crystal vase."

Laila wouldn't back down. She wouldn't leave the scene, not when her countrymen needed help. Arguing wouldn't get him anywhere. He'd seen her strength many times before. She might act like a shrinking violet in front of her brother or other males, but she had an iron core. "You're stubborn when you want something."

"So are you," Laila said, giving him a small smile.

Don't miss
PROTECTING HIS PRINCESS
by C.J. Miller,
available November 2013 from
Harlequin® Romantic Suspense.

HARLEQUIN®

ROMANTIC suspense

THE COLTON HEIR

Ranch hand Dylan Frick threatens to turn
in a gorgeous intruder, but Hope begs him
to keep her deadly secret. She isn't the only
one whose identity is under wraps.
Will the truth set them free?

Look for the next installment of the
Coltons of Wyoming miniseries
next month from Colleen Thompson.

Only from Harlequin® Romantic Suspense!

Wherever books and ebooks are sold.

Heart-racing romance, high-stakes suspense!

HHARLEQUIN®

ROMANTIC suspense

Two *USA TODAY* bestselling authors in one book!

Two deadly missions have these men in uniform putting their lives and their hearts on the line for service, duty and love.

Look for *COURSE OF ACTION* next month,
featuring *Out of Harm's Way*
by Lindsay McKenna
and *Any Time, Any Place*
by Merline Lovelace.

Only from Harlequin® Romantic Suspense!

Wherever books and ebooks are sold.

Heart-racing romance, high-stakes suspense!

HRS27845